NESTING DOLLS

a novel

Salena Fehnel

Northampton House Press

NESTING
DOLLS

For Ashlee,
my beautiful, wild, imaginative girl
who inspires me more than anyone or anything else on this green earth.

VALENTINE

"I think we dream so we don't have to be apart so long. If we're in each other's dreams, we can be together all the time."

— Bill Watterson, *Calvin and Hobbes*

Val made her entrance into the bright lights of the maternity ward, shrieking and naked, at 12:04 a.m. on February fourteenth. Her mother, Theresa, just fourteen herself, grasped at the single breath of innocent romance that had found its way into her polluted life, embraced it, and named her firstborn Valentine Saint.

The last name, printed in capital letters on the California birth certificate, was the same as her mother's: Maureino.

In elementary school, she would feel a flush of pride when pretty, perfect Lacey Penning swished her blonde ponytail at Val's grammar book, cornflower blue eyes studying it briefly. Then raised a pale, eight year old arm to announce, "Valentine Maureino has all the vowels in one name." She'd smiled, revealing a missing bottom tooth, and said two words that had stuck with Val for the entire school year: "That's neat."

At that point in her life, Valentine was attending Las Cruces Elementary. After a "turn of events," as Theresa liked to call it, Valentine, her mother, and her mother's new boyfriend of three weeks, picked up all of their belongings again, and moved into a one bedroom apartment in Mesilla, New Mexico.

Val remembered that guy well. The last decent one before the black plague that became her mother's love life. Theresa had brought him home exactly three hours after they'd met at the little green trailer converted into a pancake house where she waitressed six days a week. Val liked him immediately. He came into the ranch style house they'd been calling home for four months, squatted, and extended a hand to Val. "Hey. I'm Bernie."

He stayed less than an hour that first visit, despite her mother's invitation to stick around for dinner. As he walked out the door, he bowed, kissed Theresa's hand, and said in a goofy accent, "I bid farewell to Queen Theresa and her lovely Princess Valentine."

Over the next week, Bernie dropped by in the evenings. He stayed considerably longer every day. Bedtime was nine, consistent and unarguable, despite the freeform style Theresa applied to all other aspects of her daughter's upbringing. Most nights Val would lie on her mattress in the upstairs room clutching her pale yellow elephant, Dumpy. Her heart would squeeze just a little bit when she heard the first closing of the door.

It meant Bernie had left safely before the second closing of the door. The one that indicated Marco, the smelly, squinty-eyed man who owned the apartment and let her and Theresa live there with him, was home from his second shift at Roadway.

So it went for three weeks. Until one night, as Val lay on the carpet drawing a picture of a little gray house with lovely pink shingles, the front door swung open. Marco took four giant steps in. He staggered against the small bookcase that held an answering machine and a dirty, torn yellow phone book, then fell face first onto the musty green throw rug that half-concealed the moldy tile of the dining area.

Theresa ran out of the bedroom wearing only faded pink panties and an orange bra out of which one underwire poked. Following her was Bernie, wearing a pair of yellowing long john bottoms that Val was momentarily distracted by. Theresa and Bernie came to an abrupt stop in front of the entryway across which Marco was sprawled. Val still lay propped on her elbows three feet away, holding her pink crayon so tightly that, as Marco suddenly shoved up off the floor and stood, she broke it right in half. The pink paper split not quite all the way, creating a Crayola logo on a carnation-pink hinge.

Marco swayed, staring at Theresa, oblivious to the half-naked stranger beside her. "I knew it. I got into my truck early because I knew it." His words sounded mashed together. Spit flew with every syllable.

Her mother, glancing quickly at Bernie, said very calmly, "Marco, that's ridiculous. Don't go accusing everyone of things that aren't even real. You and I both know how you get."

"You lying, disgusting whore!" Marco screamed. A gob of spit landed on Theresa's cheek, inches away. "You ain't nothing but trash. I let trash in my house!"

"Don't you talk like that to me! Don't you dare." Theresa's voice shook as she adjusted the bra strap that'd slipped off her shoulder. Val scooted back and pressed tightly against the ratty floral love seat, eyes peeled wide. She brought both hands up just under her eyes, the way she always did when she was watching a very scary movie and didn't want to see what was going to jump out. But didn't want to miss it, either.

Marco sucked in a loud breath. "Don't talk to you?"

His fist flew in a short arc, smashing into Theresa's painted lips. She fell back and Marco lunged forward, past her, into the narrow hallway that led to his and Theresa's bedroom. Bernie sidled two quiet steps toward the front door, then stopped.

"Mama?" Val said, the first word spoken in the chaotic silence.

Her throat and chest felt so tiny, she couldn't even swallow her own spit. Theresa ran to pick her up, and held Val's head against her chest. Her mother's heartbeat thumped like a drum against Val's temple.

"It's okay," her mother breathed quietly, but Val didn't feel like it was. "It's okay. He'll sleep it off. He'll be fine when he —"

Two loud blasts rang in Val's ears. The bullets hit the wall behind Theresa. The sound they made tearing out of their steel womb rippled through Val, as her mother shoved her down onto the love seat and screamed, "You're crazy! Marco! Stop! Put that down! You'll go back to jail, you sonofabitch!"

"Hell if I will," Marco spat out, and then fired once more.

This shot traveled eight short feet, tearing into the abdomen of the little girl huddled on the couch.

As Val rolled off and fell flat on the carpet, she was vaguely aware of muffled screams. For some reason everything sounded the way it did when she went swimming at her friend Ginny's house down the street and they submerged themselves in an aqua wonderland. She'd always wanted a ruffled swimsuit like Ginny's.

The room was covered in fuzz, as if thousands of dandelions were blowing around, making the walls soft. As Val was thinking this, it grew dimmer.

When the fourth shot rang out, and Marco too dropped to the floor, Val saw the mess on the gray carpet was carnation pink like her crayon. Then, like a bedtime flick of the light switch, the pink and the dandelions and the screaming all went away into the dark.

When Valentine opened her eyes again, her head felt heavy, like shoes full of sand.

"Somebody's making my eyes closed," she mumbled. A warm hand took hers.

"No, you're okay, sweetie," a woman's voice, not her mommy's, said. "You're in the hospital. The medicine makes you feel sleepy."

An hour later, she was sitting up, chatting with two nurses, and eating vanilla ice cream out of a small plastic cup. It was only as she scooped the last of the ice cream with the small plastic spoon that she thought to ask: "Where's Mommy?"

One nurse abruptly stood and opened a cabinet, pulling out another blanket, laying it carefully over Val's legs. The other, the one with short brown hair and a kitty cat shirt Val liked, smiled. "She'll be back."

"But where is she?"

"She had to visit the police a little while. But while she's there, you and me can hang out." The nurse pulled a coloring book and crayons from a drawer next to the bed. "And color! And watch cartoons!"

"And have more ice cream?"

"Surely. And have more ice cream." The nurse tucked her legs in, taking care not to touch the bandage on her belly.

"Why can't I sit up all the way?"

The nurse laid the coloring book in front of her. "Well, because you have a boo-boo. It has to get better before you can move around."

"Oh. Okay." Val, already paging through the coloring book, finally settled on a picture of a cartoon girl dancing under a glittery ball.

"So, how does that sound?" The nurse sat on the bed next to her and pulled a blue crayon from the box.

"Fine." Val liked this nurse, and this bed with legs that lifted it up off the floor, and the window with all the sunshine. She pressed the crayon to the page and pretended that this was her home. That this nurse, who smelled so nice, was her mom, and she could stay here forever.

Chapter 1

Blueberry Lane sounded like a quaint, country dirt road leading to cozy summer cottages. In reality it was the same as Barker, Hurley, and every other pothole-plenty road in scummy Antioch, California. I threw my book bag down and sat on the curb, carefully avoiding the sticky mural of gum decorating the cement.

Spring in California always brought rain and windy days more than flowers and sun. I tucked my hands into the pockets of my windbreaker and waited for the bus. The smell of the wind on days like this always gave me this waiting feeling. I could be doing the most routine, everyday things, but one whiff of that hot, dry wind, and I had the strongest sense that some big, life changing event was about to happen.

The school bus creaked to a stop in front of me, and I stood, brushed my butt off, and smiled wide as the doors opened. Jonathon came out in his quiet, ambling way. Some kids barrel out of places, tumbling into and out of rooms like they're supercharged. Jonathon had never been like that. His sandy brown hair hung shaggy over wide eyes – the only feature we shared, really – and he was quiet right down to the way he walked, kind of slumping, without making his feet smack the pavement too loud. The bus doors slammed behind him, and he stood still for my routine afternoon hug.

I gave an extra squeeze. "How did show and tell go?"

"Okay. Brian Watters brought in his blue pickup, and we raced in the sand and everyone said our trucks were cool."

I nodded. Sometimes all I got was a shrug, so this felt like a victory.

Jonathon held my hand tight as we walked the block and a half to our house. His bus from Boone Elementary brought him back to me every day at three forty-five. The stop was almost a mile away, and being that he'd barely turned six, I broke a sweat Monday through Friday running from the last bell at my school to the stop in time to see him descend those four steps off the elementary bus.

"Think Mommy's home today?" He looked up, already knowing the answer. Every day he asked the same question as we reached the dingy house and started up the crumbling concrete steps. And every day I said the same thing: "Yup."

We reached the door, but I wanted to stall for another minute or two. "Hey," I said. "I got you something this morning on my way to school." I let go of his sweaty little hand, and he smiled up, waiting for the surprise. I opened my book bag and pulled out a sixty-four count box of Crayola crayons. Long black lashes framed dark green eyes as he smiled wider and hugged me tight. "Sixty-four! I never seen that many in one box! There's prolly so many colors I won't even get to use them all on one page! Thank you, Val! Oh man! Thanks so much!" He hugged me tighter, and I thought how wrong it was that a kid should be so grateful for something so small.

"You got it, Bud. Let's go inside and have a snack first. Then maybe we can color in my room."

I opened the front door and the smell of home surrounded us. Our house was old, as were the near-identical ones flanking it, and all the others on the same street. Everyone's house has a smell to it. Ours was stale cigarette smoke and cat pee.

I looked on the shelf in the kitchen without having to open the cabinet door, because two weeks after we'd moved in the door fell off and it'd never been replaced. I set Jonathon up with a bowl of canned tomato soup, promised we'd go food shopping tomorrow, and then headed upstairs.

I climbed the steps fast. I couldn't wait to get into my room to take my shoes off. Jonathon and I both know not to take them off anywhere but in my room because the fleas from the cats are in the carpeting everywhere else. Right after we moved in, I spent an entire Sunday afternoon yanking up the nasty orange shag carpet from my eight by ten foot bedroom. Underneath was a wood floor that, after I scrubbed it down, looked almost as nice as the ones in the courthouse. Plus, fleas don't like wood floors, so they stay pretty much out of my room.

I immediately noticed the disruption of my Russian nesting dolls. When I was in sixth grade, we went on a field trip to San Francisco to tour Alcatraz Island. I didn't like the prison because it was creepy and dirty, and I hated that people had died there. But I loved the part of the trip where we got back to the wharf and divided into groups to shop on Pier 39.

Before I'd left that morning, my mother had handed me a rumpled five-dollar bill. "Use it to buy lunch and bring me back the change." There I was, walking into the little stores on the wharf, not touching anything because the shopkeepers watched all the kids as though we were going to stuff every piece of merchandise into our pockets and then graffiti the walls and windows. Everyone in my class was buying the little plastic see-through key chains that said *San Francisco*, and I wanted one too, but if I spent the dollar left over from lunch, my mother would be really angry. So I didn't even look at the key chains.

Instead, I wandered to the far end of the store, resisting the temptation of the cheap souvenirs up front. There, in the back, were the nesting dolls. They were painted shiny bright reds, greens, yellows, and blues and set out one next to the other, biggest to smallest, five in all. I looked around to check where my teachers were, then reached out and cupped the smooth wooden head of the largest. I pinched the smallest one between two fingers; it was so tiny and cute, I cradled it in my palm like a dollhouse baby. The three in-between sizes were beautiful too, but I really loved that tiny one and that big one.

They were the most beautiful things I'd ever seen. I stacked all five one inside the other, careful to face them all the same direction as I closed the set. Then I carefully carried it to the front.

"Excuse me? Ma'am?" I waited by the register as the saleslady, a redhead my mom's age, talked on the phone.

"Hang on a sec, Marge." She covered the mouthpiece and glared like I was the most trivial interruption ever to hit her important life.

"Hi." I glanced down at the dolls and licked my lips. "I just wanted to know how much these are."

She glanced quickly at the big doll cradled in my hands. "Fifty dollars. They're from Russia." She rolled her eyes and put the phone back to her face. "So. What'd he do when he saw the stains?"

I really wanted those dolls. "Excuse me…"

The sales girl let out a noisy, exaggerated sigh and said extra loudly, "*Jesus*, hang on a second, Marge. I have a *customer*." She turned and raised her eyebrows at me. *"What?"*

"Think they might go on sale anytime soon?" Like in the next thirty minutes, before we had to get back on the bus to go home.

She huffed. "*No.* This isn't K-mart, okay? The price is what the price is. Okay?" She turned her back.

So I made my way to the rear again, stared at the empty space on the shelf where they'd first found me, and imagined placing each back on it. Taking them out of each other and letting them be their own dolls again. I thought about how they could just go back to be being in the store for their whole life, while I went home without them. Then I opened the zipper on my pink nylon fanny pack, slid the dolls in, and walked out of the store, back into the sunlight.

I stood next to the guardrail, watching the water swirl around below, and waited to get caught. I had ants in my pants, like my mom said whenever I fidgeted. I bent my knees and straightened them over and over while I stood there. When after a good twenty minutes no one said anything to me, I felt so guilty I walked back into the store, stuffed my one-dollar bill into the plastic jar that said, "Save-A-Dog," and hauled my butt up the steps onto the yellow bus.

Ever since then, I have kept any money I manage to earn hidden in the second to smallest doll, tucked deep within the others. However, last week, and again today, the moron who broke into my dolls and took the money didn't have the sense to put them back into one another correctly. So it didn't take a detective to see how the middle one sat idly next to the others. I walked over and picked them up, finding just what I'd expected: a couple of singles and thirty-two cents in change. That made a total of $209 stolen from me in the last week.

"I'm all done eating. Can we color now?" Jonathon stood in my doorway clutching a Batman coloring book to his chest.

"Yeah, Buddy. That sounds like a great idea. You sit here." I pulled my desk chair out and patted the seat. "And I'll sit on my bed and work on my English, okay?"

He smiled that precious smile and plopped down. For the next three hours we sat like that, him happily lost in a paper world of superheroes, me brooding over past participles and nesting dolls.

I draped the old bath towels over the curtain rod and adjusted the bottoms, overlapping them so nobody could see into Jonathon's bedroom. He snuggled down into the covers and nestled his head into the pillow.

I sat on the edge of his bed. "Love you, Buddy." I kissed his cheek and smoothed his messy brown hair.

"Love you, Val. Is my window locked?"

I went back over to the window and through the motions of checking it again, even though he and I both knew I'd locked it ten minutes before.

In the house we lived in right before this one, the tenants next door were drug dealers. The cops were all over them – really late in the game, in my opinion, but I guess I'm just more observant than they were, or maybe just more bored – and they watched the house from a car parked a little ways down for most of the summer. The night the police made the move to bust them, one of the dealers ran out his back door, crawled into Jonathon's window and threatened to shoot himself and Jonathon if anyone came near them.

After an hour and a half of being locked in a room with a hysterical three year old, the dealer made the fortunate mistake of letting Jonathon go out to the bathroom. The police went in and got the guy by emptying three rounds into his chest.

So now we check twice before bedtime. I turned off the lights and closed the door quietly.

"It's late for him to be getting to bed, isn't it?" My mother said from behind me. She stood a foot away, wearing a ratty purple terrycloth robe, her hair up in an orange banana clip, a leftover from sometime around my first birthday.

"No, Ma. It's only eight-thirty." I slid around her, and took a step farther down the hall.

She dragged a sleeve across her nose, the tip of it red and swollen, her eyes watery and lidded heavy. Her face sagged in ways other mothers' didn't, sometimes swollen and sometimes droopy but never quite right. She sniffed. "Did he eat today?"

"He eats every day, Ma. That's the daily recommended dose for kids, ya know?" I reached the stairs and started down, but she stayed three steps behind.

"Do your homework?" Her slippers scuffed along behind me as I went into the kitchen.

"Yup."

"That's real good, baby. I was thinking about maybe having a cake for when you get your diploma. You want that? It could be a nice yellow cake with chocolate frosting. You like chocolate."

I turned toward the sink. "I like strawberry."

I squeezed the dish soap bottle a couple of times, willing the air to push out the last couple of drops so I could clean up the soup bowl. Funny how, when you know there's nothing left in a bottle of soap or shampoo, you still squeeze it in that rhythmic way, thinking if you just do it enough times more will magically come out.

My mother opened the refrigerator and took out a yogurt and a can of beer. I gave up on the soap and turned the water as hot as it would go then held the bowl underneath. It was just tomato soup, right? How germy could it be?

She took a sip of beer and licked her lips. "Has Ernie been in?"

"I don't know, Ma. I've been in my room."

"The whole time? No, you came out. I heard. You went in the bathroom."

"Okay." I dried the warm bowl and put it in the cupboard that still had a door. "Yeah. I came out to go into the bathroom to put Jonathon in the bathtub."

"So was he?"

I gritted my teeth. "Was he *what*, Mom?"

"*Here*, Valentine. Was he here?"

"No! I don't know. I didn't see him, but I didn't send a search party around, either. I don't know where he is at any given point during the day."

She squinted. "Your hair is in your eyes. You should put barrettes in it. I have extra clips like the one I'm wearing. You should pull the hair out of your face. It's always in your face." She took another swallow of beer and shoveled a spoonful of yogurt between her lips.

"Are you going food shopping tomorrow?" I asked.

"Yeah. That sounds like a plan. I'll try to go tomorrow."

"You really have to go, Ma. There isn't anything left besides soup, beer, and yogurt."

She smiled and licked her spoon. "No more yogurt neither."

"So you'll go tomorrow?"

"I'll try. Ernie said he's gonna bring a paycheck made out just to me tomorrow. Kinda like a rent check. Good idea, huh?"

She finished off the beer and threw it at the garbage can, missed by a good six inches, and watched as it clanged to the floor. From the little pocket in the side of her robe she took out a pack of cigarettes and used her lips to pull one out. She felt the outside of the pocket and reached in to pull out a dark green Bic lighter. "He might be working at the post office now. That's a good steady job, huh?"

I picked up the beer can and dropped it into the garbage pail. "I'm going to bed." I started to walk out of the kitchen.

"Tomorrow at the store . . . we can get some of those jelly bean candies you like so much. Just gotta wait for that check, okay?"

I paused, wanting to rest my head on the doorframe and close my eyes, and sighed. "Okay, Ma. That'd be nice." I looked over my shoulder at her.

She nodded absentmindedly, staring at something invisible in the middle of the table, taking a long drag on her cigarette, not even bothering to tilt her head upward as she exhaled.

Chapter 2

The next morning, I waved and blew kisses to Jonathon as he looked out from the bus window. He smiled and gave a little wave before turning to talk to the boy sitting next to him. When he started first grade I was so relieved. I could send him off in the morning, away from home, and pick him up in the afternoon. Kindergarten had been only a half-day, and he'd been assigned to the afternoon session, which meant he was absent more days than he was there – for simple lack of my mother waking up to put him on the bus.

I watched it turn the corner, then started walking the twelve blocks to my high school. I'd been late every single day of my senior year, and today would be no exception. After the first seven weeks of me walking in to homeroom fifteen minutes after the flag salute and morning announcements, the principal had called me into her office to have a little "sit down," as she called it.

"Valentine, Mrs. Tarcell has sent a final plea of disciplinary action to me this morning. Do you know why?"

Ms. Bloomfield was quite possibly the youngest principal ever to work within our school system. She looked no older than twenty-five, and was a woman who clearly took care of herself. Her chestnut hair was always up to date with multi-faceted blonde highlights, and she dressed in beautiful pastel skirt suits that fit her slim body perfectly. As the west wing boy's locker room wall testified, Ms. Bloomfield was a *hotty with a botty*.

Fortunately, she was also very fair, and never handed out punishment unless someone was really asking for it. So there she was, French manicure-tipped hands clasped in her lap, trying to figure out why a student who remained on Honor Roll eight consecutive semesters, was acting Treasurer of Student Council, and had never so much as had a hallway write up, would blow off homeroom every morning of her senior year.

"Ms. Bloomfield, my little brother started first grade this year. His bus comes at eight-ten in the morning, and homeroom starts at eight-oh-five."

She looked at me as though I was saying two plus two now equaled five.

"I have to put him on the bus," I said, trying to make the point she was apparently looking for.

She frowned. "Well, surely one of your parents can put him on the bus. Getting to your own class on time is your responsibility, and your brother, although I'm sure you love him, is the responsibility of your parents."

That summed up all the irritating, useless thoughts that ran through my head every morning. "Yeah, I know. But it doesn't really work out like that. So if I don't put him the bus, I won't know for sure if he actually gets to school that day."

She stared for a moment, her large green eyes outlined beautifully with two well-applied coats of mascara. "Your parents don't ensure he goes?"

"Well, for one, it's just a mother. Not 'parents'. And yeah. I mean, no. If I don't put him on, I can't be sure he'll get to school."

"This sounds like a situation that maybe we should consider calling someone about," she said gently.

I knew what she was getting at. "No, listen, I'm sorry, I'll try really hard to not be as late. But I can't not be late at all." Basically I was telling her I *was* going to be late. And there was nothing she or I could do to make it different, short of me dropping out.

She seemed to understand this. "I see. Well, I will talk to Mrs. Tarcell. Though this isn't something that's normally excusable, Valentine."

I nodded. "I know. It's just . . . he has to go to school. And I have to put him on the bus for him to do that. So . . . " I hoped my trail-off said it all.

She nodded again and patted my hand. "I think I understand. Well, go back to class. I'll speak to your teacher. No more than twenty minutes late, okay? That's all I can excuse on a daily basis." She stood. "And Val? If I see a change in your grades or any other problems when you are here, I will need to make some calls to remedy this situation the way it really should be handled. Okay?"

I thanked her, and thought about hugging her. She smelled like lavender and chocolate, and she was so close. "Thanks, Ms. Bloomfield. I really needed this."

"I know, sweetie." And before I could move a muscle she leaned in and wrapped me in a hug. "Hang in there, okay? Just hang in there. You're too bright with too much to lose right now. Graduation's around the corner."

I held tightly for a moment and breathed in the smell of her fruity shampoo, then let go and walked out.

So for the last six months, this morning being no exception, I slipped into my homeroom seat with an excused tardy. Which, it should be noted, displeased cranky Mrs. Tarcell to no end.

Jonathon and I were silent on our walk back from the bus stop after school that day. He seemed down, and I was just plain tired.

We stood on the front porch for a moment, and Jonathon looked up at me with wide, scared eyes. The screaming inside escalated to a dull roar, and he held tighter to my hand. I took a deep breath, trying to stay calm. "It's okay, Buddy. No big deal. Let's scoot right up to my room, okay? We can have snacks up there today. 'Kay?"

He nodded and gripped harder. I turned the knob and pushed the door open at the exact moment something very breakable hit a solid surface and shattered. Jonathon spun into me and clutched my shirt, burying his face in my stomach.

Time to play Tough Girl.

"Oh for Christ's sake, this is ridiculous. Jonathon, come on. Let's go. Upstairs. Now!" I tugged, pulling him into the living room, toward the stairs. We were just four steps away from the landing when my mother and Ernie tumbled down the stairs in one drunken heap. Ernie slammed her body against the wall at the bottom of the stairwell. She scratched and smacked at him like a cornered raccoon, landing a blow to his ear. He stumbled backward, flailing, knocking over the lamp on the beat-up chrome end table. It broke into jagged pieces.

Jonathon began to cry.

My mother's sloppy, strained voice filled the room. "Get out! Get your stuff and get out. I hate you! You hear? I hate you! Get out, you scumbag!"

I bent and scooped my brother up, pressing his head to my chest, and used my free hand to cover his other ear. "It's okay, Buddy," I whispered. "Up we go." I took another step up. For a kid who hardly ate a full helping at any meal, he sure felt heavy, clinging to me like a baby chimpanzee.

Ernie's nasal voice was almost too slurred to understand. "Don't you ever touch me again, you nasty bitch! I'll kill you. I'll kill you!" He grabbed my mother's neck and slammed her against the wall again. This time she yelled in pain.

"Hey!" I screamed at the top of my lungs.

Jonathon cried even harder, twisting his fists into my damp shirt. My voice momentarily pulled Ernie and my mother out of the private hell they both dwelled in when they drank. Ernie paused with a hand locked on my mother's neck and turned a disgusted face up at me.

"Get your hands off of her!" I shouted again. "I mean it! Right now, Ernie!"

He looked at me for a moment, blinking with eyes that couldn't focus. Then with one meaty hand he shoved my mother over the back of the couch. "You, huh? A big girl now, aren't you?" He grabbed onto the banister railing at the bottom, and my knuckles turned white holding onto my end at the top. "Real pretty, like your mama. Pretty, but you women all got the same problem. Can't keep your fuckin' mouths shut when they should be shut!" He planted one foot on the bottom step.

I pried Jonathon's fingers out of my shoulder and shoved him behind me, holding him with one hand behind my back. Then bared my teeth at the filthy, enraged face below. "Don't come up here, Ernie. Stay down there. I mean it." I stood still on the top step as Jonathon's hands wrapped around my leg. "Leave! Leave this house. Get out."

"Oh, get out, huh? Little girl, you gonna tell me what I do or ain't do? You know what your problem is? That mouth. Just like your mother. Think you need lessons on talkin' to men. I think you do."

He vaulted up two more steps in one motion, bringing him almost to the top.

I backed up, pressing Jonathon into the hallway wall behind me. "I'll call the police, Ernie. Get out! Now!" As a last resort, I screamed, *"Mom!"*

She didn't appear, and my stomach flipped. He took one more step up, making the distance between us just two tiny risers. His eyes were glazed and crazy looking, like someone ready to kill. Or worse.

At that moment, Jonathon jumped out from behind me with what I can only imagine must have been six years of built-up courage, and lobbed a huge wad of spit right into Ernie's deranged, red face.

Call it reflex, call it instinct, call it whatever you want, but I took that glorious instant of opportunity to kick Ernie square in the chest, knocking him right back down to the first floor. He lay at the bottom, stunned and wasted. We didn't wait to see him get up. I grabbed Jonathon's hand and yanked him down the hall and into my bedroom, frantically turning first the doorknob lock, then the deadbolt I'd installed just six weeks before. We were both dead silent, holding our breaths, listening for the thunder of footsteps. I only heard silence.

I looked down at Jonathon, who stood straight as a board, his forehead crinkled, arms pinned to his side. "Okay. We're okay, Buddy." I kneeled and held him tight. He wrapped his fingers in my hair and laid his head on my shoulder.

That night, I pulled out the milk crate I stashed food in for just such special occasions, and we dined on peanut butter and jelly on Ritz crackers, Fruit RollUps, and two Capri Suns each. Around 8:45, Jonathon confessed that he had to use the bathroom, so we hustled across the hall and back into my room in record time, relocking the door behind us. I gave him one of my t-shirts, and we crawled into my twin bed. He snuggled close and draped an arm and leg over my body before quickly falling asleep.

I lay awake long enough to hear my mother two doors down, loudly making up with Ernie, before I fell into a restless, uncomfortable doze.

Chapter 3

W henever Northern California gave us an early summer, the last weeks of school felt like eternity. That May the air conditioning was broken for the third school year in a row, so the teachers resorted to swivel fans they plugged into one corner of the rooms in hopes that some sort of air would be circulated. With only two weeks left before graduation, real teaching ended and the afternoons were spent "reviewing" for finals, and watching any movies even slightly related to the subject matter.

I clicked my pen in and out as Mr. Brookes used the remote to turn up *Forrest Gump*, which he said would give us an idea of what the Vietnam War was like for soldiers. Jonathon was at home with the remains of the flu. I was thankful he'd gotten sick on Friday afternoon, spent the entire weekend throwing up and feverish, and was practically well enough to go back to school by Sunday night. Practically. This morning he'd asked to stay home one more day. "My tummy still feels yucky," he said, and he was never a faker, so I had reluctantly left the house without him. All for a movie.

"Val," the only girl I would ever consider my best friend stage-whispered across the aisle at me. "Here. Take this." Angela held out a folded piece of notebook paper. I took it and glanced over at Mr. Brookes, who was watching the game highlights on his laptop, completely oblivious.

Inside the paper she'd written, *Let's go out after school? Mom said I can use the car now that Penelope has her fabulous new Jetta. Just go shopping or something...Wanna?*

"Can't," I whispered, lifting one cheek into my sort-of smile.

She sighed and frowned at me. "Fine."

Angela Scarpelli knew me better than anyone. We'd met three years earlier when she'd sat down next to me at lunch, cracked open her chocolate milk carton, and blurted, "Justin White is the dirtiest, rudest, most obnoxious guy in the entire school *district*." I'd raised my eyebrows at the emphasis on district. She nodded, as though she couldn't believe it herself. "He dumped me yesterday."

For the rest of that day, we'd met between classes to hand each other multiple-page notes with detailed outlines of our most private lives. I'd kept it surface, of course. I didn't really detail *my* most private life until nearly six months after we met, while we sat on the cool November grass behind the maintenance building on school property. The homecoming pep rally was going on at our football field, and I could vaguely make out the sounds of cheerleaders offering school spirit by the mouthful. I pressed my hand against the stucco wall until I could feel and see little pocked imprints on my palm and the pads of my fingers.

Angela sat across, Indian style, the caps of her knees touching mine. She painted my fingernails with one hand and held a Black and Mild with the other, bringing it up to her lips every few minutes as though it wasn't an action but simply instinct. She hummed *Amazing Grace*, her choppy black-streaked hair blowing lightly, messily in the breeze. When she paused to take a drag, smiling from bare, unglossed lips and slate blue eyes simultaneously, I fell in love with her.

She flicked her thumb to ash the stick and, in the blatant manner I'd already come to know as Angela, said, "So what the hell is wrong with your family, anyway? Your mom seemed totally out of it when we were at your house the other day."

I looked down, expecting that burn of humiliation across my cheeks I usually felt when someone realized my mother and I were related. But with Angela, I didn't feel anything but agreement and a weird sense of relief, like I wasn't the only one that saw what Theresa was really like. "Yeah," I nodded. "She is. She always is, sort of."

"Why?"

"Well, I mean she wasn't always like that. She used to take me on picnics and stuff, out on the water on these stupid little row boats, shit like that." I blew on my nails.

Angela continued to paint my other hand.

"Man, I can't picture her on a picnic *anywhere*."

I thought about it for moment. "Yeah." The only thing that came to mind.

"Oh yeah and *ew*. Who was that *guy* at the table? I swear to God he had pedo written all over him."

I pulled my hand away for a moment and looked hard at her. "What? You think so? Do you really?" My stomach tumbled over itself as I searched Angela's eyes for the truth I knew they'd smack me with.

She shrugged bare shoulders and took another long drag. "Eh. He could just be your run of the mill perv. Who knows? Why was he in your house, anyway?"

"It's my mother's boyfriend. Dino."

She wrinkled her nose. "Ew."

I smiled. "Yeah."

"I have a creep alert that goes off like this." She snaps her fingers. "My dad was a creep, but I barely remember him. Penelope remembers more."

"Oh. Did he leave your mom?"

She shakes her head. "She left him. Doesn't talk about him, like, ever. But when I was little she always told me and Penny that he 'just wasn't a nice man.' So she left. And took us with her."

I thought of her mom, Kate. "That was brave. That takes a lot of guts." Guts my own mother will never have, I thought, envious of Angela and not for the first time.

"So." She put the brush back into the small bottle and turned the cap until it was tight. "How come your mom is so messed up now if she used to be like, you know, like *you*?"

"Her whole life, I guess. Her whole life has been, like...it's one thing after another with her. She doesn't really talk about it. Like, life before I was born, I mean. She had me when she was in 8th grade, so she dropped out of school, and then she started dating these guys that were horrible..." I stopped because I was out of air, and because tears were coming out of my eyes, slowly, but at a consistent pace like tiny streams running through muddy ground.

Angela kept silent across from me. Her thin neck was bent slightly, her eyes squinted just enough to let me know she was intently listening.

I swiped the back of one hand across my cheek, holding the fingers spread apart so I wouldn't smudge.

"Anyway, yeah. So she screwed up a couple times, and God probably hates her now and is like 'That's it, no more chances for you.' It wouldn't be so friggin' bad if she just didn't bring the scumbags into our house."

"Do they hurt you?" she asked casually, quietly, and with the force of ten thousand warriors.

I laughed and lifted the corner of my shirt up three inches.

Angela put one finger out and touched my skin there, tracing the ragged edges of the gunshot scar. She said nothing, just put the cigar back to her lips and breathed in, then handed it to me. I inhaled, holding it until the charred-leaf smoke burned my throat and gums and nostrils.

I walked into the kitchen carefully holding a container of veggie soup I'd picked up at the deli. I hoped the broth would kick the last of Jonathon's stomach bug. My mother was standing in front of the open freezer, holding a bag of frozen baby carrots in one hand and a cigarette in the other. She turned quickly when she heard my footsteps on the linoleum.

"Valentine." She said my name like a discovery. I noticed the clarity in her voice, and, upon closer inspection, in her eyes, too. She was sober. Completely sober.

"Hi." I looked at the carrots in her hand. "Are you…making dinner?"

She looked down at what she held and stared at the bag for a moment, as though deciding whether she really wanted to cook carrots this evening or if peas might be better. I could remember the two times in my life my mother had cooked dinner, and neither one had been fun for anyone involved. "Yes. No."

"Okayyy…" I walked toward the doorway that connected the kitchen with the living room.

She jumped toward me, blocking the doorway. "Valentine, wait! Just wait. Listen to me, baby. Listen, okay?"

It could've been the fact that she called me baby, or the panic I saw flash across her face. Whatever it was made my lunch of tuna salad lurch dangerously toward my throat. "What?"

"Now, let's just wait a minute, okay?" She looked around like she was waiting for that minute to reveal a way out.

"Mama, what's going on — where's Jonathon?"

It was the magic question. My mother grimaced, then attempted to look carefree. Both expressions scared the hell out of me. She said, in a high-pitched voice, "Val. There was a little accident, no biggie really."

I didn't even hear the rest. I tore through the living room and took the steps two at a time, pausing just long enough to turn the knob before flying through the doorway into his room. He bolted upright in bed and I stopped in my tracks at the sight of his face.

"Oh my God, Jonathon. Oh my God." I knelt next to his bed.

"Hi." He put his arms around my neck and held onto me.

"Oh God, I'm sorry, Jonathon. I'm sorry. Let me see you." He leaned away, and I looked at his battered little face. His left eye was swollen shut, the eyelid and soft skin around it a nasty bruised mess. His bottom lip was extra plump, darkening to purplish red, and I could make out a split where blood was crusted over. I stared at that face, not believing it was my little boy. "Oh, Buddy…"

"I'm okay, Val. I'm okay. Mama said the cold will make my eye feel better. Then I'll be good as new, she said."

I started to cry, trying not to sob loudly, though I wanted to bury my head in the pillow and soak it right through. I didn't even bother wiping the tears and snot, just held Jonathon's skinny body and thought about how I'd finally, finally made the biggest mistake ever.

"Valentine, don't cry." He patted my back the way I pat his when he's upset. "I'm okay, look. Look. I'm okay."

I glanced at his face and bit my lip. He started to smile, but it stretched the torn skin on his lip, and he winced. I'm pretty sure my heart broke right down the middle then. "No, Buddy. No. Tell me. Just tell me what happened."

He looked down and picked at the edges of the tattered afghan that we'd had since I was little. "I said bad things to Ernie," he mumbled.

Yeah, right. I smoothed the hair back away from his eyes. "What bad things, Jonathon?"

"The F-word."

My ears must've been deceiving me. I could count the times he had ever even disagreed with me on one hand. And now he'd dropped the F-bomb on a two hundred and fifty pound alcoholic on the one day he was alone with him in the house?

"Why'd you say that?"

He glared down at the yarn strings on the blanket's fringe. "He made me mad."

This was not my sweet boy. I closed my eyes for a moment and took a breath. "Jonathon, just tell me exactly what happened, okay? I need you to tell me."

My mother's voice came from behind me. "It was just a little run-in. Stop being dramatic, Valentine." I turned to see her still holding a bag of frozen vegetables. She'd chosen the peas. "Jonathon here was mouthing off, Ernie was in one of his moods. We can just chalk it up as a bad day." She eased my brother back against his pillow and laid the bag on his face.

I stared at the thing that used to be my mother. Jonathon peered at me out of the good eye that wasn't beneath cold peas.

"Don't touch him." I stood up and spoke evenly, even though I felt like my body was shaking uncontrollably. "Don't you touch him. Get away."

My mother looked up, baffled, like we'd been having a lovely day at the beach and I'd just announced I wanted to go home. She stood on one side of Jonathon's twin bed, and I stood on the other, facing her. "Valentine, what in the world – "

This, I thought, must be what it feels like to have high blood pressure. My temples suddenly housed a tiny but ambitious drummer boy doing his job far too well. I swallowed hard before I screamed, "GET OUT! DON'T TOUCH HIM! LEAVE RIGHT NOW!"

And with that, I leaned across the bed and shoved my own mother backwards. Actually pushed her, hard. My own hands, the hands I wouldn't even have if it weren't for her, reached out and slammed into her shoulders.

She took two teetering steps backwards. "Valentine!"

"Mama. *Leave*." I sighed heavily, suddenly too tired to move.

She reached down to take Jonathon's hand, but he yanked it away. "Leave me alone," he said, each word deliberate and leaden. He reached for my hand and held it tightly.

My mother held my stare for an eternity, and then turned slowly and walked out of the room. We sat silently, me and Jonathon, until my palm started to get sweaty from the tight grip of his small hand.

Graduation was stressful. I put Jonathon in the bleachers next to Angela's family and didn't hear a word of the ceremony because I was watching to make sure he was there and okay. His face was almost back to normal now, except for a little bit of shading under one eye. He'd grinned at me the whole time, waving every few minutes. When it was my turn to walk up, he stood up on his own and clapped. We stayed only a few minutes after because I wanted to get moving.

Now, I checked the red blinking numbers on the clock that sat on my dresser: 10:17. My purple duffel bag sat on the bed, chock full of...well, of everything. My closet looked like a style-crazy thief had paid a visit, leaving only the never-to-be-worn-again clothing on the floor below the wire hangers. I stripped my bed of all the linens and stuffed the sheets and as many blankets as I could find in two pillow cases. A mustard yellow suitcase sat next to my bag, filled with the contents of Jonathon's drawers. The things I wanted to keep for us, like the few baby pictures we had, his crayons and coloring books, and the rolled-up piece of paper the school had handed me to keep while my diploma was being printed.

I passed by my dresser one last time and picked up the nesting dolls, handling them as carefully as the first day I'd brought them home. I laid them inside Jonathon's suitcase before moving all of the bags into the hall, flicking the light switch down, and shutting my bedroom door.

I walked at a normal pace down the hall. My mother and Ernie had yet to come home from whatever bar they were at tonight, and so I didn't even attempt to be quiet. I opened the door to her bedroom and went right to the small top drawer of her nightstand where she kept her lingerie and bags of potpourri. The smell of her, a mix of flowers and Banker's Club and a certain other bitter scent I never could identify, wafted up, and I reconsidered my plan for a minute before pulling myself together. I slid the drawer open, pushing some bras to the side, and then yanked my hand back like a snake was sitting there. I opened the drawer wider. A gun – small, kind of plump, black – sat there, and it scared the shit out of me.

Why would she keep a gun in this house again? Anger pooled in my chest and crawled up my neck. I shook my head to clear it, and focused on my job. Reaching past the gun, careful not to touch it, I pulled out the small cedar box engraved with her name, a gift from Jonathon's father. It took less than ten seconds to unlatch it and scoop out the roll of money nestled under some pearl necklace, Jonathon's birth announcement, and a silver Zippo lighter embossed with red rose. Inside the box went the letter I'd done in my best handwriting.

Mama,

I love you so much.

I'm taking him away from here, Mama. Somewhere else, where he can have a real chance. No one should be hurt like he was, Mama. I know that somewhere in you, you know this too. Do you remember when we snuck into the Holiday Inn when they were having breakfast time? Remember how we filled our backpacks with muffins and bagels and little boxes of Frosted Flakes, and you took me all along the sidewalks in Santa Cruz, and we passed out one or two things each to the hobos who sat on benches or just the ground? When I asked why we were giving all the food away to strangers, you told me that sometimes people hurt so bad on the inside they can't even help themselves get better. I think you're one of those people now, Mama. And I wish I could just hand you a blueberry muffin and make it all better, but I can't. So I'm doing what I know I can do. I'm taking him away, to be safe.

I love you, Mama. I love you.

Love, Your Valentine

p.s. I took the money to help us. I took the car to get us out of here. I took Jonathon because I love him too much to keep him in this place. Please don't call the police about the car. If you do, I'm going to have to tell them about Ernie, and then they'll take Jonathon away from me and you both. I'm being his family now.

I shut the drawer and looked up to see Jonathon standing in the doorway in blue cotton pajamas, holding his stuffed giraffe, Lisa, in one hand, his pillow tucked under the other arm.

"All set, Buddy?"

He nodded, face somber.

"Okay then, let's do it." I pushed up, palms against my knees and stood, went over and ruffled his hair. "You sure Lisa is the only thing you want to take? We can fit whatever you want."

"I'm sure."

"You can bring a couple other stuffed animals, if you want."

"No, it's okay. They can stay with Mama. In case she needs someone to snuggle at night in her bed."

I suddenly couldn't swallow. But there was no more time for second guessing now. I thought for a moment of the dark red suitcase in my mother's closet, a piece of my childhood that felt warm to me. I had always waited until she was passed out to open it quietly, tucked deep into a closet or behind a wall of junk in a nook somewhere. It had pretty clothes in it. Clothes that would never have been my mother's. I would put on the dresses and the scarves and dance around in them, folding them back up carefully before rezipping the suitcase. Sometimes the sweet flowery smell would linger on me for hours afterward. A part of me wanted to take the whole thing with me, but it was just one more piece of this life we didn't need to drag along.

"Well, okay then, Buddy. Let's go," I said.

He followed me down the stairs, carrying one of the pillowcases, and I stepped outside the house into the perfect June night air. I shut the front door and put my key under the mat. It was just a spare now. We walked out to the driveway, and I opened the trunk of the nine-year-old white Mercury. I stuffed everything in, except for a red LunchMate cooler that held salami sandwiches on rolls, Doritos, Reese's Peanut Butter Cups, Capri Suns, and some other favorites of Jonathon's.

I slammed the trunk shut, then got in the driver's side. Jonathon was already seat-belted into the passenger seat, clutching Lisa.

I turned the key and thanked someone that, for as much as it looked like a piece of shit, the car ran alright.

"You be my navigator, okay?"

I saw a little spark of brightness in his eyes. "And you'll be the pilot?"

"Yup."

He smiled. "Does the navigator get to push the buttons on the radio?"

"Of course. What kind of navigator would you be if you didn't do that?"

He laughed. "Maybe a not good one?"

"Nah, you're the best probably in the whole world."

He grinned, shrugged kind of conceitedly. "Maybe." That made me laugh. He cracked me up sometimes.

Jonathon poked decisively at the buttons on the radio, pausing only slightly before settling on an Elvis song. I put the car in reverse and pulled out of the driveway.

Chapter 4

W e'd very nearly made the Nevada state border by two a.m. By then, the neon-orange glare of the gas warning light forced me to pull into a Shell. If you've ever driven at night for a long distance without stopping, you know how your eyes feel like old wool socks by the time you finally take a break and blink. I pulled next to the pump and turned the car off, blinking gratefully.

Jonathon, noble navigator that he was, had pooped out around midnight and was curled up on the reclined passenger seat. I'd untied his sneakers and pulled them off. He opened his eyes a bit and mumbled, "We there, now?"

I tucked Lisa into the crook of his arm and whispered, "No, Buddy. Not yet."

He pulled his knees toward his chest. "When will we be there?"

"Not for a little while."

"Where, Val?"

"Where what?"

He opened his eyes again. "Where's *there*?"

I stared at him for a moment. "Home, Jonathon. A new home."

He smiled. "A new one with just you and me?"

"Yeah, Buddy. And Lisa. Don't forget Lisa."

He kissed her neck and squeezed her tight. "Oh, I didn't forget you, Lisa."

"I'm going to buy some gas, okay? I'll be right back."

"'Kay." He yawned, nestling back to sleep.

I grabbed the loop of wire connected to what used to be the door handle. If you didn't pull on it just right, you had to climb out the passenger door. It had taken me a long time to master, but I'm proud to say I hadn't had to climb across the stick shift for nearly five months.

The sign on the pump read, *Please pay with Card-O-Matic or Pre-Pay inside* so I walked into the square, brightly lit building. The guy behind the counter was playing some war game on a laptop. When I walked up he turned his head toward me but kept his eyes on the screen. He had absolutely nasty green hair spiked up to ungodly heights and a gold hoop in one eyebrow. I'm pretty sure he had the beginning of a beard but then again it could've just been all the acne playing tricks on my eyes.

"Hi." I had to start somewhere.

He tapped a key and the noises ended. "Hey." He grinned, revealing teeth that seemed to be wearing little yellow velvet jackets.

I looked down at the lottery tickets under the glass and tried not to breathe in what I expected to be putrid air. "Um, can I get a fill-up at pump four?" I handed him a twenty.

"Sure. Will that be all?"

"Yeah, thanks. I'll be back for my change."

He nodded absently and eyed his laptop.

I stood by the car and held the nozzle in, waiting for the click. $20 flew by. Then $30. Then $35. Finally at $37.44 the shut-off click came. I couldn't believe my eyes. Forty dollars on gas? I peeked in the window at Jonathon sleeping soundly, then went back into the gas station.

The guy had taken advantage of the Slurpee machine and was now staring at something on his screen, helping the drink live up to its name. I pulled another twenty-dollar bill out of my envelope and handed it to him.

He smirked. "Fillin' a gas tank on twenty bucks. Haha. That's a good one. What do you drive? A lawnmower? Haha." His laugh was a cross between a chimp's hoot and an asthmatic's wheeze.

"Yeah, right. Thanks." Ugh.

He took another cherry-red slurp. "Hope you're not goin' too far, gas prices the way they are."

"Actually, yeah. I am going far...I think."

"Oh yeah? Where you headed?"

"Massachusetts." It just popped out. The name sounded pretty nice though.

"You're driving all the way east?" He leaned to the side and looked out at my car. "By yourself?"

I pretended it was absolutely the most normal idea in the world. "Yup." I relaxed my face, trying to look casual, and paged through the first thing I got my hands on.

"You need that map?" He nodded toward the book I was holding. "It's a U.S. road map. All the states. You probably do need it." The hooting laugh came again.

I probably did. Now that I was going to Massachusetts, yeah, road maps were sounding pretty good. I handed it over and he scanned it. I pretty much choked on my own saliva when the register blinked $23.99. I did a quick mental tally. If gas was going to be forty bucks a pop, all the way to the East Coast…no. No road map. I didn't even know if I could afford food at the rate I was going.

"Um, sorry. No thank you. I really don't need it, actually." I turned to walk away.

The boy squinted at me. "Yeah, you do. Trust me, right around Nebraska in the middle of nowhere, you are gonna be like, 'God damn I wish I listened to that punk at that gas station and got the freakin' map.'"

I smiled. "No. Thank you, though."

He stuffed the book in a plastic bag with the red block letters THANK YOU spaced across it. "Here."

I sighed. Clearly, it was time to just suck up my pride. "No. I really don't want it, no thank you. I can't, I don't have enough…I mean, it's more than I thought it would be."

He shrugged. "Yeah. The old man has no mercy when it comes to prices around here. Good thing I do the inventory." He held the bag out. "Go on. Have a safe trip. Send me a post card or something."

I thought briefly of what Angela would say about this guy asking me to write to him from another state. But then I took the bag and smiled wider. People surprise me sometimes. Once in a while, anyway. "Thank you. Thank you so much."

He shrugged again, and I pushed out the glass doors to the car. Jonathon didn't even stir as I started the engine again and pulled back onto the highway.

We drove 'til Nebraska. I was nodding off at the wheel and considering how my drowsy driving was not protecting Jonathon any more than being at home. I eyed up the signs for the Howard Johnson, next exit. I glanced down at my purse, wedged between console and seat. Home to all the money I owned. We could afford it. It would be worth it. I flipped my blinker on and pulled off at the exit.

"Are we there?" Jonathon's sleepy murmur caught me off guard.

"Stopping at a hotel, Buddy. Doesn't that sound like a good idea?"

"How come?" He sat up a little and looked out the window. "Are we on a vacation like Brandon went on with his mom and dad?"

"Not really…I'm just sleepy. Hotels have cozy beds." I passed the Denny's and pulled into the adjacent parking lot.

"Does it have a pool?" He now looked fully awake, and I was thinking about how I wished he would be as tired as I felt at the moment. "Does it have a ice machine that lets me fill a little bucket up? Brandon said that they give you an ice bucket and there's a machine that you just, like, push the bucket into and it fills up. Every time." He sat up taller and grinned at the prospect.

I rubbed my eyes. "I don't know. Let's go take a look." I climbed out of the car, and my ass almost fell off. I had forgotten how to straighten my legs. I imagined myself walking into the hotel in the crouched driving position, hands jutted out in front of me at ten o'clock and two o'clock. Or, as the trip had progressed, just at six.

Jonathon, on the other hand, had just slept soundly for roughly fourteen hours, and had plenty of energy for him and the rest of the hotel occupants. I held his hand as he bounced across the parking lot, past a grimy-looking in-ground pool surrounded by a couple of broken plastic lounge chairs. "We get to go swiiiimmmming," he sang out.

Even the lounge chairs looked inviting at this point. I could barely imagine having the energy to walk up to the room. Swimming was the absolute last thing on my mind.

Jonathon grinned up again, still bouncing.

The lobby was a polyester-blend heaven on earth. Air-conditioned to the point of frigidity, familiar in the same way that a McDonald's, no matter where you are, always cures homesickness for a little while. We walked to the desk. A woman with platinum-blonde hair and two-inch black-as-night roots, cut into a blunt bob reaching just to the chin, greeted us. She wore no eye makeup but her cheeks looked like someone had colored perfect circles of red onto them. Her mouth was painted messily in a thick abhorrent purple. Her black nametag read *Carol*.

"Hello. What can I do for you?" She smiled. Two front teeth struggling to free themselves from her mouth, jutting out past her bottom lip.

"Hi. I need a room for one night." I smiled back, glad to be talking to someone other than myself, not just silently in my own head.

She kept the buck-toothed smile in place and glanced at Jonathon. "Are you two on vacation with your mom and dad?" She spoke in a high-pitched, syrupy sweet voice that could've been directed at Jonathon if it weren't for the direction of her eyes, still staring at me.

I put my shoulders back and tried to imagine Miss Bloomfield's posture if she were in this moment instead of me. "No. Actually, we're traveling together. The two of us. We've been on the road for quite some time," I sighed dramatically and plowed on. "And we would really like to just kick back for a while and relax."

"Mm-hm." She nodded. The smile lessened a bit. "Alrighty. Well a room with two double beds, television, air conditioning, microwave, and other amenities will be..." She tapped her fingers on the computer keyboard, looking up what I presume was absolutely nothing, "Sixty-nine forty-nine."

She put the smile back on.

I opened my purse and pulled out four twenties, wincing on the inside. Seventy dollars for a room with two crappy beds and itchy blankets? Still, the thought of lying down was too tempting. The thought of a hot shower was controlling my hand. I handed her the cash.

"Oh. Cash. Okay. Well, I will need to see your ID, too."

"You need my ID because I'm paying cash?"

I was suddenly too irritated to function. Jonathon looked up at the tone of my voice.

Carol smiled wider. Her voice took on the sugary quality again, as she spoke slowly, tilting her head to one side. "No, sweetie. I need your ID to check to make sure that you are of age to rent a hotel room by yourself."

News to me. Here I was, being too big for my britches, as my mother would've said, thinking I look older than I really am. That didn't matter, though. I'd turned 18 months ago, and my driver's license proved it. I opened my purse and handed her my license. Take that, sucka.

She nodded and handed it back. "Sorry. You must be twenty-one years of age or older to purchase a hotel room without your parent or guardian."

Jonathon's voice broke through my disbelief. "Val, I have to go pee." He looked up with the eyes of a boy who had already held it for as long as he could.

Carol came around the desk, and knelt down in front of him. "The potty is over there, sweetie. See it? You go right on ahead." She waited 'til he had closed the door behind him before standing up and brushing her hands over the front of her tacky zig-zag patterned skirt. "So, you and your little brother traveling far?"

"Yes." I tried to focus my gaze on her eyes instead of that bruised-looking mouth. "Going to Massachusetts. We have family there. My aunt and uncle." Where was this coming from? My *aunt and uncle*? "Listen, we really need to get a good night's sleep. Jonathon...he is so tired. He can't sleep too good in the car, what with his...scoliosis. Sometimes, it hurts him so much he can hardly get a good night's sleep in a comfy bed, much less –"

"Cut the bullshit."

I stopped at the sharp voice, absolutely devoid of sweetness now, blaring from its fuchsia prison. "I don't want to hear your sob story. I don't care. You have money, you can stay." She walked around the counter again.

"Thanks..." I tentatively handed over the twenties again.

She let out a single "ha." It wasn't a laugh. Just a single monotone syllable. "No." She pointed to my purse. "You have *money*, you can stay."

At that moment, Jonathon came out of the bathroom. And I finally understood what she meant. Sometimes people surprise me, but most times, they're just as sucky as I expect.

So we got back in the car. Me gripping the steering wheel, seething. Greedy, selfish bitch. Who the hell took advantage of a young girl and her little brother? I mean, didn't we look helpless? Didn't we look like orphans? Who did that to orphans? Bitch.

Jonathon was looking out the window at the golden arches in the distance. I hated how he handled disappointment – like it was never a surprise, like he didn't even think anything would go right in the first place. Sometimes I wished he would just throw a fit or something.

"Can we get an Egg McMuffin?" he asked quietly.

"Yeah. Next exit." Why the hell not? I'll load up on coffee. It'll be fine.

I pulled into the parking lot, got Jonathon settled with breakfast, and watched him through the window as I poured quarters into the pay phone outside.

It rang twice and then I heard Angela's heavenly, soothing voice.

"Where the *fuck* are you, Val?"

"Calm down, Angie. I'm in Nebraska."

"*Nebraska*? You're in fucking Nebraska." She was silent on the other end for a long moment. When she spoke again, her voice was full of tears. "What are you doing in Nebraska, Valentine?"

"I ran away."

"You ran away. You ran and didn't tell me you were running? You're a billion miles away and you didn't tell me, *me*, that you were even leaving." Her voice cracked, and I couldn't believe my ears. Ange is really compassionate about animals. Sometimes she cries at the SPCA commercials, when the dogs are looking at the camera and are all scruffy, and I laugh at her. But when it comes to life and humans and other stuff, she's really tough as nails. So this was weird.

"Don't cry, Angie. I had to take him away." I listened to her sob on the other end. "She would've ruined him. He's so little, he still has a really good chance."

I was crying then, too.

"Val." She stopped, and I prepared myself for a lecture, but then she was crying again, too hard to talk.

"My mother would've wrecked his whole life, Angela. She would've just…"

"She's dead, Valentine."

I couldn't find my voice to ask what she meant. To ask *who*.

"Val?"

I gasped, and suddenly realized I wasn't breathing in or out anymore.

"She threw herself in front of a train. Last night. The police were looking everywhere for you…they needed…they needed someone to ID the body. Your mom. Her *body*."

One word leaked out. "Ernie?"

The silence was unbearable.

"*Ernie?*" I screamed at the receiver.

"His wife came to your house. She followed them home from the bar two nights ago and saw where he's been going. She – the wife, I mean – came to catch him. The front door was open and – she found him. Said he was shot once in the chest." She took a breath in and lowered her voice. "Twice in the face. She called the police. They had a woman who – they didn't know who it was, but she was found on the tracks. It was on T.V. I saw it on *television*, Val. They couldn't find you. They couldn't fucking find you, I didn't know where you were. God." She starts to hyperventilate over the watery sound of crying.

"I'm right here, Angela. It's okay. I'm right here."

Jonathon was popping a hashbrown into his mouth. His Happy Meal toy was a NASCAR racecar that he zoomed around the table.

"Come home, Valentine."

"Angela, I can't come home. I can't come back."

"I need you. Please, please come back."

It did occur, in case you're wondering, how odd it was that my mother had just killed her boyfriend and herself, and that my best friend was telling me how much she needed *me*, instead of vice versa. In her Angela way, though, she knew it was vice versa just as much as I did.

Chapter 5

C an we go *now*?" Jonathon whined. I sat behind the wheel, and he fidgeted in the passenger seat, bored with his Matchbox toy, uncomfortable from sitting still for the last hour with no view but the dumpsters behind the McDonalds.

I couldn't tell him. I couldn't even tell me. What did this mean? What did the words mean? I suddenly thought back to when I was nine years old, and the concept of death meant something to me for the first time. I wouldn't go to sleep alone anymore. I made my mother lie by me until I fell asleep, and even then I wanted to make sure that she didn't leave me, so I wrapped a few strands of her hair around my fingers, thinking that when she got up, it would tighten and pull, and alert me to her escape. She always outsmarted me, unwrapping it carefully before getting up, and in the morning, I never remembered her not being there.

One night she had a visitor, a man, and when I asked her to lie with me she said it would be rude to her guest to leave him alone for so long.

I'd cried. "Please, Mama, just for a little bit."

She looked at me for a moment, and then shut my door gently and sat on the bed next to me, pulling the blankets up to my chin. "Valentine, tell me what's wrong at night now. Why you won't go to sleep on your own anymore."

I wanted to blurt it all out, but didn't even know why myself. "I'm afraid you'll die," I said, eyes burning with tears. "I'll wake up in the morning, and you'll... be dead."

She didn't roll her eyes or scoff. She was always understanding in that way. If one good thing can be said about my mom, it's that she never made me feel stupid or small. Instead, she nodded gently. "I see," she said. "Why're you afraid I'll die?"

I snuffled the tears loudly. "Delia Brown's dad died in a car accident on the way to his work last week, and now Delia doesn't come into school anymore. And she said her mom is in the hospital." I thought, *You could die too,* and fresh tears burned my eyes and overflowed onto my cheeks.

My mother reached over and pulled an undershirt from my top drawer and wiped my tears with it. "Ah, I see, Jellybean. You're afraid I'll die in a car accident, too?"

"No. It's not that." I thought of the long night, and the ten feet that separated my storage-closet-turned-bedroom from her room. "I'm afraid you'll kiss me goodnight, and then in the morning…when I wake up…*you* won't wake up." I cried even harder, and she hugged me tight against her. We sat like that for a minute.

"Valentine, let me ask you this…do you think you'll go on a rocket ship to the moon, and walk around collecting moon rocks?"

This took me off guard. For a few moments I stopped crying and thought about it. "No…" I said slowly, considering the dim possibility of this.

"Hm. What about going down into the ocean, *allllll* the way to the bottom, and collecting ocean rocks?"

I smiled a little, considering that too. "No…I don't think so."

She smiled brilliantly. "No? Hm…well, what about climbing to the tippy-top of the most gigantic pyramid you could find in Egypt? Do you think you'll do that?"

I laughed at the silliness of me, a skinny nine-year-old girl, climbing to the top of a pyramid. Pictured myself waving from the little point on top. "No, I don't think I can do that."

She kissed me three noisy kisses and squeezed me tight. "Well, I'll tell you what. There's a better chance of you doing all three of those crazy things in *one* afternoon, all by yourself, than of me ever dying at night."

I stopped smiling at the mention of her dying at night, but then thought about what she was saying. I could never do all three of those things in one afternoon. Which meant that, if I could never do them, then she could never die in the middle of the night. For the first bedtime in weeks I felt my stomachache subside.

"Okay." I smiled at her.

"Plus, you know, mommies don't leave their little girls. And since I'm a mommy, and you're a little girl…I think you're stuck with me for a while." She tickled me, and I screamed and flailed around, laughing.

She tucked me tighter under the covers and kissed my forehead. "Goodnight, silly. I love you too much."

"Love you too much," I said, snuggling into my bed, feeling safe and happy. I fell asleep before the smell of her perfume even had a chance to fade.

And now she was all gone.

I looked at Jonathon, who was looking at me, waiting. I couldn't tell him. So I started the car, and got back on the highway, going back exactly the way we'd left. I was no longer sleepy.

When we cross over the California border, Jonathon finally notices.

"Where are we?" he asks, looking outside. "Is this Alabama?"

I sigh. I don't even know where he got the idea of that particular state. "No."

"Oh. Cuz...Alabama looks just like home, kind of, I thought."

"This isn't Alabama, Jonathon."

We're two hours from the driveway in front of the house where my mom no longer lives. I stopped once more to call Angela, a few miles before we hit California, to tell her I was almost back. She wasn't crying anymore.

"My mom is so worried about you guys, Val." Then she'd stopped, because, after all, I have no mother to worry about me anymore, and she knew she had just pointed that out.

Mama didn't worry about me before this, I keep telling myself. I keep telling myself life will be no different than if Jonathon and I had succeeded in running away and starting up a new one together. She would've died someday, anyway. And we, being far, far away, would never have known at that moment. So someday is simply today, and we now know. Or I do. It's exactly the same.

"What is it?" Jonathon is staring from the passenger seat.

I glance sideways. "What is what?"

"This state we're in now."

So this is how it's going to be forever. No getting around it. I can't even have a damn minute to myself to think. For a moment, I want to just snap at him, to yell "SHUT UP!" as loud as I can. I picture myself swerving, slamming on the brakes, jumping out of the car, and screaming my head off.

"California," I say calmly.

After a couple minutes of silence go by, I sneak a peek. He's casually looking out the window, hugging Lisa. When he sees me turn, he turns too, and smiles, that sweet little boy smile that he's been giving me since he was six months old.

"Okay?" I ask.

He smiles again. "Yeah. It's okay, Val. I missed Mommy too."

It feels like someone punched me in the stomach. I look straight ahead again and nod. If I talk, I'll cry. If I look at him, I'll cry. I just nod.

The next two hours go by too quickly. When I see the One Stop Mart that marks the entrance to our neighborhood, I keep going. I drive on to the one house where I know I'll feel safe. When I park in the driveway, Jonathon jumps out of the car and runs up to the door, which opens before he can even knock.

Angela's mother, Kate, picks him up in a hug and squeezes tight. She's crying, holding him against her and looking out. At me, still sitting in the driver's seat, my car door shut. I shake my head, no. She nods, looks into his face and smiles, saying something I can't hear.

He yells, "Yeah!"

They turn and go inside, probably to eat cookies and play with Kate's finches, a thing Jonathon loves to do.

I see Angela come to the doorway. She walks down, opens the car door, and gets in the passenger seat. When she finally looks up and meets my eyes, I realize how incredibly insane this situation is. She leans across the middle and hugs me tight.

"My hair smells pretty nasty," I say.

"Yeah. It's okay, though. I've smelled worse." She lets go of me and sits back in the seat. "The car smells like feet and burritos."

"Five year old boys are smellier than you'd imagine," I say, drawing circles in the dust on the dashboard.

"Sure. Blame it on the kid. It's probably you."

I start to cry. The tears roll hotly down my face, which scrunches up. Angela leans over and pushes my head onto her shoulder. "Oh, it's okay, Val. I love your smelly ass."

I smile in spite of the world crashing down outside of this car. "She's really dead, Ange?"

"Yeah."

She takes my hand, and we sit like that for I don't even know how long.

When I walk into the Scarpelli house, the smell of garlic and oil paint overpowers me. I love this smell. The living room is beautiful, decorated right down to the little glass artsy ornaments on the coffee table, and always kept impeccable. The kitchen is big and roomy and the appliances are all black. The house looks like someone from *Better Homes and Gardens* comes in regularly to keep everyone on task.

But I know better. The basement is Kate's studio, and at any given time it looks like a tornado just hit in there. Paint cans sit everywhere, splattered canvases are propped up on every wall. Some lie flat on the floor. Jars of brushes and weird wooden stencils are scattered all over the place. But Kate's paintings are nowhere to be found in the upstairs part of the house. When she graduated from the University of Maine with a B.F.A. in studio art, the university galleries signed her on for a one-year contract to display her work. That turned into a national thing, and now her paintings, all of women and little girls, are in galleries from here to New York. She flies out to Manhattan and Boston and Chicago every other month. Jennifer Aniston saw one of her paintings at a gallery in Syracuse and bought it on the spot. Kate's pretty famous, but nobody would ever know that from the way she's sitting at the kitchen table now with my little brother, dunking Chips Ahoy in milk and sharing the mushed cookies with him and the three birds that are scuttling around the tabletop.

Jonathon holds out a crumb. "Here, Dante, take some, it's good." The bird scoots closer and takes the crumb from Jonathon's fingers. My brother looks up at me. "See Dante? He eats cookies, too."

Kate turns around and sees me. She wipes her mushy-cookies-and-milk hands on her gorgeous linen pants and stands up. Jonathon watches as she puts her arms around me and quietly says, "We missed you so much. The spare room is made up, fresh sheets, everything."

Jonathon asks the start of questions I do not want to answer. "Are we having a sleepover at Kate and Angela's?"

Kate looks at me expectantly, but I just can't do it. Not yet. So instead, I take the cowardly, easy way out, and feel just a little better. "Would you like to have a sleepover for a few nights? Think you'd have fun?"

I already know the answer, but he whoops anyway. "I want to! I want to stay here!"

Good, I think, *because you have no other choice. You're an orphan now.*

"Okay then, I guess we'll stay for a few days," I say, with a smile that feels like an open wound and a voice that sounds as sweet as funeral flowers.

Kate walks into the living room, looking back to tell me to follow her. I already know, and don't want to hear it.

I plop down on the loveseat.

"Valentine."

I stare at my lap before finally looking up. "Kate."

She presses her lips together and crosses her arms. "Val, would you like me to tell him? I can do that, you know. You don't have to bear this alone." She comes over and sits down next to me, covering my hand with her own. "We can do this together. Or you can do it alone. Or I can do it alone. But no matter which way we do it, it needs to be done."

I sigh. "I'll do it."

She nods. I know she's waiting out that awkward silence that hangs when you want to ask a question but also know it just might be the straw that breaks the camel's back.

She pats my hand and gives in. "When, Valentine?"

Jonathon squeals in the kitchen, then erupts into hysterical laughter. "Val! Val, come here! Kate!" He laughs too hard to talk. "DANTE IS EATING MY EAR!"

Kate smiles at me, kisses my forehead, and goes into the kitchen. I hear her laughing with Jonathon as I sit on the loveseat and think about when, exactly, will be the right time to tell a five-year-old that his mother is never, ever coming back.

I climb the stairs up to the spare room, which is not at all like most people's spare rooms, with a twin bed pushed against the wall and some extra mismatched quilts. This one has a king-size bed and dressers and a full closet. The sheets are so soft that when I lie down and close my eyes, I feel like maybe dying wouldn't be so terrible after all. Maybe it feels just this peaceful and wonderful to finally, finally give in.

Chapter 6

I slept a sick, deep sleep. I dreamed my mother was knocking on the door to the Scarpellis' spare bedroom, but every time I got up to answer, the knocking stopped and every time I opened the door, she wasn't there. I don't even know how I knew it was her on the other side. When I wake up, it's black sky outside, and the room is the kind of dark that makes you feel like your entire day is gone. That perhaps there won't *be* another day coming.

I stand and stagger downstairs. My body feels shaky, heavy. The stove light glows green in the kitchen, and the clock on the microwave says 4:47. In the morning? It's five in the *morning*? I didn't even put Jonathon to bed. I slept for twelve hours.

I open the fridge and pull out leftover barbecued chicken. I sit at the table and take a messy bite. Somewhere upstairs a door opens, and five seconds later Angela appears in underwear and bra and a giant, fuzzy pair of duck slippers.

"Sexy," I mumble, mouth full of chicken.

She looks at my gooey hands and face and smiles. "Likewise."

"Can I have some juice?"

"Apple, orange, or cranberry?"

"Cranberry."

She pulls two glasses down from the cupboard and drops ice cubes in both. She pours half-glasses of cranberry and looks over one shoulder at me. "Vodka?"

I consider my day and the fact that this is technically breakfast. "Yeah."

"Yeah," she says, agreeing, and fills the crystal glasses the rest of the way with Grey Goose. She plops down in the chair next to me and slides my glass across the table.

I take a big gulp, clenching my teeth as I swallow. "Brutal," I take another sip.

"Well, it is breakfast, you alky."

"How was Jonathon? Did your mom have a hard time putting him to bed?"

She reaches for a drumstick and takes a bite. "Val, this is Jonathon we're talking about. He basically flew himself up to the Blue Room with his little angel wings and was sleeping within minutes."

The Scarpelli house has four spare bedrooms, each one decorated in a main color. Jonathon likes the blue room, and Kate knows that, so she purposely put coloring books and stuffed animals in there for whenever he comes.

"So." Angela takes another gulp of her drink.

"So I'll tell him in the morning." God, it *is* morning. I wince at the thought and take another sip.

She nods and stares at me over the rim of her glass. "Do you want my mom to do it?"

"Yes. But, unfortunately, it seems that what I want and what is currently happening in my life are two different things. So…I'll tell him in the morning." I don't want any more chicken. In fact, all of a sudden the chicken seems absolutely repulsive, and I want to get the sticky sauce off my hands and face immediately. I beeline for the sink and wash furiously.

"Whoa, Val."

"What?"

"I didn't realize chicken carried the plague. My bad."

I dry my hands and sit back down. "Why are you up?"

"Why are you?" she counters.

"Well. I just slept for twelve hours. I was worried about Jonathon. And my mother is dead."

She nods and swallows the last of her drink. I do the same.

"So, it's easier if you keep saying it aloud?"

"Maybe. Yeah. I think so."

"Because then it doesn't seem like some weird, terrible dream-slash-joke that might be a huge giant mistake."

"Right."

"So, just keep saying it then. Whenever. To me, or whoever."

"Okay. I will."

"Okay."

"My mother's dead."

"Yeah."

We leave the glasses and the chicken on the table, and I follow Angela back to her room, a gorgeous master bedroom with cathedral ceilings and skylights. I peel off jeans and shirt and crawl into her bed. She pulls the covers over us, and I feel like I haven't really slept any of those twelve hours after all.

When I wake up the second time, the room is brightly lit and Angela is still sound asleep next to me, hair spilled out across the pillow. I get up and yank on a pair of her shorts and a tank top, pull my hair into a ponytail, and head downstairs. I glance in the mirror as I head down the hall, but really, does it matter how I look when I tell him? Will he for the rest of his life have a nervous breakdown whenever he sees a ponytail?

I don't know.

It's quiet downstairs. I listen for Jonathon's voice but don't hear anything. The kitchen table is clear of our crack-of-dawn snack, and a vase of fresh flowers sits in the center. I walk out the sliding glass doors and onto the stone patio. Kate is lying on the lounge chair in her bathing suit. Jonathon's head pops up out of the pool. He is wearing green goggles and holding a neon-pink ring triumphantly.

"Val!" He waves crazily, then dives back under.

Kate turns when she hears him call me, and smiles. Her oversized white sunglasses sit on her head and she squints for a moment, then pulls them down. "Good morning, Sleeping Beauty."

"Morning." I sit on the chair next to her and lean back. "What time is it?"

"Oh, just a little after noon."

"Wow, I'm sorry. I've basically abandoned Jonathon with you for the last twenty-four hours. I never sleep this late."

"I know, honey, and it's no big deal at all. Besides, after that little nightcap, I'm sure you girls conked out as soon as your heads hit the pillow." She grins, but shakes a finger at me.

Sometimes I forget she's someone's mom. "Oh yeah. Sorry about that. It was all Angela's idea."

She laughs. "Somehow that is totally believable."

We're quiet for a minute.

"I guess I'll do it when he's done swimming," I say.

She nods and reaches over to hold my hand. "Whatever you want to do. If you want me to sit there with you guys, I'll sit there. If you want to be alone, I'll leave the house to you for a while. Whatever you want, honey."

I must've thought about this in my sleep because I know exactly what I want. "No, I want you and Angela to sit there with us."

She looks surprised but agrees immediately. "Sure, sure."

"I think it's important to have people with him, safe people, who love him. That way, you know…it's not like that's *it* for him, like him and me are the only two people left in the world. He could feel that way, you know? Like his entire world is crushed and we're the only two left trying to survive."

She squeezes my hand. "It'd be easy to feel like that. So, we'll sit with you, and then he'll know we're here all the time. That it will never just be him and you alone. That family isn't just people who share the same blood."

I link my fingers in hers and think about how that is exactly the right thing for a mom to say.

When Jonathon is finally tired of swimming, three hours later, he dries off. Then we sit at the patio table and eat watermelon chunks Kate cuts up for us. Angela sits across, and Jonathon next to me, and when Kate comes out with a tray of peach iced tea and sits down on the other side, I feel like it's now or never.

"Jonathon." I take a breath in.

He looks up with watermelon juice on his chin. "Huh?"

"Jonathon, I have to tell you something. And I just want you to know that me and Kate and Angela are right here and that you're okay. Alright?"

He stops eating watermelon and looks at me. "'Kay."

I pretend like I'm in front of the class giving a speech on something like the Salem witch trials or North American environmental risks.

I steel myself. "Mommy had an accident and she got hurt very, very badly."

Jonathon doesn't say anything. He doesn't blink. I reach across the table and hold his hand.

"She got so hurt that she…she…she's not *here* anymore."

He looks at me like I'm completely crazy. Then he says, simply, "Well, this is Kate's house. Mommy has to be at the doctor's."

I shake my head. How am I not crying? "No, Jonathon. No. She was too hurt even for the doctor. She died. She…she's dead."

He sits like a stone, staring at me, his hand limp in my own tightened squeeze. He looks at Kate and then over at Angela. Like it's a joke, and he's making sure we all aren't in on it. God, do I know how that feels. We sit in silence, like statues of people enjoying a summer day.

He won't be able to eat watermelon now, I think. *He won't be able to swim without having panic attacks. Oh my God. This was a horrible way to do it.*

Kate speaks up first, thank God. "Jonathon, would you like me to hold you on my lap?"

He looks at her for a second, then shakes his head. "No thank you, Kate."

Then he opens his mouth and howls. Cries that echo through the upscale neighborhood, so imprinting themselves in my mind, that five hours later, when he's tucked into bed, I still hear them rumbling in my ears, the sound of someone who doesn't know what else to do but scream.

I sit downstairs on the cream-colored couches that seem too nice to use, watching television without even knowing what I'm seeing.

"The secret life of sea anemones, huh?" Angela plops down next to me. She squints at the television, despite it having a fifty-inch screen. "Are they…is that some anemone love going on right there, is that what I'm seeing?"

"They're floating in the water current, perv."

She holds out a bowl of pistachios, and I take a handful. They calm my nerves, for some reason, those little nuts. I crunch down on the first one. "How's Jonathon?"

"Sound asleep. There's something to be said for the way crying makes you so exhausted you actually conk right out."

"Yeah. It's like the only way your body can protect you from your mind."

She nods. "Yeah."

"Your mom told me about how they need a relative to ID her." I swallow some pistachios too fast then, and they stick in my throat where apparently no saliva was available to help them down. I cough, swallowing hard to clear them.

"Are you going to go?"

"Who else, Angela? Who else can go identify my mother? There isn't anybody but me."

"Are you going to, though?"

I stare at the sea anemones billowing on the screen. "Yeah. I have to."

"Do you want me to come with you?"

"Yeah. But I want you to stay with Jonathon more. He needs somebody to be with him tomorrow."

"My mom will go in with you."

"*In* in with me?"

"Sure, if you want. I know she will."

I think about this. Should she be there with me? Come in to see my mother dead. But what if she looks cold and freaky? What if her eyes are open? I've always hated that – eyes being open on dead people on TV. I can handle dead people with their eyes closed because it looks like they're sleeping. But the dead, open ones…it haunts me at night.

"What if her eyes are open?" I look away from the anemones at Angela.

She stares at me. "What do you mean?"

"I mean, what if I go in and see her lying there with her eyes open, and I totally freak out? What if her eyes give me bad dreams for my whole life?"

My mother's eyes are green, not brown like mine. They used to have a sparkly quality to them when I was little. When she was laughing, they would change just a little to look even more sparkly. "What if they're staring wide open?"

Angela reaches over to the remote and clicks the television off. "Valentine."

I get scared because she isn't sounding cynical or sarcastic or ironic or funny at all. She's using a tone of voice that I never wanted to hear coming from Angela's mouth. One that's gentle and calming and scary as hell.

"What?" I whisper.

She brushed the bangs out of her face and then says, calmly, so very calmly, "Valentine, she was hit by a train. She didn't die from a heart attack or something. Her eyes…she's not going to look like she's sleeping. She's not going to be…okay to really look at."

Colors flash in my mind. Just colors. Disgusting red and black and mutilated colors of rotting flesh and blood. I feel my stomach sicken and turn, and wonder if I need to get up and try to make it into the bathroom.

"Oh," I say, digging my fingers into one of the soft pillows.

"I told you, on the phone. I told you that's how it happened." Angela sounds like she's begging me to remember.

I nod quickly. "Yeah, you did. You're right. I just – I forgot, I guess. I forgot."

She takes my hand in hers. "That's okay. Don't feel bad about it. It doesn't matter."

The flashing images make me sicker now. "So. She'll be, um, a mess, then, right? A mess of just…stuff."

Angela shakes her head. "Maybe."

"Then how do I…I mean, how do I identify her? If she's a mess…if she's, oh fuck, she'll be like squished, like something hit on the road. Oh my God."

I throw up all over the cream sofas that really are too nice to even sit on. I throw up until tears run down my cheeks from the force of the heaving and Angela holds my hair back and doesn't even move to get a bag or a bowl or anything to keep me from ruining the sofas. When I'm done, she stands me up and walks us to the bathroom, hands over two fresh towels, and tells me to take a shower, because, "You smell like puke."

It makes me feel better for her to say this, like things are okay. Like she can still say whatever she wants because our lives are still normal. Like I'm a normal girl, sleeping over at my friend's house, just puking from a wild night of partying. And not at all a girl about to see her mother's trainwreck of a corpse.

I shower, wrap my hair in a towel, and go out to survey my vomity mess. "God," I mutter and walk into the kitchen for paper towels. Kate and Angela are sitting at the table there with glasses of wine. Kate pours me one as I walk in.

"Kate. I'm so sorry. All over the couches."

She finishes swallowing some wine and shakes her head, smiling. "No, no. Don't be silly. The cleaners will be here within a half hour. No harm done." She hands me my glass. "Here. Some Pinot will calm you."

I smile. "Whatever happened to warm milk before bedtime?"

She shrugs. "I was never the warm milk kind of mom, I guess. I can take a stab at boiling some, if you'd like." She winks, and I take a sip.

"So," Angela says. "My sister's coming home next weekend. That should be fun."

"Angela," Kate says in a warning tone. "We'll *make* it fun, won't we?" She looks at me. "I thought we could have a spa day. What do you think?"

It feels weird now, planning a spa day, which is one of Angela and Kate's favorite things to do on boring summer days. "Sure. Sounds nice."

Kate nods. "It *will* be. Just us girls. Mani-pedi, facials, a nice, *loooong* massage by a gorgeous guy. Or gal."

Angela smiles encouragingly. "With Penelope being a frigid, know-it-all priss and complaining about the quality of the bottled water."

I laugh. Kate smiles and points one long finger at Angela. "We all have our flaws, Miss Vodka-and-Cranberry-at-four a.m."

Angela presses her lips together and raises her eyebrows at me. "It was Val's idea."

"Hey!" I'm laughing full force now. Too hard, I think. And then suddenly not laughing at all. Kate notices and sets her wine glass down.

"We'll go first thing in the morning to do it, okay? And I will stay with you every second, you understand?"

"Yeah," I agree. Then say what I don't even want to think about: "She's going to be destroyed from the train, isn't she?"

Kate puts a hand over her mouth and leans on one elbow. She doesn't speak for maybe a half a minute, and then says, "I don't know how she's going to look, Valentine. I don't know how bad the accident was, or how fast the train was going..." She closes her eyes. "I don't know how this works, or what the procedure is for identification, but I promise I will find out all of that before we even set foot in there tomorrow morning. Then we'll be as prepared as we possibly can be."

I nod, relieved. "Okay."

She kisses me and Angela both on the forehead, then goes up the stairs. We go to our separate rooms, but after twenty minutes of seeing my mother's cold, wide-open eyes in the dark, I climb out of bed and pad into Angela's room. She scoots over and pulls the quilt back for me. We sleep there all night together, but neither of us really sleeps at all.

I hear Kate's voice all tense and formal, swallowing irritation, as I enter the dining room the next morning. The perfectly-round marble clock with no numbers, only hands, tells me that it's nine-twenty.

"I understand that, but what I am *trying* to do is contact someone who can help prepare me and the daughter for the traumatic responsibility that's been placed upon us. Please get me someone who *can* answer my questions. Thank you. *Thank you.*"

She looks up from her spot at the table with the phone cradled between shoulder and ear, hand poised with a pen over a notebook. She smiles at me. "There's fresh bagels on the counter in the kitchen. Cream cheeses and lox, if you want it. Make yourself one."

I walk into the kitchen and cut myself a bagel. I put it in the double toaster and push the button down. Here's a crazy thing: in your mind, when everyone is alive, and you're okay, and you picture something like this happening (something being, your mother getting killed by a train), you picture the whole world stopping. Picture hearing the news, crying, and then...that's it. No more world. Maybe a few little visions of your grief at a funeral, but then nothing.

Nothing. Yet, here I am prying the lid off the strawberry cream cheese container while my sesame bagel toasts, and that's just how it is. You still eat bagels and you still watch documentaries on sea creatures and you still have to take a shower when your hair smells like throw-up.

I hear Kate's voice again. Then she lowers it, which, of course, only means that I have to listen harder.

She doesn't sound annoyed anymore. "Yes, thank you...I'm a close friend of the family. The daughter and son are staying with me until future arrangements are made. What I want to know is," she lowers her voice a few more notches, "what...*condition* will her mother be in during the identification procedure?"

I spread the cream cheese on one warm bagel half and run the butter knife back and forth, making tiny grooves in the pink.

"Yes, please check, I would be very grateful. I'll wait, take your time." Then, in the same very quiet voice, Kate says, "Valentine?"

I stand still in the kitchen. She calls my name again quietly. I don't answer. I don't want her testing to see if I can hear, and more than that, I don't want her moving somewhere else so I really can't hear at all. I stand on the other side of the wall, my shoulder pressed against it and hold my breath.

"Yes?" She speaks louder now, probably because she thinks I'm on the patio or that I went back upstairs through the other hallway. "I see...yes, yes, I'm just fine, thank you. Well, what can we do instead? I mean, what are our other options? Dental records? Fingerprints? DNA? I mean it's the new millennium, don't you people have some kind of technology for this stuff now?" Her voice cracks.

I put my bagel down and walk into the dining room. She looks up and wipes her eyes quickly. "Yes. I would appreciate you looking into that. I'll wait. Thank you."

She hits a button, and I hear soft music playing on speakerphone. She tries to smile at me.

I sit down on the other end of the long glass table, about ten feet away. "So, is that the place where she's at, or whatever? The police station or the hospital?"

"Yes. It's a morgue, actually." She lets the word hang in the air for a moment. "Val. I'm trying to find a different way to do this. To ID her. The woman there feels that..." She clears her throat and looks at me squarely. "She feels your mother's condition could be very disturbing. She's looking into other possibilities for identification."

The on-hold music plays quietly. I pick at my pinkie nail cuticle and then yank it off. It bleeds. "Okay." I think of blood again, as I watch it seep into the little crack between my nail and my finger. Lots and lots of blood. I plop the bagel down. Don't want another episode like last night. I push the thoughts, the colors, the blood, out of my mind and stare at Kate to calm myself.

She runs her hands through highlighted blonde hair. "Okay. So, we'll know in a few minutes what else we can do."

"Okay."

"Why don't you go take a nice hot bath?" She smiles coaxingly. "I have the most delicious lavender bubble bath. You should go up to my bathroom, run a full tub and put three of those beads under the faucet while it's on. You'll feel amazing afterward. Go on. They're in the top cupboard, right next to the washcloths. Fresh loofahs in the drawer next to the sink."

She looks at me, waiting. And so I do just what she suggests because somehow it's easier for her to do this without me here, and all I want right now is to make the whole thing go away, for all of us.

I run the bathtub, which shouldn't even be called that because it's a four-person Jacuzzi that is beyond wonderful to sit in. I put three of the bath beads in, and watch as the bubbles creep up with the water.

Did my mother take a shower before it happened?

I step into the water. It's a little too hot, but I sit down anyway. The bubbles rise up to my chin. And then, just like that, I'm thinking about being little and taking a bath. How my mother would drain the whole bath except for the tiniest bit of water on the bottom, then let me use the bar of Ivory to soap up the whole tub. Once it was really slimy and slippery, I'd push myself all the way to one side of the bathtub and then use my legs to kick off and glide across to the other end. She'd sit on the toilet and laugh hysterically as I slipped around like a skinned chicken. She always said that. "You look like a little skinned chicken, Valentine." When I'd had my fill of slipping around (which was usually not for a good half hour), she'd stand me up and turn the shower on to wash me off, and then I'd put on my pajamas. I don't know when the last time I did that was, but it had to be before I was big enough to realize that the giant slippery expanse that I was gliding around on was only three feet across.

Someone knocks and I remember the dream of my mother knocking, then disappearing. Kate's head pops around the door. "How's the bubble bath coming along?"

I smile. "Great. Thanks."

She puts the toilet lid down and sits on it. "Well. Here's the scoop, honey. They have no dental records showing for her. Maybe she just didn't like the dentist." She smiles a little smile at me and I feel like I have to at least give her one back. "They did find fingerprint records from the Los Angeles police department and also a police department down in Arizona. However, they can't use those either because…her upper body – her arms and hands – they're not in a condition that allows them to verify prints."

So, she's smushed. Actually smushed into nothing. I turn the faucet on and run cold water into the hot bath. I feel nausea creeping up again, and the cold water calms it a little bit.

Kate takes a deep breath. "So, what they *can* do is ask a family member or a close friend to identify a special mark or scar or mole or something else they made note of while doing the autopsy. The woman said they were only able to find one identifying mark on her body, other than the cesarean scar on her abdomen. Can you think of what that mark is, Val?" She blows out another long breath. "This fucking system is ridiculous, you know that? Absolutely ridiculous that you should even have to deal with this on top of everything else."

I run my wrists under the cold water. "She had a scar on the bottom of her foot. It looked like a sunburst. It was really deep. I used to tell her she needed a matching moon on her other foot."

Kate looks up. "Are you sure it was a scar? Not a birthmark? Scars aren't usually shaped specifically."

"No, a scar. She got it a long time ago. She stepped on a broken sprinkler head that looked like that, round and jagged and symmetrical, and it cut into her foot and left that. I know that scar." I think about how, when I was very little, I wished to have one just like it on my foot so we could match.

"Do you know which foot?"

I pretend I'm sitting on the bed with her, our backs against the headboard, in just our underwear because it was summer time and we didn't have air conditioning and it felt too sweaty for clothes. I picture her pulling her leg up, half Indian-style and showing the scar to me. Under the hot water that's quickly turning cold and the bubbles that are dissolving, I cross my own leg. "Her right."

Kate sits quietly for a minute and then nods. "Okay. So. You don't have to see her now. Just tell them, and if it matches, then…that's that. We'll go down to the office whenever you're ready." She takes two fresh towels out of the cupboard and sets them on the toilet seat. "Here. Stay in as long as you want."

I wait until she closes the door and then stand up and dry off. What should you wear to a morgue? I go to the spare room and open my suitcase and pull out a sundress bought two summers ago when my mother got a job at the department store in the mall, and we planned a celebration dinner at Sizzler. I put it on, and it still fits. Actually, it fits looser than back then. I guess that's because other than the barbecue chicken and the watermelon, I haven't eaten a damn thing in four days. It still feels like new clothes, since I only wore it for one night, sitting on our living room couch with Jonathon, waiting for my mother to get home and take us to dinner.

She'd finally come in around one in the morning, sickly drunk and loud, with a man who, the very next morning, took off with the only cash we had in the house: her entire paycheck's worth. Three weeks later, she got fired for showing up to work drunk, four hours late, and wearing two different shoes. I mean, they actually wrote that on her termination slip – that she was wearing two different shoes. As if it was the final determining factor, the straw that really broke the camel's back. We never went to Sizzler, then or after.

I wear the sundress, and Kate wears a white Versace suit and a turquoise scarf tied around her neck. She looks like she should be strolling Rodeo Drive, not hauling some scummy orphan girl to the morgue.

The building is huge and white and only has one door that I can see. When we go in, the waiting room smell makes us both clench our teeth and take tiny shallow breaths in through our mouths.

"Crap, what is that *smell*?" I feel sick enough without this room closing in and suffocating us with a disgusting reek of rotten chicken sprinkled with…perfume or something.

Kate discreetly cups a hand over her nose. "It's just…it's the smell of preservation liquids and stuff."

Stuff. The smell of dead bodies. And the juice they put the dead bodies in to keep them from smelling worse than they do right now, if that's even possible. My hands start to shake. I squeeze them into fists and fold my arms across my chest. Kate walks to the front desk and asks for someone named Linda. The secretary disappears through swinging double doors. Two seconds later a tiny Asian woman appears wearing a white lab coat and chocolate-colored linen pants. She barely clears the counter, so it makes sense for her to walk around it to shake our hands.

"Hello. You must be Kate." She smiles warmly, and really, considering the grim line of work she's in, I have to give her some credit. She puts her hand out to me next. "You must be Valentine. I'm Linda Cash, the county medical examiner. Would you care to sit for a moment?" She gestures at the tacky burlap chairs behind us, so we sit down.

She opens a file on the table between us. "As I said on the phone, Kate, there are a few things we need to take care of before you can be on your way." She looks at me. "I'll need to see your driver's license or state ID proving you are eighteen years of age or older. Also, I will need to see your birth certificate, proving that you are in fact related to the deceased. Also," she says, pulling a typed packet out of the file. "I will need you to correctly identify the mark we noted during the autopsy to confirm the deceased's identity."

"Theresa," I spill out.

Kate nods and takes my hand. "Yes. Her name is Theresa."

Linda looks uncomfortable. I guess when you work with dead bodies all day, you have to stop caring what their names are and just view them as work. Linda clears her throat. "Of course. In any case, are you able to provide those three things today?"

"Yes," I say, but the truth is, no. I don't even know if I own a birth certificate.

Linda pulls a pen from her front coat pocket and looks at me expectantly. "All right then. Go ahead."

I hand her my driver's license. She looks at it briefly, then hands it back to me. This is it. I just have to say it, and it'll be over. My hand shakes violently in Kate's, and she squeezes it. I close my eyes and remember.

"A sunburst-shaped scar on the bottom of her right foot, about this big." I touch my thumb and pointer finger together in a circle and then tuck my pointer finger into the first crease of my thumb.

Linda nods. "That's correct. I'll just need to make a copy of your birth certificate, have you sign a few things, and you'll be all set."

I look at Kate. "But I don't have a birth certificate. I mean, at all. I never saw one. I don't know if I do have one, or where it is."

Linda purses her lips. "Are you sure? You were only born in the late eighties. Certificates were issued on a mandatory basis for every birth."

I feel anger pushing up and somehow it makes me shake less. "Well, I don't have one. She's my mother. I don't know what else to say."

Linda looks down at the file in her hand and sighs, and I wonder if she just wants to go home and order a pizza or something. Maybe she has a husband or a boyfriend or kids that make her job not so horrible once she leaves. I wish I had the damn birth certificate to hand over so we could all go home.

Kate leans forward. "Is it absolutely necessary to have the certificate?"

"Well, honestly, yes. We need legal documentation showing that Valentine is related to the deceased." She tapped the pen on the file.

I slam my fist down on the small table between us. "THERESA! My mother's name is *Theresa*! Do you really think I would be here if I wasn't related to her? If I didn't have to be? If there was even *one* other fucking person in the whole world who could do this instead of me? Give me a break!"

Suddenly the smell of the bodies, of my mother's body somewhere back there, and Linda's small face looking startled and put out – and Kate, Angela's mother, not mine, looking beautiful and vibrant and alive – is all too much. I throw up for the second time in two days, all over the other brown seats next to me and the faded yellow linoleum floor. And when I have thoroughly vomited out everything in me (which isn't much, really. A quarter of a bagel and some still-pink cream cheese), I jump up and walk out the doors. I go and stand next to Kate's car, trembling, hating the sour-milk taste clinging to my mouth.

Five minutes later she comes out and unlocks it.

We sit in the car without her starting it. Finally she speaks first. "You sure have a thing for ruining upholstery, huh?"

I smile. It could be Angela sitting there next to me, and I understand how they're related. "Well, I figure anything would've been an improvement on those disgusting brown seats."

"Agreed," she says, and turns the ignition key. "They're getting your birth records from the Department of Public Health. It's done. They're sending us the papers in the mail to sign." She puts the car in reverse, and we pull out of the parking lot, away from the smell, away from Linda, away from my mother. "What will they do with her now?" I feel my chest squeeze shut in a panic. "Kate. Where are they going to take her?"

"She's staying right there until we make some arrangements, sweetie."

I picture where she is, cold like a giant refrigerator, and even though I have absolutely nothing left in my stomach, the heaving threatens again. I press it down and turn the air conditioner vent to blow on my face. "What arrangements?"

"Whatever you'd like to do, honey. It's up to you. You're her family."

"Do you mean…I mean, what do you mean?" My words are broken. Like there's a shorted-out circuit in my brain that doesn't let me connect ideas.

"Burial, Valentine," she says gently, glancing at me before looking back out at the road. "Do you want to have her in a casket? If so, where? Would you rather not make any decisions? I can have everything handled if you'd like that instead. Whatever you want."

"I don't know what to do, Kate. I don't even know where to start. Seriously. Seriously, am I really supposed to be picking out, like, what exactly? Coffins? I don't know what to *do*." The tears feel hot coming from my eyes. They feel foreign running down my cold, air-conditioned face and onto my sundress and seatbelt. "Please tell me what to do."

"It's going to be okay," she says quietly, but in the Kate way – the same way that Angela has – that makes me believe her.

She drives silently the rest of the way home, as I cry, and neither of us knows what to say, so we don't say anything at all.

Chapter 7

I stand in the bathroom of the funeral home. In front of one of those mirrors that aren't real silvered glass, just weird distorted cheap metal that only really kind of show an outline when you look at them. I hate that sort of mirror. I can make out the squiggly line of myself in the new blue dress Angela and I found when we went shopping last night. I tried on three, and on the third dress, found this, the perfect one. I smooth out the knee-length skirt and lean toward the warped mirror to fix smudges in my mascara.

The funeral has been in process for forty-five minutes now, and I know that when I walk out, it will still only be Kate, Angela, Jonathon, Penelope, and the funeral director standing in the room.

Oh, don't think that nobody wants to come. Thanks to the fantastic reporting job done by the newspapers and the news stations, every five minutes or so a new freak or group of freaks shows up and tries to get in. I know why, too. They think maybe it's open casket, and that maybe, if they're lucky, they'll get a glimpse of what was left of someone after a train has hit them. The funeral director or Kate or someone apparently knew this would happen, and, lo and behold, my mother's funeral actually has bouncers at the door. She probably would've loved that.

I haven't looked. I haven't opened the pale birch coffin to look, and I won't. I don't need to. I know she's in there, I can just tell.

But when I push open the bathroom door and walk out into the room, it's not just the five us any more. There's a sixth, and she's standing over my mother, looking down at the closed coffin. Her back is to me. Her dark curls are pulled back in a long, silver barrette, and she's wearing a pretty gray skirt and jacket. And when she turns, I grab the wall because it's my mother staring back at me, and I can't even move my legs, or speak.

Chapter 8

I 'm rooted to the spot, staring at my mother's new, nice clothes. At how silky her hair looks, smoothly brushed and pulled back. Kate and Angela are standing stiffly to one side, facing her as she stands over her own coffin. When they see me, their faces change, and I guess she notices because she turns toward me. When she does, for the second time in one minute, my knees almost drop me to the floor. It is *not* my mother. It's a woman who looks just like her minus the sagging skin under the eyes, the droopiness of the jaw, the ratty hair. It is my mother, come here from a whole different life.

"Valentine," she says softly, carefully, and her voice is familiar. Not in the way you recognize somebody you hear all the time. Familiar in the way you feel a sound as some part of your life you don't quite remember. "Valentine, I'm sorry." She says my name again, and then I realize that her voice is my mother's voice from when I was a little girl. Before the smoke made it raspy and the booze made it slurred and sloppy.

Kate is at my side in an instant. I turn my head slowly to stare at her, and she explains. "This is your mother's sister, Val. Your aunt, Abigail."

I try to take it in. I really do. But all I see is the cinema in my head replaying a scene from seventh grade. I'd brought home a genealogy chart from history class but didn't have anything to fill in the blanks with. I didn't know the names of anyone other than my mother, and this realization simultaneously startled me and made me feel like a complete freak. I found my mother lying on the couch, her stomach bulging, seven months into her pregnancy with Jonathon. She'd draped a washcloth over her eyes.

"Mama?" I whispered because I didn't know if she was asleep or not. I knew she hadn't been sleeping much at night and didn't want to wake her up.

"What?" she murmured without moving or uncovering her eyes.

I sat down at the edge of the blue paisley couch. As I did, the movement knocked over a glass leaning against my mother's thigh and the last drops of the clear fluid leaked out onto the tattered carpet. I picked it up and smelled it, and my anger overflowed. Health class told us about crippled babies who were born after their mothers drank too much. "*Mama*."

She lifted a corner of the washcloth off one eye and saw me holding it, a perfect testimony to her bad choice. "Don't start." She put the washcloth over her face again. "What do you want?"

I gripped the glass, furious, and vowed to search the cupboards and under the bed for yet another bottle to pour into the toilet. "I need to know my family history. It's for *school*."

She was quiet for so long I thought for sure she'd fallen asleep. Then, "What do you want to know?"

"I have a bunch of spaces to fill out. And I don't know what to put in them."

She sighed heavily, and I felt the weight of the glass grow in my hand. "What kind of spaces? What do you mean?"

I just didn't feel like taking the time to explain. "It's a thing, for school. A paper that shows my family tree. I have to fill in the spaces with my family starting at the top and ending with me."

"Okay," she mumbled.

I felt exhausted. "Mama! Please just sit up a second and help me so I can finish." I pulled the cloth off her eyes and eased an arm under to lift and prop her against the back of the couch.

"Okay, okay, Pushy Pants." Her words were sloppy, but still understandable and relatively coherent, a good day if I ever saw one. "What? What do you want to know?"

I leaned the family tree chart against her stomach. "Well, I have me. And I have you. But I need to fill in the father space…with a name."

My mother shook her head. "You know the answer to that."

"Mama! Am I supposed to leave the entire left side of my chart empty? I don't know *anything!*" Tears stung my eyes, and I had no idea why because really it was just a stupid family tree, and I hadn't missed a single homework assignment all year, so even if I didn't turn it in at all, who really cared? But still. More was at stake than just the stupid grade. "You have to tell me the rest of my tree, Mama."

"Valentine. I told you already." She smiled suddenly and shakily pushed my bangs off my forehead. "You and me, we're from another planet. We got bored on our other world, so we decided to explore. But our ship's steering broke, and we got launched here, to Earth."

I threw the empty glass against the wall and listened to it shatter. "Mama, come on! I'm not five anymore! We didn't come from a different planet. I don't know where we came from. I don't even know where I was born. This is so stupid! I don't want to hear your stupid, lame story about stupid planets."

The tears burned my cheeks, and remorse immediately hit my stomach. I ran into my room, launched onto the mattress on the floor, and curled up into a ball. I slept the whole night.

When I woke in the morning, my mother lay on the mattress next to me, sound asleep, hair matted against her forehead, skin oily. I ate a half-bag of sour cream and onion chips from lunch the day before, dressed quickly and tiptoed out to leave for school. On the counter lay my chart, with two names in my handwriting. And now two in my mother's, next to her own in the sibling branch space: Abigail and Patrick. All the other spaces were blank, but I didn't care. Somewhere, some place, there were people related to me.

Patrick. Abigail.

And now here she stands. One of the filled spaces, right in front of me. I nod like I understand, but I don't really. "Hi."

She smiles, my mother's smile, then breaks into tears. "Oh, I'm a mess. I'm sorry. You're just...you're what I always imagined." She cries harder. "I never knew, you know. Our mother...well, I never knew about you, or where my sister went." She glances toward the coffin and takes out a tissue from her purse. "You have to know that, Valentine. That I never knew. That I'd never leave my little sister to fend for herself with a child, that...you're beautiful, just like your mother."

She is crying so hard, but her face is beautiful still. Beautiful, but just so sad. I suddenly feel more sorry for her than for me, which is a nice change of pace. "I believe you," I say, because I do.

She nods and dabs her eyes. "I'd like, if it's okay with you, to have some time – I mean, if you don't have other plans – to just sit down, and maybe talk. After, of course," she adds hurriedly.

I am reminded that my mother's mangled body lies in the box three feet from us. And that at some point there will be an after, and that point is coming up quickly.

I close my eyes for a second and nod quickly. "Sure. Yeah."

"Okay." She reaches out to gently touch my arm. "I'll stay, if you don't mind. For the burial."

I nod again. Abigail turns back toward the coffin, Kate takes my hand, and we all wait, together, to bury my mother.

Theresa

"We all have our time machines, don't we? Those that take us back are memories...And those that carry us forward are dreams."

— H.G. Wells

The two figures in the stands sit close to each other. Theresa, a pretty brunette of thirteen, taps her maryjane-clad feet nervously against the metal. Her knees are pressed together, hands folded neatly in her lap. She smiles often, looking shyly at the boy seated next to her. Her purse, a small designer bag, is a present from her father, Police Chief Bruno Sepuchelio. He often brings gifts home, seeming to forget she is no longer a child. She shops where she pleases, her mother, Caroline, accompanying her when her ailments were not taking away all of her energy. Their home on Burbank Drive has a yard envied by most. The perfectly-manicured lawn is bordered by a garden of petunias and lilacs that Caroline tends to with devotion. Theresa is the youngest of three children. The elders are away at college dappling in art. Her birth status, ten years younger than the next oldest, has put her in a position of reverence. What her father lacks in compassion toward her mother, he makes up for in his dedication to his daughter. She revels in her pre-teen life, unbothered by the lack of happiness in her parents' marriage. Ignores the frequent arguments, tunes out the screaming, and completely erases the beatings her father doles out to her mother alone.

The boy, Charlie, lounges back against the metal seats, one arm draped over her shoulder, legs spread. He takes swigs from a soda bottle periodically, and smiles a lot at Theresa. She is everything functional in his life. The third youngest of seven children, he approaches his graduation a year later than scheduled. On the day of the graduation ceremony he will forego his robe and diploma and sit on the back his brother's truck, drinking beer that is freshly stolen from the 7-11. His father, a large, violent man with an unnatural proclivity for performing sexual acts with his children, will discover them drunk and knock three of his brother's teeth out. His mother, still thick with the German accent she has never lost in the years since the war, lives to cook and clean and obey. He found Theresa at a football game nine months prior to this day. A rabble-rouser classmate dropped a lit cigarette in her cashmere sweater pocket when she wasn't looking. Their meeting took place after Charlie pulled the lit cigarette from her pocket and left the perpetrator bloodied and burned in the school parking lot. A knight in shining armor, Charlie found a person who could use his protection as much as he could use her love.

He wipes his mouth and hands her the Coca-Cola bottle. She takes it from his hand and sips.

"*Thanks.*" *She smiles at him.*

"*Sure.*"

"*So, are you excited about graduating? I mean, in just five months. That's pretty lucky.*"

"*I can't wait to get the hell out of this dirthole.*"

"*Oh...yeah. Paradise Valley isn't so bad though, you know? I mean—*"

"*Yeah, coming from the police chief's daughter, I'd expect some bullshit like that. Rainbows and sunshine and puppies.*" *He playfully nudges her under the chin with his fist, and she smiles despite the insult.*

"*The park is nice. The ducks are nice. They always...eat bread and quack. They're nice.*"

"*Are you always so good, Reesie?*"

"*No. Well. Yes.*" *She sits up a little straighter and meets green eyes with brown.* "*Are you always so bad?*"

He laughs and throws an arm around to pull her close, kissing her temple. "*Where would you be without me?*"

"*Lost.*"

"*Yeah. Probably. What time we gotta be at the hospital to pick up your mom?*"

"*Five-thirty...thank you, Charlie, I mean...thank you so much. I don't know what would have happened if you didn't get there so fast yesterday. My mother...she just would have been...I don't know. Thanks, though.*"

"*Babe, don't even worry about it. It's nothing. She is okay, and it was no problem, and you don't need to worry about stuff.*"

"*I know.*"

"*I always tell you the same thing. You don't need to worry about stuff. You don't need to cry and panic. I'll take care of it.*"

"*I know.*"

She opens her suede pocketbook and takes out a tube of cherry lip-gloss. "*So then I guess you're probably gonna leave town when you graduate, huh?*" *She presses her lips together to even out the balm.*

"*Leave you, ya mean?*"

"*Oh. No. It's just that you want to get out of here, don't you?*"

"*Yeah. But I'll wait a little while for you. Then when you graduate, we'll jump on the first plane we can catch and blow this stinkin' town.*"

"*Five years is a long time to wait.*"

"*Nah. I can't just leave ya out in the cold, right?*" *He pulls her tighter against him.* "*Right, Reesie? You need me around, keep ya out of trouble.*"

She smiles, showing her teeth. "*Oh, yeah. Right.*"

He tips the pop bottle all the way toward the sky, swallowing the last of it.

Chapter 9

I'm sitting in the waiting room of the clinic, and the pink walls are making me sick to my stomach. The magazines are from last winter, and the idea of reading an eight-month-old *Time* while I wait with strangers to have my vagina prodded at makes me feel sick. I pull my neon-green mini-skirt down another impossible inch. Sitting across from me is a young woman wearing a UCLA Berkley sweatshirt and holding the hand of a boy wearing the same thing. Their heads are bent close. He's tucking her hair behind her ear and smiling gently.

No one is tucking my hair behind my ear. No one is holding my hand.

God, I'm scared.

"Theresa Maureino?" The nurse holding the clipboard is calling my name through the plastic window. I blink twice, not recognizing my mother's maiden name at first. But I thought it'd be best to use hers when I filled out the form, since pretty much everyone in the area knows my dad's name from the paper, and the last thing I need is for someone to mention that the Chief's daughter was at this place. God. My stomach cramps up just thinking about it.

I stand and try to hold my head high, but for some reason all I can think about is my mother bathing me and putting my pajamas on, then sharing a bowl of kettle corn while we watch Johnny Carson. Was that forever ago? A decade at least.

The white-uniformed nurse doesn't smile as she puts me in the little room and tells me to take off my clothes and put on a pale green papery robe. "The doctor will be right in," she says, never making eye contact, shutting the door firmly behind her.

I undress self-consciously. I'm fat now and afraid that the door is going to fling open any minute. The robe gaps in the back. I sit down and tuck it under me to try and make it like a real covering.

The table is cold.

The door opens and a man in his late fifties walks in. White coat, silver glasses, black loafers and khakis. I notice this kind of thing because, as my older sister Abigail always says, I have an eye for style. I'm going to New York when I graduate, to work for *Vogue*. And to Paris to eat snails, which I doubt I'll even like, but I'm going to eat them anyway so that when I come back to the States – that's what people who travel to places like Paris call the United States – I can nod thoughtfully and declare how I feel about eating snails in a foreign country.

"Ms. Maureino," he states.

I nod. I'm thinking about snails when he clears his throat.

"Age?"

"Uh, thirteen." I hold out my hand to shake, but his remains by his side as he peers hard at me over thick glasses.

"What seems to be the problem?"

"I'm not," I start, then clear my own throat, and start again. "I'm not getting my period at all."

"Lie back, feet in the stirrups." He puts the clipboard down on the counter with a thud. I wait uncomfortably as he calls the rude nurse in. She stands, face blank, to the side of me.

"Um, so, this is my first exam…is it going to hurt?" I'm nervous and my knees won't relax. I'm holding them together despite my feet being miles apart in the metal stirrups.

"Well," he says, bringing a bright light to shine you-know-where, "God doesn't make these things easy for whores."

I cry during the whole thing, but never say another word. The tears fall silently, running over my chin and splattering without sound onto the paper robe. When he pulls his rubber gloves off and asks me to pee in a plastic cup, I cry on the way to the bathroom, then the entire time while I pee, and when I hand it back.

Ten minutes later he comes in again.

"Your results came back positive. When would you like to schedule a termination?" He clicks his pen expectantly.

I don't know where to look or what to say. Is he really talking to me? *Positive?* Maybe that means positive news…maybe it's good. Termination doesn't sound good, though.

"Clarissa?" He's talking to me again.

"Um, it's Theresa. And, uh, does that mean…?" I sit up straight and try to look professional. Like an adult. Not the trembling kid I am, sitting naked on a metal table, feet dangling without touching the floor. "What, exactly, does that mean, Doctor?"

He stares long and hard, then clears his throat again. The scratchiness of the cough feels abrasive on my skin. He pinches the bridge of his nose for a moment, eyes closed, then opens them and looks at me again.

"What does it mean? That your sinful actions have manifested themselves in your womb." His voice is angry, burning and I feel hot waves passing from him to me. He squeezes between his eyes again. "It means you are pregnant."

He turns away, and I feel stupid and ugly and worthless. I think of my mother, probably setting the table for dinner right now. All I want is to be home, in my bed, near my mommy. I pick up my purse and slide the strap over my shoulder.

"Thank you," I say to the bastard. "Have a nice day."

Two months have passed since I was handed that news. I hardly recognize my normally neat bedroom: a pigpen, as my mother would call it. Except she's the one making it that way, tearing clothing out of drawers and off hangers, throwing them on the yellow carpet, like a toddler having a temper tantrum.

"Mama, please." I cry, with no effect. She is turned away, folding my shirts and skirts and putting them into a large maroon suitcase. *"Please."*

She stops momentarily, maybe because of how desperately pathetic I sound. Then continues putting things into the suitcase. My socks. My underwear. My shoes and belts and tights. She shuts the case and zips it.

"Carry it out to the car," she orders, without looking me in the eye.

I pick up the suitcase and carry it out, heaving it into the trunk of the Mercedes. I stand at the back passenger door for a moment, looking at the yard my mother takes such care to make beautiful. I want to lie down on the grass. I want to dig a hole there and get in it.

I hear the clickity-clack of my mother's heels against the paved driveway. She opens the driver's door, gets in, starts the car. I keep looking at the grass. I want to cling to something. My front door, my kitchen sink, my mother. Anything.

"Theresa!"

The sharpness makes me flinch. I get in the passenger seat and stare straight ahead. Once more, I'll try. Just once more. "Mama, please, I'm so sorry. Please, don't do this. I love you. Please."

She slams the car into gear and then sits with her foot jammed on the brake, holding the steering wheel tightly with both hands, staring straight ahead just like me.

"You – you could have had anything you wanted," she finally whispers to the windshield. "Your father…" She stops for a moment and covers her mouth with one hand. It seems like she might start crying, but she takes a huge breath in and holds it. She doesn't look at me, but exhales shakily and smoothes her hair back with an open palm.

"He would've given you anything. Do you understand that? Do you even understand what you gave up?"

I am so relieved she is talking to me again that I reply too fast, too eagerly. This is hope. "Yes, Mama. And I am sorry. I'm so sorry. I'll make it better. We'll get through it. We'll be okay." I feel hope, I see a light. I'll be okay.

She shakes her head slightly, and then so, so quietly, says, "You don't deserve it. Neither of us do."

I say what I've been dying to say since I first found out, since my mind first stayed awake all night trying to figure it all out. A solution. An offering. "I'll give you and Daddy the baby. I'll give it to you. You can be its Mama and Daddy."

She slaps me hard across the face then. The first time in my life she's ever laid a hand on me. It stings. I hold my hand against my burning cheek.

"We," she says through gritted teeth, "will not be okay. We will not get through anything. You ungrateful little bitch! You did this to yourself and you will deal with it yourself!" She stops and puts a hand over her mouth again, closing her eyes. "You will *not* prolong this life for me. You have – you have *no idea!*"

She stills for a moment. Then looks right at me, her eyes red-rimmed,frantic. "You will disappear, Theresa. You will not do this to me. You will go."

More than the sting of her palm across my cheek, I feel the words striking my skin, like rocks flung hard. I say the rhyme involuntarily in my head: *Sticks and stones can break my bones, but words will never hurt me.*

Except they do.

Is this actually happening? Didn't we just spend Saturday afternoon having brunch at the bistro in the mall? Weren't we just talking about whether I wanted strawberry cream or chocolate pudding filling in the cake? The cake she was ordering for my eighth-grade graduation party. My party dress is packed. It burns me from the trunk.

She takes a deep breath full of hissing rage and backs methodically out of the driveway, adjusting the rearview mirror as she goes. She winds through town, waves at Mrs. Garrison, the woman who walks the dogs in our neighborhood, then turns onto the highway.

Ten minutes later we're at the train station. My mother drives the straight and narrow lane until it splits. The left is for long-term parking, the middle is for day parking, and the right is for drop off only. I feel my body lean toward the door as we veer right. My insides slosh, liquid, as we pull to a stop at the curb.

I am silent for what feels like eternity. Then I have to ask, quietly. "Where will I go, Mama?" I flinch inwardly, wondering if she'll hit me again.

She glances into the rearview and adjusts her sunglasses. "I don't know."

I get out of the car and grab hold of my suitcase, fully expecting my mother to laugh her chipper, high laughter at any minute. To say, "Get back in the car. I feel like a turkey club and some fries."

I pause at the revolving doors and look back, but her taillights are already indistinguishable from all the others leaving. I push against the glass door ahead of me and disappear into the crowd.

I buy a ticket to Los Angeles. The train ride is numbing. I open my purse and find an envelope with ten hundred dollar bills in it, and a note from my mother, folded carefully into quarters. The rumble of the train makes my hands shake as I open it. I tell myself it's the train's fault.

Theresa,
Spend it wisely. If you are in a fix, be sure to send me correspondence through my post office box ONLY. Do not – I mean it, Theresa – do NOT send anything to this house. I have set up a box in my name. If an emergency arises, and you need assistance, contact me through the post office. I am sure I need not tell you that you are not to call the house ever. However, I will save you the trouble of trying. I had our phone number changed this morning, and it is unlisted. Here is the address:
> *Caroline Eaton*
> *P.O. Box 214*
> *Grass Valley, CA 95945*
The post office box is for <u>emergencies</u> only.

The note is unsigned. Where did Eaton come from? Maybe it's the nausea creeping up from my stomach. Maybe it's just the sheer stress of this completely unreal situation. Either way, I begin to cry. *An emergency?* I want to scream. *I am thirteen years old and pregnant. How can that not be an emergency!*

I rock back and forth crying, wrapping my arms around my middle, thinking about the time before.

Six months ago my hands would have touched each other around my back. Now my stomach is huge, fat, bulging out from the stretch pants I wear under a loose flowered dress that comes down to my knees. My mother, beautiful and thin, saw this before anyone else, though it took three whole months for her to actually notice anything was wrong.

I'd thrown up this morning after eating a bowl of Cocoa Krispies, and the smell, as usual, clung to my hair and my clothing. I couldn't go to school like that, so I got in the shower. My sweet mother, not thinking any better of it, opened the bathroom door to deliver fresh warm towels from the dryer, and saw me looming, naked and disgraced.

Her disbelief was brief. Her resolve whole and unshakeable. This morning she discovered the secret I had endlessly tried to make myself tell her, and this afternoon I am on the train.

Snot is running down my nose, over my mouth, onto my chin, mixing with the tears, but I can't stop rocking to get a tissue. As I think this exact thought, a tissue appears in front of me, connected to a hand belonging to someone standing in the aisle. I take it without looking up, wipe the snot the best that I can, and then look at the giver. A middle-aged woman, around forty-five, long blonde hair pulled back by a barrette. Her face is kind, gently worn. I think somehow of a cowboy when I see her, but instead of a hat and spurs she wears a floor length skirt with palm trees covering it, and a worn-in t-shirt that says "You can always die tomorrow" with a big yellow smiley face under it.

I am temporarily preoccupied with the saying. Does that mean you can always die tomorrow, so make the best of today? Or does it mean you can always die tomorrow *instead*, so why kill yourself today? Five months ago, the second one wouldn't have even crossed my mind.

"Well, you sure do leak, don't you?"

I snap back to look into the face of the woman, who is now holding out her entire travel box of tissues. She smiles warmly.

"Hi," I snuffle out. I don't want to talk to anyone. I don't want to see anyone. I am hideous and gigantic and completely alone. So I ask her to sit down. She takes the seat next to me, and opens her tote bag, pulling out a plastic baggie full of nuts, which she begins to expertly shell.

"Pistachio?"

I hate pistachio nuts. But she holds out the bag to me, and for no other reason than that I am completely alone, I eat pistachios.

"I'm Lorrie," she says.

I continue to crack open the shells, chewing the nuts quickly so I don't have to taste them as much. I just like the crunchiness. The noise is loud in my head, drowning out the sounds around me.

"Thank you…for the tissues…and for the nuts. I'm Theresa."

She nods, looking out the window. "Have you thought of a name yet?" She lifts her eyes to the sky watching something I can't see. It's a question that should set me off, turn me into a new puddle, but she asks it calmly and clearly, like she's not even being mean or judging me.

"No," I say. "Not yet."

She nods again. "Any ideas?"

I'm not sure what to say. How could I have thought about names when I just ignored the entire situation? How could I ever even imagine calling this kid anything when I'd insisted there was no kid at all? That's the thing with me. My mother always said my head was in the clouds, to keep my feet on the ground. My whole family's feet are always on the ground; I was the only one, she'd say, smiling sometimes, shaking her head, who liked to live up in the clouds.

"Sarah," I say, half-heartedly, giving her my own middle name for lack of anything else.

"Oh, lovely. It's a girl, then?" She hands me another heap of pistachios and, I break them open slowly, one by one.

"I'm not sure. I don't know." I focus on the crunching again, counting my chews out in rhythm. *One, two. One, two, three. One, two. Swallow.*

"Well, Sarah is a good, strong name. From the Bible, did you know that? It's the name of Abraham's wife. And when they were so old, and thought for sure they couldn't have children, God made Sarah pregnant with a precious gift." She smiles, and the lines around her mouth stretch out in soft, creasing rivers across her worn cheeks. "Sarah is a strong name."

"Theresa is not a strong name," I tell her, thinking of the absolute fear that grabs at my chest when I wake in the middle of the night with back pain that shoots down my legs. Then it occurs to me that I don't know where I'll be waking up tonight to suffer through that pain. I push down panic and eat another pistachio nut.

"Oh well, that's not true," Lorrie says, shaking her head. "Theresa means 'to harvest.' Harvest time in a lot of cultures is a time of joy and strength and unity. It makes people feel successful and hopeful. It brings families together."

My throat swells with a lump. I close my eyes and nod. She seems to understand and we ride the next hour in silence. Then she dozes off, leaning her head against the window. I sit awake with my eyes closed, my fingers splayed widely across my belly, holding tightly to the bump. The only family I have now.

Chapter 10

I'm watching the ball drop on a black-and-white television that runs on batteries and belongs to a girl who scratches bloody lines into her forearm with a paperclip she bent into the shape of an S. I think her real name is Cammie, but I can't be sure because when she isn't sleeping on the cot next to me, she's out on the main avenue trying to get guys to pull over their cars and have sex with her for money. Right now she is sitting on the cot, her knees drawn up against her chest, staring at the little television with me.

Two of the other cots are occupied, one with a woman much older than me. Older, even, than my mother. The other with a tall black girl who periodically comes back here to sleep, but who, for the most part, is not one of the core residents at the fabulous Saint Peter the Savior Second Chance Shelter.

If anyone needs a savior right now, it's me. My belly is humongous. Every night I go to bed with the hope of sleeping, and every morning I wake up from eight hours of nonstop tossing and turning both inside me and around me.

Nothing's like it seems on TV. Every time I flip the channel and see some after-school special about pregnant teens who run away from home, I want to punch the screen and cry. The writers or television producers or whoever does the whole TV thing, they make it look so amazingly easy. Girl gets knocked up. Girl runs away from home. Girl wanders around on the street scared and lonely. Girl's parents find out, come looking for her, and find her. All before nighttime. There is never a damned nighttime in those movies.

I've had a billion nighttimes since the train station. I stayed with Lorrie for a month. She smoked pot and read the Bible every night with her boyfriend, Roger. Her house was nice, cozy. It didn't have couches.

Instead there were big, puffy pillows all over the living room floor, and the lights weren't tall floor lamps like at home. Half the time the glow came from the 5000 or so Christmas lights strung around the corners of the rooms, and the other half the light came from candles. She didn't have a TV.

She gave me a journal and told me to write letters to God whenever I felt lost. I didn't write any letters, but every morning I woke up, I drew a line on the first page. Some days Lorrie left for a while and came back with a few friends, who usually stayed until late at night, sitting on the pillows, smoking, and talking about God and Jesus and the Apostles and Jonah. I remember Jonah because he got swallowed up and landed in a whale's stomach, and he stayed inside for a lot of nights. In the Bible, it makes it sound like he just sat there twiddling his thumbs, waiting for God to get him out. But really, I bet he was having a total fit in there, flailing around, banging his fists against all the slimy insides, screaming 'til he lost his voice and overall making the whale want to vomit.

Sometimes I feel like Jonah and sometimes I feel like the whale.

I made thirty-two lines on the page at Lorrie's house. Then one morning, as she and Roger and I sat at the wooden picnic table in their dining room, eating oatmeal, they told me they were moving to Arizona. "The following's good down there," she said, "We want to go where the need is plenty."

They'd already been to look at houses before they met me, I guess, and found a really great one, with a backyard that had no fence, and a little pond the owner said they could fish in.

I nodded, holding the maple and brown sugar lumps on my tongue even though they burned. I waited for them to talk about how my room would be just the right size, and how the school district was a really good one, even though the town was small. When my bowl of oatmeal was empty, and they still hadn't mentioned me, I understood. I had made my thirty-second line that morning. When I woke up the next day before the sun even came up, I took a minute to draw one dark diagonal line on the front page across all the others, and then I walked out the front door.

My envelope still had $952 in it. In the whole thirty-two days I'd been there, Lorrie had never asked me for a penny. The missing money I'd spent on clothes that fit over my huge stomach. Nothing nice. First, I went into the Macy's Maternity section, but one shirt cost forty-eight dollars, and the pants with the weird stretchy pouch thing cost seventy. So then I found a Salvation Army on Dartmouth Avenue, and got six shirts, three pairs of pants, and a jacket for twenty-six dollars. I bought new underwear. The pack of six at Wal-Mart was expensive, but I decided I deserved brand-new underwear, that I would always have brand-new underwear for myself, dammit.

"I wanna be at Times Square." Cammie is staring blankly at the screen. She talks without separating her teeth, kind of. Her lips move, but her teeth stay pretty much gritted together, so she always sounds bored and mumbley.

I look at the television. Dick Clark is counting down.

"So go to Times Square next year," I tell her. "Go watch the ball drop in person."

She laughs quietly, and I know why.

"I think I'll do that," she says. "You should come, too."

I smile. We say things like this all the time.

Times Square explodes with noise.

"Happy New Year, kiddo," she says, turning to lie on her side, facing the wall.

"Happy New Year," I tell her.

When I first got to this place, this Second Chance house, I figured I'd stay overnight 'til I could figure out what to do. The building itself was small. It had a kitchen like a cafeteria, and we got fed on trays, and the food tasted like Satan himself had concocted it. But the Coop, as the girl's dorm was so kindly named, had ten beds in it, and they weren't too uncomfortable, and the bathroom was clean. When I first lay down on the cot, all I felt was relief to not be walking. I'd never understood why pregnant women waddled until I felt how much it hurts to be on your feet, trying to walk, carrying three bowling balls in front of you.

I'd stretched out on the scratchy brown blanket and calmed myself. I could call my aunt, I thought, for the ten millionth time since I got on the train. I could call her and tell her what happened, and she would come pick me up in a flurry of hugs and big breasts, smelling, as always, like coconut and vanilla. I thought of this on the train, kind of. And then Lorrie offered to let me stay with her, and for the next thirty-three days I didn't have to think about anything that already had happened in this nightmare, or what to do next.

Lorrie and Roger were probably in Arizona, having a wonderful life.

I could call my aunt. No, I would call her. I'd just call now. I heaved myself off the cot and walked toward the front door. There was a pay phone on the outside. Someone had written "Shoot 'til your minds are open" on the side in thick black marker, and for some reason that side seemed dirty, so I stretched the cord as far as it would go and dropped quarters in the slot.

It rang twice before I heard her voice.

"Hello, Dominik's." It always sounded like a pizza place when she answered the phone.

"Aunt Liz? It's me." I felt like I couldn't even swallow.

"Theresa?" she whispered. Not the kind you use when telling a secret to your best friend over the phone. The kind of whisper when you're afraid the curtains in your room are blowing because the neighbor kid who got killed by the garbage truck has chosen you to haunt.

"Hi. It's me."

She was quiet for so long I thought I got disconnected. I dropped in five more quarters for good measure.

"I know who it is," she said. "I've held you since you were born, in case you forget."

I felt the hotness of tears, and was mad because I'd done so well with not crying these past few weeks. "I didn't forget, Aunt Liz."

I heard her take a deep breath. "How could you do this to your mother? To your family? How could you ever, ever do this?"

I didn't want to hear, but just the familiar sound of her voice made me sick for home, for my room. For my parents and my bed with the satin sheets that my mother got me as my First Day of Eighth Grade present.

"I know, Aunt Liz. I'm so sorry." My voice cracked. "I'm sorry, I don't know what else to say."

She screamed suddenly. "You don't know what else to *say?* How could you even do it? Do you have any idea what you are? Do you have any idea what this makes you? How could you do this to your mother?" She cut herself off, and I heard her start to cry.

The baby was kicking me like there was no tomorrow.

"Aunt Liz, please don't cry. Please. I'm sorry. I know, and I'm sorry. I'm going to make it better."

"What?" Her voice was a yelp. "How could you ever make this better, Theresa? You're a *murderer!* You *killed* an innocent baby! For what – for your mistake? You can never make this better. That child is dead because of you. Nothing you can ever say or do will make that better."

I was too stunned to say anything. My vocal cords were paralyzed. I didn't even know what she was talking about. And then, suddenly, I did.

My calm tone scared even me. "Aunt Liz." I was trying to force the calmness through the phone. The message I wanted to get through was so important I was afraid it somehow wouldn't fit through the payphone holes. "Aunt Liz. Please listen to me. I…did not…kill…a baby." The relief at getting the words out exhausted me. I leaned against the dirty side with the black writing.

"No, you listen to me. I don't care what you call it. I don't care how you want to think about it to help you sleep better at night. Your generation is so...so selfish! Your mother told me everything, and somehow, somewhere along the way, her values did not cross over into you. I do not ever, EVER want to hear your excuses. Abortion is *murder*. You killed another person, and don't you ever, ever forget that. Do not contact this family again. You made that choice."

I hung up the phone before she could hang up on me, and then I held my stomach until the kicking stopped.

When I got back into the Coop, my suitcase was moved to another cot. A short, thin girl was sitting on the cot I had claimed earlier. The liner was thick around her eyes and her mascara clumped too much. She was braiding her three-toned hair into dozens of small braids. She looked up when I walked in, and said, through closed teeth, "This is usually my cot, so I moved you to the next one."

I nodded. Who cared? Who cared what cot was mine. Brown rectangles in a brown room.

"Cammie," she said, her fingers still working quickly in and out of the braids.

"Theresa." I sat with such a heavy thud that I was afraid it might break the flimsy cot.

"When are you due?"

"Not sure. In February. I have a doctor's appointment." I didn't but made up my mind in that moment to schedule one the next day. Who even knew what was going on down there, anyway, with all the kicking and moving around?

"That's cool," she said.

Yeah, I'd thought, closing my eyes. *It's fucking awesome.*

But it was all I had.

Chapter 11

The Planned Parenthood here is from a completely different planet than the clinic I went to at home. The building is new and white, the inside roomy. The chairs have padded leather seats, and (trust me, I could hardly believe this myself) every magazine issue is current. The most amazing thing of all is that my doctor, Dr. Hicks, is a woman who never once made me cry. I went the day after I spoke to my aunt, and Dr. Hicks met with me, referred me to the Healthy Lady Healthy Baby clinic, and had her equally nice receptionist Hilary call to make the appointment for me. When I left, she gave me her pager number and told me to call if I felt anything odd, or even if I just wanted to talk about something I was worried about.

I wanted to say, Lady, I'll be calling you every minute if that's the criteria.

My baby is healthy. The HLHB clinic assigned me a doctor, another woman whose name was Colleen McDonnelly. She lets me call her Colleen and did tests that didn't hurt, and didn't scare me except for the fact that nobody was there to hold my hand but her.

This is the news: my baby is a girl.

I am growing an actual GIRL person inside of my fat stomach. Colleen said that I'm due on or around February 20th. That's twenty days from right now. I feel kind of the way you do when you're going on a plane to go on vacation, and even though you packed all your clothes and are holding your tickets in hand, you still don't really *believe* that in just a few hours you're going to be somewhere completely different from where you are at that moment.

I know twenty days isn't a few hours, but trust me, after this hell of a year, it sure feels like it. I have to stop cursing. I never did 'til these Coop girls started rotting my brain – something I jokingly tell them all the time.

And Becca, another one of our roommates, spews out the vilest words I have ever heard anyone say, and that's including the maintenance guy who comes in to mess with the heat and hit on the other girls who aren't fat and disgusting like me.

But I can't have a dirty mouth. For one, ladies don't *have* dirty mouths. For another, I don't want my little girl to ever hear a curse word. Not *ever*. Especially not from me. I want her to only hear nice things, and know only good things too, like poetry and history, and I guess maybe classic movies like *Gone with the Wind*, because Scarlett's dress is so beautiful, and I want my little girl to have everything beautiful, you know?

"GOD! What the FUCK is going on with this cheap-ass heater today!" Becca slams her fist against the thermostat, and the boxy plastic cover pops off and lands on the floor. She pulls roughly at her neon yellow shirt, exposing one brown shoulder. "I feel like my fucking skin is melting off. Theresa, you're about a hundred times fatter than me, how aren't you sweating like a pig?"

"Oh, Becca, take a chill pill. She's not fat. She's having a baby." This from the ever loyal, infinitely cool Libbie, who is sitting on the bed across from me, reading a battered copy of *The Sun Also Rises* from the book box in the hall. Libbie moved in two months before me, around the same time Becca did, and between me, them, and Cammie, we make up a pretty steady family unit...if you can consider four girls under the age of eighteen who have no parents and no money, steady.

"Libbie, I don't think I was talking to you. Put your goddamned nose back in the book." She smacks the thermostat one more time for good measure, then flops down on her bed and sighs loudly. "You guys, what're we gonna do tonight? I'm *so* bored."

Without looking away from her book, Libbie reaches under her cot and feels around for a moment before pulling up another book and throwing in the direction of Becca. "Here."

Becca picks it up and reads the cover with a look on her face like she's actually holding something rotting and dead. "What the hell is *In Our Time*?" She turns it over and reads the back cover for exactly 1.2 seconds before throwing it down on her bed. "Why would I want to read this shit, Libbie?"

Libbie stops reading and looks up, blue eyes wide, blonde hair pulled back in a long ponytail locked into a tie-dye scrunchy. "It's Ernest Hemingway, Becca. Why would you ever call it crap? For Christ's sake, it's Hemingway."

Becca stares at her, face blank.

"Okay, wait. Do you not even know who that is?" Libbie laughs as she says it. Obviously Becca doesn't. Libbie looks at me, and I want to not be included, for once. "Theresa, you know who Ernest Hemingway is, right?"

I look at Becca staring at me, and nod slightly.

Libbie keeps going. "Okay. Right. So...Becca..." her voice light with amusement and laughter. "You DO know who Ernest Hemingway is, right?"

Becca shrugs. "Yeah. So? That doesn't make him less shitty." She turns over on her side. Libbie looks at me and bursts out laughing.

"Theresa, do you like Hemingway?"

"I guess." I nod, not wanting to say anything, either way, even though honestly, I sort of like him, but not nearly as much as I love Emily Dickinson. Because, I mean, she just sat in that room by herself for years and years and never wanted to leave or get married or anything. Just write. What a total weirdo. You have to love that.

Libbie smiles at me. "Well, who do you like then, if not Hemingway?"

Becca lies very still on her cot.

"Emily Dickinson, I guess." I didn't know really. I'd stopped paying attention in class when Charlie started buying me ice cream if we skipped together.

Libbie's smile turns into the toothiest grin I've ever seen on her delicate, tan face. "Dickinson! Nice, Theresa! Very nice." She winks at me, then turns toward Becca.

"Becca – "

I guess sometimes it's the little things that finally make people crack right open.

Becca jumps up from the cot so fast it makes *me* jump all the way over on my own cot. "WHAT, Libbie?" She leaps toward Libbie's cot and stands inches from her face. "What you got to say to me, huh? WHAT do you got to say to ME?"

Libbie's smile disappears. She doesn't move her face away, or back up, even though Becca's nose is about half an inch from her own. "I say," she says calmly, but through a very clenched jaw, "that you should move out of my face right now."

"Oh, is that a threat? Are you fucking threatening me? I will beat your white ass down like *this*." She snaps her fingers violently. "Fucking threaten me, go ahead. GO AHEAD!"

Libbie, for her part, looks about one million times braver than I would, in her place. I hold my breath. Becca never calls any of us white, and we never call her black. We're the same. What does it matter? We're all the same, on the same cots, in the same damned situation with nowhere else to go.

I watch as Libbie stares at Becca unblinking, not saying a word, not moving away.

Becca reels back suddenly and makes a scoffing sound. "You're worthless, know that? You're fucking worthless, Libbie. Go ahead and keep reading your fancy college shit and sleeping on a cot in a homeless shelter. I'm sure you'll go far in life. Send me a postcard from your mansion on the hill." She laughs, a barking sound with absolutely no happiness in it.

Libbie deliberately opens up her book again, licks one finger, and turns a page. She glances over at me and says, "So, Theresa, do you want to take our *white asses* down into town to get some food? My treat."

Becca whips around, and I think G*eez, here we go again.*

"Oh, you think that's funny?" she spits out, staring at Libbie. "Think it's funny to joke about you all being white and me being black? It's fucking hilarious, isn't it?"

I don't even know why I say something. It just comes out the way you scratch mosquito bites, consciously making an effort not to, but then your hand just moves up and scratches anyway. "You're the one that started saying stuff about white and black, Becca. Not Libbie, and not me."

Becca stares at me for a minute, then carefully starts to speak. Which, might I add, is way scarier than any of the screaming that just occurred in the last few minutes. "Theresa, you have a mouth after all. How fantastic. Let me tell you a little something about who started what, okay?"

As if I have a choice.

She continues, her scary voice sounding on the edge of flipping over into psychotic. "You have no fucking idea what you're even talking about. You sit here on the cot, crying wah-wah-wah about who knows what, and don't think nobody notices your suitcase is Donna Karan. That all the little skinny-ass clothes in that suitcase are expensive designer shit. So what's the deal with Theresa, hm?" She makes her voice sound fake-confused, high-pitched, annoying. "Did you run away from your big pretty house with your pretty backyard and your pretty little dollies to have a special adventure, hm? Maybe your life was just too gosh-darned boring over there in suburbia? Too many slumber parties and days at the beach and straight-A report cards?"

My mouth hangs open and nothing comes out.

Libbie speaks up then, blessedly, because I sure can't. "Becca, knock it off."

"Libbie, shut up." Becca keeps her eyes on me even as she snaps at Libbie. "Do you really think for one second you're anything like me? Or even like Libbie or Cammie? How could you for one fucking minute ever think your life is anything like ours?"

She stares like she actually wants an answer, so I give her one. "Because," I say slowly, obviously. "We're all here in the same situation."

She laughs. Libbie looks down at her hands. "Oh come ON, Theresa!" Becca says. "You never for one second been in the same situation as me. Out on the streets when I was nine. Wanna know why? Because my daddy went to jail for killing somebody else's daddy, and my mommy blew her fucking brains out all over the kitchen table. So, 'stead of spending the next ten years getting raped in good old California's foster care program, I left on my own." She takes a breath and scowls at me, willing it all to settle in and scare the bejesus out of me. Which, of course, it already has.

"Libbie, over there." She jerks her head toward Libbie. "Reading her classic shit. You ain't nothing like her either. She didn't get out of foster care fast enough, you know that? Didn't do like me and leave before it was too late. Nope. She only ran after bashing her foster father's head in with a hotel lamp. Right, Libbie? It's cool, though, you know? Fuckers like that rape a kid one too many times, they all gonna get a lamp to the head at some point."

I stare at Libbie. "Is that true?"

She looks at me without nodding or shaking her head, just looks, and that's plenty.

I put my hand over my mouth. "Oh my God."

Becca nodded her head vigorously. "Yeah! Surprised, ain'tcha? Cammie, she don't say much, but she carves those nice little pictures into her arm to remember, or maybe forget – who the fuck knows? – how many times her brother sold her to his friends for free blowjobs before she got ten candles on a cake. So tell me, Theresa, what's *your* story? Go ahead. I'm just dying to hear how you're in *exactly* the same situation as us."

My eyes sting from the tears. All I can see are images of Libbie getting raped, of Becca finding her mom in the kitchen, of Cammie as a little girl being forced to…I start to cry, because really, how much worse can people be in life?

Libbie scoots off her bed and comes over to mine. "Oh for Christ's sake, Becca, you didn't need to do that." She sighs and puts an arm around me. I cry harder, my hands over my face. When I finally look up, Becca is sitting on her cot, but with no nasty fire left in her. She just looks sad. Stares down at her hands for a minute, then gets up and sits next to me and Libbie.

"I'm so sorry," I say, like it will make any difference at all. "I don't – I mean, my situation isn't like yours. I see that. I'm so sorry." I start crying again, because what else can you do when you don't have anyone but damaged people to take care of you, and you're feeling too sorry for yourself to help anyone else out?

"Well, what *is* your deal, Theresa? I mean obviously you're all knocked up with nowhere to go." Libbie asks gently, and smiles a sad smile at me.

"I didn't get raped. I didn't – my dad never touched me...like that...ever. Nobody ever touched me like *that*. I just loved a guy, Charlie, and he loved me."

Libbie and Becca look at each other, and I know exactly why. I'm sitting here with a fat belly, and no guy.

"He was my only boyfriend, I swear. I mean, the only guy I ever even kissed or, you know, did *anything* with. We were going to just wait 'til I finished high school and then get married. We were going to Europe to see everything there, you know?"

They put their arms around me and nod. A cocoon of understanding.

"It just happened one day. And then I started to get fat. And then when I stopped by his house on the way home from school, before I told him about the baby, you know? I stopped by and some woman answered the door – she was old, too. Like, way older than us. And she told me to stay away from him."

"Did you fight her?" Becca jokes.

I shake my head at the memory. "No. I asked to see him, but before the woman could call him or anything, he came out. And he saw me, and I asked what was going on. I wanted to tell him right then, to just, like, blurt out: 'I'm pregnant! I need help!'"

"Well, did you?" Libbie asks.

"No. He put an arm around that woman and she kissed his neck..." My chest feels tight. I haven't said this aloud to anyone, ever. I never even told my mother I was dating him. And Charlie didn't like me hanging out with other people, so it was just me and him.

"Holy shit! Tell me you decked her. Or him. Or both of them!" Becca fidgets next to Libbie, like they're watching a soap opera unfold. *Drama is only fun when it happens to everyone else*, I think.

"I didn't. Deck her, I mean." I try to shrug the way Becca does when she hides how she feels. "He said, 'This is the girl.' And then he looked at me, and they had their arms around each other and stuff, and he says, 'Quit stalking me or I'll call the police.' And they both just stared at me, and then she slammed the door."

I sigh.

"And that was it. But I still kept getting fat. And sick. And then I went to this doctor, he was a real asshole, I mean a really big one...anyway, then my mother found out when she walked in on me naked in the shower. She was just putting away some fresh, warm towels for me to use." I start crying yet again. "And then –"

Libbie smoothes my hair away from my wet, sticky face. "Yeah."

We sit like that for a few minutes, quietly, holding on to each other. Then Becca stands abruptly. "Well this place is too fucking depressing for three hotties like us. Let's go get some food."

We put our shoes on, and walk out into the sunlight.

"Hollywood is the place to be, if you ain't got nowhere else to be." Becca looks up at the blue sky and smiles.

"I don't have anywhere else to be," Libby says, linking her arm in mine.

"Me neither," I say.

But I think I'm the only one who wishes it wasn't true.

When we get back from dinner (hot dogs from a vendor on the strip who loads on the chili and cheese and doesn't charge us for it at all), Cammie is back, sitting on the bed. She's holding a wad of toilet paper against her nose, which is bleeding pretty hard. Her sleeve is soaked red from what I guess was before she could get to some toilet paper. The three of us stop in the doorway, no small feat, by the way, considering that I alone almost take up the entire opening.

Becca, not surprisingly, is the first to speak. "What the fuck's going on?"

Cammie looks up, still holding the stained wad of tissue against her face. She slowly pulls it away from her nose and waits to see if the bleeding has stopped. When nothing else runs out, she looks at us and shakes her head.

Libbie goes over to her bed. Becca and I crowd around, until the four of us are sitting on the one tiny cot, and Cammie's little pile of bloody crumpled toilet paper topples over.

Becca tries again. "Girl, you better speak up right now. Who done this to you?"

Cammie looks down at her lap. That's how we know it was one of the jerks who picked her up for sex, because whenever something about that kind of stuff comes on TV, Cammie always looks down, and it always takes her a long time to look up again.

"Jesus!" Becca explodes for the second time today. "What the fuck is it gonna to take to make you stop doin' this shit? Wait 'til some pervert knifes you up or bashes your skull!" She stands and puts her hands on her head, pacing around the tiny room. "You coulda DIED, Cammie. Some fucker coulda killed you, that what you want? That what you fucking want to happen to your ass?"

"Maybe." Cammie's voice is sickeningly quiet.

Becca stands there with her mouth hanging open. Libbie and me just stare at the blackening bruises under her eyes.

"Don't, Cammie." Libbie reaches out and takes her hand, and I take the other one. "Don't say stuff like that. You don't want to die."

She presses more folded toilet paper to her nose, dabbing at some leftover blood. "No," she says, calmly, decisively, in the same kind of voice you use when you tell someone, *Yes, I'll have fries with that.* "No, I think I do."

Becca slams a fist against the wall. "Cammie! Knock it off! Don't start pullin' shit like that." She sounds angry, but more, she just sounds scared, which I guess is okay, since Libbie and I are petrified holding Cammie's hands. But not okay, since it's Becca, who just doesn't get scared.

I squeeze her hand. "No, Cammie. It's okay; you're just really upset. Anybody would be after something like this. Are you okay? Do you want to go to the hospital? Is your nose…is it broken?"

Cammie stares at me as she talks from under the toilet paper. "Theresa. Where do you think we are? What do you think this is? Do I *want* to go the hospital? Yes, please. I'd love to go the hospital and have them fix my nose, which is broken, judging from the piece of bone that ended up in the first tissue I used to soak up the blood."

Even though her voice sounds kind of mean, I take this as a good sign. The first step to helping someone recover, I remember from my health class with Mrs. Lesbian Carlson, is getting them to admit they have a problem. So I smile. "Okay. Good. Let's go to the hospital, then. Come on. All of us can go with you." I heave myself off the cot.

Libbie sits there looking down, shaking her head. Becca just stares up at the ceiling from her place lying down on her cot. Cammie's face softens then, and when she opens her mouth again her voice isn't mean anymore.

"Theresa. I want to go to the hospital. But I *can't* go." She sighs and throws the bloody tissue over the edge of the bed. "It's not in the cards, baby. Just not in the cards."

I don't know what to say, and I look to Libbie for help. She presses her lips together. Trying, I can just tell, not to hurt my feelings, which I guess hurt pretty easily, judging from how much Libbie tries to take care of me. "She can't go to the hospital because she's a minor, Theresa. She's too young. They're going to ask where her parents are. That's problem number one. Then, they're going to ask how she got her broken nose. She can't tell them she got it being a hooker and some guy beat the crap out of her as payment. That's problem number two. They're going to look into where she really belongs after she gives her name. Cammie, where do you belong?"

"In a foster home on the West Side. I left after they locked me in the bedroom without food or anything, and I ended up having to pee standing up, halfway out the window. It ran down my leg and onto my socks. I busted the window after three days and left."

Libbie nodded, not looking surprised, because this was, of course, just a normal story from a normal girl. "Right. So she gives her name, she has no parents, but she has a broken nose. They're going to start poking around, find out she's in the System, and two hours later they'll take her back into custody and put her back in the foster home." She looked at me, eyes wide and bright. "Do you understand now?"

I nod, feeling stupid that I'd never thought of these things. Becca stands up and starts out toward the door.

"Where are you going?" I ask.

"Cafeteria. Steal some bags of ice to put on her face."

Libbie goes to her cot. She reaches underneath and pulls out a tiny travel first aid kit. "I have gauze, if you want to pack it up there, Cam. It'll hurt pretty bad, but maybe it'll help."

Cammie nods. She swings her legs over the side of the bed and faces me. I plop down on my cot so our knees are practically touching.

"Sorry I was bitchy, kiddo. That's just the way it is."

My face heats up. "It doesn't have to be, though. It doesn't have to be this way, Cammie. Libbie." I look at both of them, feeling enraged. I turn my gaze back to Cammie, whose eyes look sad above the dark circles. "You don't have to do…that. You can find another way to get money. You don't ever have to do that again."

She stares at me without saying a word, and I see her. I mean, I really see *her*, a little girl who's ruined, and want to kill someone with my own bare, swollen hands.

I lie down on my cot and fold both hands over my enormous stomach because suddenly the little girl inside me is moving around like crazy. Kicking right at my belly button. I yank up my shirt. "You guys! Come here! Quick, quick."

Becca walks in with two ice bags and drops them on Cammie's cot.

"Come here! Put your hands on my stomach and feel this. You gotta feel it."

Becca puts a hand on, then jerks it away. "Holy shit! That is some freaky ass something going on in there." She carefully sets her hand back on the baby again.

I smile enormously. "I know! And don't curse in front of the baby."

She nods at me. "Sorry."

Libbie crawls over from her cot and puts a hand on. Cammie leans over and sets her hand next to the three of ours.

"It's so alive in there right now... just jumping all around, waiting to get out." Libbie's smiling. We all are now.

"She," I say.

"She?"

"It's a girl in there. She's a little girl."

We sit like that until she falls asleep and stops kicking. Probably because four hands are holding her and she couldn't have felt safer anywhere else in the whole world.

Cammie's nose started to heal, but only after her whole face swelled like a balloon and the black and blue faded to a really gross green. A few weeks later, the four of us sit on the floor of the Coop playing Uno. I dipped into my precious envelope and bought us pizza, which we had delivered. I even tipped the guy, because, as Becca put it, "He ain't going home to sleep on a bed made of money either."

Libbie pulls the cheese from her pizza and eats that first.

"That's a waste. It ruins the whole pizza," Cammie says.

"What're you talking about? It's delicious. The cheese is the best part." Libbie pulls another glob off.

"Exactly. Why would you pull off the best part and eat all of it at once? That doesn't make sense." She shakes her head and throws down a wild card. "*Green.* If you leave the cheese on, then each bite is just as good as the last."

Libbie puts a card on the pile and shakes her head stubbornly. "No. It's delicious this way. Why don't you concentrate on your own pizza? I'm not picking on you for folding it up like a retard."

Cammie opens the second box and gets another slice out, creasing it down the middle, long ways, and taking a giant bite. "It's double as good this way. See? Because it's double layers of pizza. It's like eating two slices right on top of each other."

"You eat it twice as fast that way," Libbie points out. "The goodness is over in half the time."

Becca huffs. "Just eat the damn pizza!" She throws the rest of her cards down in the middle and leans back against the end of one cot. "I can't play one more game of cards."

The rest of us pile our cards in the middle and lean back with our pizza. We're completely used to sharing quiet time together without having to do much but just be there. We sit silently for a minute, eating.

"Have you thought anymore about a name?" Libbie says at last.

It never fails; one of them asks me this every day since we all felt her kicking. "No."

"Come on, Theresa. You're due to be havin' this baby in ten days. Whatcha gonna do? Say, 'Oh hey, welcome, you ain't got a name, but it's cool' when she pops outta there?" Becca eats her pizza with a fork and a knife, cutting out triangles and chewing each one neatly.

I laugh. "I don't know. I mean, how do I give her a name? It's not like giving someone a shirt they can just try on and not like and get a new one. I don't want to be the one to give a person a crappy name and have them hate me forever."

"What's *your* whole name?" Cammie asks.

"Theresa Constantina Sarah Maureino."

Becca snorts. "What the hell kind of name is Constantina?"

"Nice catch, Bec," Cammie says. Becca is practicing not swearing in front of the baby.

I pretend to be indignant, which I figure is putting my nose up pretty high in the air and raising my eyebrows to a point I deem snobby. "It's Spanish."

Cammie raises her eyebrows. "You don't look Mexican."

Becca shoves her arm. "You idiot. Mexicans aren't Spanish. People from Spain are Spanish." She takes a forkful of pizza and sneaks a glance at Libbie, who is beaming at her for willingly contributing knowledge to the conversation.

"I'm Spanish, a little," I said. "And Constantina was my grandma's name. But *see*? I don't want to name someone something and have them get made fun of their whole life."

"So don't name her Constantina, and you'll be in the clear," Becca shot back.

"Fine. What's *your* full name?"

She puts down her fork and picks up the crust to eat with her hands. "Rebecca Lynn Vermont."

"Oh, that's pretty," Cammie says, and we all agree. "Mine's Kimberly Anne Detweiler. What's yours, Libbie?"

She smiles. "Elizabeth Eleanor Eden. Three Es all in a pretty row."

"Whoooaaaa," Becca says. "You sound like a queen or something. We all kind of sound like royalty, you know? Except Constantina here." She pokes me and grins.

"My mom's name is Caroline, like the real princess." I don't know where it comes from, but I just say it like the most natural thing in the world. The other girls look at me and I feel the surprise. "I'm...I'm just saying. Caroline Kay Maureino." I say it again to make it real, because it's been months since I've even thought her name in my own head, much less said it aloud.

Libbie nods. "That's pretty."

We sit quietly for another minute, chewing, deep in thought.

"'Kay. So, a name then. Figure one out," Becca prods.

"I can't handle that kind of responsibility." I take a swig of soda and let out a disgustingly loud, gaseous burp.

"Charming." Libbie wrinkles her nose. "Just think of a name you really like to say because you'll probably be saying it for the next eighteen years, at least a hundred times a day."

I let this sink in. The next EIGHTEEN years? I'd be...I'd be thirty-two freaking years old! Ho-ly shit. My stomach suddenly feels bad. Bad bad bad. I put my hands on it and breathe out slowly.

All three of them lean forward at the same time, like synchronized surveillance cameras.

"What's wrong?" Becca gasps.

Libbie frowns. "Are you in pain?"

"What's going on? Is she kicking?" At this last suggestion, courtesy of Cammie, three hands join mine on my belly.

I swallow and try to calm the sick feeling. Maybe it's the pizza. Maybe the soda. Maybe the reminder that whatever is growing in there, *whoever* is growing in there, is going to be my responsibility all by myself until I am a wrinkled, shrively thirty-two-year-old old lady. Oh God.

"Theresa! Talk! What's wrong?"

"Oh God," I say. "This is really it."

"You're having the baby! This is it?" Libbie jumps up.

"No! *No.* I mean, God. This is *it.* What if this is the last day I have before the baby is here? The last day anything is normal?" I feel my heart speeding up. "This could be the last...everything...okay?" I crumpled into tears for what was probably the five thousandth time in the last month.

Libbie sits down next to me and puts an arm across my shoulders. Becca takes my hand.

"No, no, honey. It's not like that. We'll be fine," Becca pets my hand.

I cry harder. "It's not *we,* Becca. It's *me.* I'm alone. I'm supposed to push a whole baby out of a place that, oh my God, I just can't push anything out of, and then I'm going to have it forever. For my whole life. What if I don't want it? What if I don't want it sitting next to me because I just have a day where I want to sit by myself, and it sits next to me anyway, and there's *nothing I can do about it. Oh my God!*"

"Her," says Cammie. "Not 'it.'"

Libbie breathes out. "All right. Calm down. That's enough. Theresa. *Theresa!*"

I smear the tears across my face and look at her. "What?"

She smiles and smoothes the hair away from my forehead. "You aren't alone. Look at us. We're right here. We're all here, and we'll be there the whole time, and we'll hold your hand while you push it out, and we'll hold her on our laps on the days that you don't feel like having anybody sit next to you. Okay? You're not alone."

Becca and Cammie nod. My cocoon is around me again, and the whole thing doesn't feel as bad as two minutes ago.

We sit like that for a minute, and then Becca sighs. "Well, that's enough After-School Special shit. What's next? Somebody gonna offer you a hit off their cigarette and we're all gonna break into song about just saying no?"

She's always good for easing tension, in her own crazy way. We laugh, and I look up at the ceiling. "I like the way 'Sandra' sounds."

Libbie smiles and says, "Yeah!" encouragingly just as Becca shakes her head and says, "Uh uh. No way."

"Why not?" We both ask together.

"Because I had a teacher, Sandra Smarts – you know you're in for it when your teacher's name is 'Smarts.' She taught me first grade, that gigantic, frizzy-haired bitch, that's why not."

"What'd she do to you? And, for the record, I'm sure you were a peach to have as a student." Libbie smirks.

"What'd she do? Everything to make us miserable. The woman shoulda never been allowed near kids, much less to teach 'em. She smacked me across the *back of my knees* with her pointer. 'Cept she didn't have a real pointer, so she used the little twirly thing for opening and shutting blinds. She pointed with that. And whacked me with it at least once a week for a whole miserable year."

"Why?" I ask.

"Why you asking me why? I don't know why. Only one time I knew, and it was cuz I licked her stockings."

I screech. Libbie and Cammie yell, "*What?*"

Becca shrugs. "They looked like they'd feel weird on my tongue. They were all, like, bumpy-looking and dark."

We can't stop laughing.

"So you licked them, then?" Libbie snorts out.

Becca starts laughing too. "Yeah. And you know what? They did feel weird, just like I thought."

"Gross, Becca. Really, really gross," Cammie says.

I feel so much better, sitting there, giggling on the floor with these girls who love me. Nothing is as bad as it felt before, and I'm going to be okay. We'll all be okay.

Chapter 12

The thing about lights-out at the Coop is that nobody makes the lights go out at any certain time. Becca says this is one of the perks of lying about our age. That if we went to one of the shelters for kids, they're up your ass all the time about school and bedtimes and curfews and stuff.

The four of us usually agree on when to go to sleep instead of just fighting about staying up. The problem comes when it isn't just my girls and me. Other women come. Strangers who show up in the middle of the night or the middle of the afternoon, choose one of the cots the four of us haven't claimed, and stay for the night or five nights or, sometimes, for a couple weeks at a time. We all hate that. It feels like an unwelcome guest sitting right smack dab in the middle of our home, and so, in the spirit of keeping things normal and L.A.-ish, we all choose to completely ignore the strangers. And unfortunately, right now, despite it being almost eleven p.m., usually a small sign of hope that we got through another day without a stranger, Libbie and Cammie and Becca and I are sitting in the dark, listening to the desk worker check in someone new.

We can hear the faint questioning. And then, dammit, the shuffling of feet toward the Coop. The door opens and it's not one of the girls who has ever been here before. This girl is really not a girl at all; she's this dumpy forty-something woman who wobbles as she carries a dirty yellow duffel bag with *Brian* stitched into one side. I highly doubt she's Brian, or that she even knows him. And then I'm lying here thinking about who he is and whether he left his bag somewhere and when he came back to find it, this hag of a woman had already stolen it. It makes me hate her immediately.

"Hey, shut the lights!" Libbie yells at the woman, who has flipped the switch up and blasted the room with light. We get a better view of her overweight, dirty body, and the day-old bruise across her left cheek. She mumbles something none of us can even begin to understand and then collapses on the nearest cot. Which, unfortunately for her, has Becca already in it.

"HEY! Get your fat ass off me, grandma! What the hell! Jesus, you reek like piss. GET OFF ME!" She shoves the woman, who, oddly enough, seems like she doesn't even notice anything has happened. Instead, she flops down over an empty cot and looks completely asleep before any of us even have time to react. We sit there absorbing the pee smell and the fact that we won't have a night with just the four of us.

"Ugh, disgusting." Becca gets up out of bed and tears her thin blanket off, throwing it onto the ground and yanking a clean one off of one of the other cots. "Pig," she grumbles.

"Shut the lights again, Becca," Libbie directs.

"You shut them, Libbie, you're closer to the damn switch."

"You're already up. Don't be unreasonable."

Becca grumbles a little more then moves three feet to flip the switch down. We lie like that, the four of us in the dark, with a urine-stained stranger snoring a really gross snore two feet from me.

"I hate strangers," I say to nobody.

"Me too," Libbie says.

"Me too," Becca says.

We're quiet for a minute, waiting.

"Cammie, do you *love* strangers or something?" Libbie asks, because the silence is noticeable when one of us doesn't speak up.

Cammie's voice comes quietly from her cot. "No. I don't love strangers. I don't hate that woman either, though. She just doesn't have anywhere else to go. How is she different than us when we're all laying on these stupid cots under these stupid brown blankets?"

"Uh, hello?" Becca starts up. "She's like fifty and pissing herself and hideously disfigured on top of being fat and greasy."

"Oh, Becca, you're such a bitch. It's a bruise on her face, not a disfigurement," Cammie shoots back, but really, with not much power behind the harsh words.

"She's not the same as us at all, and you know it."

The only sound we hear for a moment is the snoring.

"Cammie!" Becca doesn't want to let it rest for the same reason I don't. "Cammie, she's not the same as us. You know that."

"No, but that's where we'll be at that age," Cammie says quietly. "I don't want to be that."

Libbie, always the peacemaker, chimes in. "Cammie, none of us will be like that. You're talking crazy because you're tired and we're all inhaling piss fumes, which is making our brains not work right. Just go to sleep, and she'll probably be gone in the morning. Goodnight."

"Night."

The other girls fall asleep almost immediately. I'm the last one to drift off, so when I feel the twist in my belly and open my eyes, I'm sure I haven't fallen asleep yet. I squint at the old digital clock with the red letters that Becca keeps under her bed: 3:20. My stomach lurches again, and the baby moves around doing somersaults in there. I sit up and press both hands on my stomach. This calms her down a little bit, and I sit in the quiet for a minute, feeling her settling. Except, then it isn't quiet. I hear a sound, really quiet and unfamiliar, and hold my breath to listen better, but then the baby kicks and I get worried I held my breath too long and didn't give her any air. That can't be good. The sound comes again and I look to the other girls to see if they're hearing it. That's when I notice Cammie's cot is empty. I ease myself out of the bed, no small task considering I'm absolutely gigantic and my back hurts too bad to even stand upright. Sometimes I feel like I should tip over forward from how heavy my belly is. I waddle to the door and open it. Sitting out in the hall, against the bathroom door, is Cammie, sobbing muffled cries into her red 49ers t-shirt.

"Cammie?" I whisper, even though nobody else is around. I feel like, since it's the middle of the night and we're in our pajamas, I should whisper. She looks up, face swollen from crying, eyes puffy and red and bloodshot. I heave my body step by heavy step toward her. "Cammie, what's wrong?"

She shakes her head, breathing in crazy bursts the way you have to when you cry so hard your chest just doesn't go at the right pace to keep your body going. She gasps in these breaths, then wipes her eyes.

"Well…I'd love to sit here with you, but I can't get my fat ass down on the ground and I sure as hell won't be able to get it back up once it's down there."

She smiles a little and stands. "Go back to bed, you need to rest and stuff." She motions at my belly.

"Nah. I'm not even tired. Let's go to the swings." We always go to the swings at night when there's nothing else we can do and we don't want to sleep. The elementary school built a new playground on the other end of the grounds, so the old one, which holds only six rusty swings and a super rusty slide, sits open for us to visit whenever we want. The two of us make our slow way there and each takes a swing. I'm really being serious when I say I have to squeeze into the banana seat. The chains on either side cut into my body, because I'm too wide to even sit in normal chairs and things anymore.

Cammie pumps her legs gently, but I sit still without swinging. "You want to talk about it?"

She pumps a little more and leans her head back to look up at the sky as she swings forward. "Nothing to talk about."

"Well...crying in the middle of the night on the scummy floor is a start."

"Scummy floor, scummy bed. Doesn't matter."

"You're having some kind of I-Hate-the-Coop-Day, huh?"

She stops pumping her legs and slowly swings to a stop. "No, Theresa. It's not that. It's that I hate my whole life. The Coop. This city. The sickos who pick me up. Not having the shampoo that I want to just wash my hair when I want to wash it. I hate it all."

I don't have an answer to that, so I say the first thing that pops into my mind. "So, change it, then. If you don't like it, change it."

Cammie smiles at me, a sweet smile; one that's older, so much older than her fifteen years. "What do you want to do with your baby?"

I think about that. I have about a thousand ideas about what I want to do, only none of them actually apply to a baby. They all apply to a non-baby, like a little girl. Swings, for one. A My Little Pony party. First-day-of-school shopping. I tell these to Cammie, and she smiles and pushes the mulch around with her foot as I talk.

She pulls herself to a stop and looks over at me in the dark. "Are you happy?"

"Right now? Yeah." And it's true. I am happy sitting on those swings in the middle of the night with the air smelling warm and clear, and the baby not moving around, and Cammie swinging next to me. "Are you?"

She starts twisting her swing around so the chain winds up tightly. "No. I'm not, Theresa. I'm sad."

"Why?"

She pulls her feet off the ground and spins as the chain untwists. When she wobbles to a stop, she looks at me again. "Because I'll never be any better than exactly what I am right now. What that pee woman is, in there. And that's just how it is."

"Why do you say that, Cammie?" I try to keep my tone light, but I feel angry. She doesn't even have a baby to worry about. How can she feel hopeless?

She rubs her arms and sighs. "Because, it's just how it is. This is the best part of our lives, right now, you know? This is the youngest, best part, and look at us. Imagine how much worse it'll get from here on out."

Something thick clogs my throat. "No, that isn't true. This is just a little...kind of glitch, a little bad part, and after this, when we're older, we'll have everything we want to have. You can do whatever you want.

This, the Coop, the everything, it's just, like, a stupid bad chapter in life, but your whole life book will be great. You just have to wait a little while."

Cammie starts pumping her legs again. "What do you want, then? When this bad chapter is over. What will you do?"

I smile. "Everything I want to do. Probably something in the fashion business. I definitely want to go to Europe and work there for a while, maybe Italy or something, like Milan, where all real designers start out. And other stuff too."

She gets off the swing, lies on her back on the brown mulch below it, puts an arm behind her head, and closes her eyes. "What other stuff? Tell me about it."

It's nice to talk about something other than the normal everyday crap we all deal with. Wonderful to talk about where I'm going when this is all over. "Well, my sister, Abby, always used to tell me about how I should design clothes, you know. Because I'm good at putting together outfits and stuff, and people pay other people to do that for them. Did you know that? I could actually get a job to make people's outfits. It's rad."

Cammie smiles. "That's awesome. I wonder if it pays good."

"Probably. I mean rich people probably don't want to pick out their own clothes so they just hire someone to do it."

"What else?"

"Well, I saw this one thing on TV last year where you actually go to Florida and they let you go into this big, like, *gigantic* pool, and you swim with dolphins. They're all swimming free around you and you can touch them and pet them and stuff."

Cammie opens her eyes. "Seriously?"

"Yeah! It's so awesome. I'm definitely going to do that."

"What if they bite you or like freak out or something?"

"No, no, they're really nice. They don't bite."

"Wow. That's really cool then."

"Yeah." I kick my feet against the mulch and swing the tiniest bit. Feeling free and light even though I'm a whale. "Oh! And there's this place down there, too, where you go on a boat and the whole bottom is made of glass, and you get to stand on it and look down at alligators and fish and stuff swimming under the boat."

"Now that is definitely too scary. I wouldn't want alligators swimming right under me. What if they broke the glass?"

"They can't break the glass. It's really super-thick glass, totally safe."

"Florida sounds cool."

"Yeah, I might live there for a few years just to see what it's like, you know?"

Cammie closes her eyes again. "Yeah. And what about the baby?"

"What about it?" I mean to say *her* and not it, but at the moment it feels like there is no baby, and I like the feeling so much I don't want it to stop.

"I mean, how will you do all those things with her?"

"I'll just...do them. I'm sure they let kids in the pool with the dolphins. And she can fly places with me on airplanes."

"Yeah."

My great feeling is fading, though, and I try to catch it again. "And I'll just do whatever I want to do, and have someone to do it with."

Cammie smiles without showing her teeth. "Yeah. And they make those cute little baby carriers that you wear like backpacks."

I feel better again. "Yeah! And she'll just, you know, chill out as we go."

"Yeah."

I am exhausted all of a sudden and want to be back in bed, sleeping a whole night's worth of sleep. "You ready to head back? I'm really tired."

Cammie opens her eyes and looks at me. "I'm comfortable right here, looking up at the sky. And it's nice and breezy out."

"You want to stay, then?"

"Yeah. I'll be in a little later."

I haul myself off the swing and start walking back toward the Coop. "Okay, see you later."

"Night."

"Night, Cammie."

I crawl back into my cot as soon as I get home and fall asleep before the snoring even has time to annoy me.

"I hate the eggs because they're runny. That's all. It has nothing to do with anything else they serve, I just hate those eggs," Libbie's voice breaks through my sleep.

Becca's voice comes next. "Fine. Then don't eat them."

"I won't."

I pry one eye open and look at them. "Um...what time is it and why are we talking about eggs?"

Libbie fluffs her pillow and pulls the scratchy blanket up to the top of her bed. "It's quarter to eleven, and we're talking about eggs because Becca wants to go to Saint Paul's for breakfast. *Which is fine.*" She shoots a look at Becca. "But I was just commenting on how the eggs there are absolutely disgusting."

I nod, awake now. "Yeah, they're all slimy."

Becca lets out a loud sigh and Libbie grins. "See?"

"Fine, then neither of you gotta eat the eggs, okay?"

"Okay," I say, easing myself up. "Somebody's a grump this morning."

Becca gestures toward the empty cot. "Gee, I wonder why. Maybe it's 'cause the pig lady kept me up all night with her nasty oinking, then woke me again at the ass-crack of dawn when she stumbled out and left."

"At least she left," Libbie points out, and neither of us can disagree.

I open my suitcase and pull out a pink, flowered maternity shirt. It barely fits over my belly, and still kind of smells like armpit from the last time I wore it and didn't wash it. Oh well. Who would I impress at a soup kitchen?

Libbie and Becca are waiting out front by the pay phone.

"Where's Cammie?" I ask.

Becca shrugs. "I don't know. She was already gone by the time we woke up."

"She was up before you?"

Becca looks impatient. "I guess. Didn't see her when I got up. Let's go. I'm starving here."

We start walking down the avenue toward St. Paul's, but I just can't let it drop. "Did either of you hear her come back in last night?"

"What're you talking about? She went to bed with us. Are the hormones messing with your brain?" Libbie pokes my belly gently.

I feel...uneasy. My stomach feels weird. Not the weird I've been feeling for the past six months, but the kind of weird I used to feel before there was ever something in there. "No. You guys, she was crying in the hallway in the middle of the night."

"Why?" Libbie wants to know.

"Because, she just was. It's a long story. Anyway, we went to the swings, and were there a little while. Then I was tired, so I came home, but she stayed."

"By herself?" Becca asks.

"Well, I was tired." I feel guilty because I left her alone at night and any one of her so-called sickos could've found her before she came home. "And she said she was comfortable outside." Like that made a difference.

Becca grumbles. "Fine. So, then, where'd she go? Who'd she go with?" She stops walking and kicks a rock across the street. "I'm sick of this shit with her!"

"Becca, calm down," Libbie says. "We don't even know if she went with one of them."

Maybe we don't know, but we're all pretty sure. Anytime Cammie disappeared in the middle of the night it was because she was out of money and needed to get some more. So she waited by the park six blocks away from the Coop, and eventually someone came along, and sometimes they smashed in her face, and sometimes they didn't. Sometimes she came back within an hour and sometimes she didn't come back 'til morning.

Well, it's morning now. The guilt drops low in my stomach and I feel sick. "You guys...what if that same guy who did that to her nose found her again?"

"You're the one who left her," Becca snaps, and then looks like she immediately regrets it when the words hang between us like a giant, terrible blame.

"Becca," Libbie says quietly.

"I was *tired!*" I yell. "Tired and wanted to go to bed and she seemed happy to lie there and sleep by the swings. I was tired." I start to cry, and Libbie puts her arms around me.

"Sorry," Becca whispers. "Sorry."

Libbie breathes out. "Let's just go get some breakfast. We'll check the Coop again when we get back. Becca, you're always a beast when you're hungry."

Becca stares in the other direction, and even though she said she was sorry, and I know she probably is sorry for making me cry, her eyebrows are furrowed and she looks more angry than anything else.

The thing about St. Paul's is the volunteers. They're always just so...*sorry* for us. Which I'm usually fine with, except that the last few weeks one of the volunteers there has been Matthew. He somehow always manages to get the bacon station, and, okay, yeah, I love bacon, but how am I supposed to ask for extra slices when I'm a walrus who obviously does not need any extra bacon, and then to top it off Matthew is the one holding the tongs over the bacon bin. He's gorgeous. I've managed to find out four things in the little bits of conversations I push out while he's tonging bacon onto my Styrofoam plate: he's a sophomore at UCLA; his major is psychology; he volunteers here for extra credit in one of his classes; he wakes up every morning and thinks, "Today is going to be another gorgeous day filled with amazing opportunities because I am so good looking that nobody could possibly resist my charm or dimples."

Okay, I made up the last one, but figure it's got to be pretty close to the truth. Unless, of course, he's even more perfect and doesn't realize how gorgeous he is. Then I guess he wouldn't do that last thing at all.

"You're looking blue today." Matthew smiles the million-dollar smile. His teeth, all in perfect rows, gleam at me from behind the sneeze guard over the bacon bin.

I know I blush because I can feel it. A hotness creeping up my neck and into my face. "Yeah, it's been a long day."

He laughs. "It's not even 10 a.m." He picks up three pieces of bacon and puts them on my plate.

"Three?"

He grins again, eyes so sparkly green and those dimples winking at me. I almost swoon right into the sneeze guard. "An extra piece to cheer you up."

I stare at him. "I love bacon." Oh my God. I love bacon? Ah! I pick up my plate and turn away as quick as my giganto belly will let me.

"Cheer up. I hear it's supposed to be another gorgeous day in Los Angeles. Enjoy it." When I peek back over one shoulder, he winks at me, then tongs bacon for the next person in line.

"Thanks," I mumble, then kick myself the entire way to the benched table for not even smiling or saying something like...well, here I am, after the fact, and still can't even think of something witty to say. Still, just once, I'd like to know what to say exactly when I need to say it.

We eat, the three of us on the bench, Cammie's spot noticeably empty. Becca got the eggs, Libbie didn't, and I got pancakes already doused in syrup to keep us from using too much, so they were soggy and wet. I didn't taste them anyway. I ate the bacon slowly, savoring the salty greasiness.

"Extra bacon, huh?" Becca raises her eyebrows.

I blush again. "Yeah."

"Hm. Girl's got a way with the bacon guy."

"Matthew," Libbie and I say at the same time.

"And I don't have a way," I add, but smile as I say it because maybe he didn't just give me more bacon to cheer me up. Moments like this (and I could count four of them since the whole thing started) make me feel like I used to feel before I looked like this. "He just gave me an extra piece to cheer up my day."

Libbie grins. "I'd take a piece from him any day."

Becca tilts her head back and laughs. "Ha! Yeah and Miss Theresa here would too."

And just like that, like a light switch, the funniness turns off and my happiness turns off and all I feel is sick. "No, I wouldn't." I see a flash of Charlie's face above mine, pleading with me. Of loving his hands on me but feeling nervous, then so afraid.

Libbie raises an eyebrow. "Oh no?"

I put down the last bite of bacon and stare at her. "Do you really think that I'd ever want to...ever again? Seriously. Jesus, look at me. The last thing in the entire world I ever want to see or have anything to do with is...you know what."

"Dicks?" Becca offers.

I take a sip of the watery orange juice. "Yes."

Libbie shakes her head. "You just feel like that now."

"Yeah! And I think with good reason, Libbie!"

She blinks at me. "Whoa, calm down. You do have good reason. I'm just saying. Don't shut the door on man parts altogether just because one bad guy got you into this mess. Someday you'll find a good one."

I stare at her. "Penis?"

"Guy. A good guy." She smiles and takes a bite of the barely-browned white toast she's eating.

We finish up. Matthew gives us (me, I think) a little wave as we walk out.

Becca wipes her hands down the front of her black jeans. "So, let's go by the swings."

I'd temporarily forgotten the current crisis: Cammie. We walk to the playground and, like we pretty much expected, it's empty. I stare at the swing I sat on next to her in the middle of the night. Look at the mulch lying under the swing and picture her lying there with her eyes closed, smiling at all the things I was saying. And suddenly feel real, honest-to-God panic.

I grab Libbie's hand. "You guys."

They stop walking and look over the same way they look at me every time I ask for their attention: like I'm about to pop out a kid right there on the spot.

I shake my head. "No. It's not that. I'm worried about Cammie." My eyes fill up with tears that sting and burn. "I'm worried one of the crazy guys got her last night. I'm worried that..." The tears start coming down my face, and my chest gets tight.

Becca rubs my back soothingly. "Oh, knock it off. She's fine. She's probably back at The Coop already."

I don't feel better, and really, neither do they. We walk faster, and then Libbie stops suddenly, making me and Becca stop with her. "You guys!" She smacks a hand to her forehead. "I totally forgot! She had that appointment at the crisis center therapist today, remember? Wait, it's the thirteenth, right? Yeah! Duh." She shakes her head and smiles, then starts walking slowly again.

I feel a weight lifting off me. "It was today? This morning?"

Libbie nods. "Yeah, I totally forgot. Apparently a chick there sees patients who can't pay anything, and she gives them, like, an hour a week for free. Cammie saw a flyer for it on the pay phone outside, and she was all about going and, like, getting it all out."

Becca sighs disgustedly. "She coulda left a note."

Libbie rolls her eyes. "Oh yeah,'cuz it's just like her to leave notes before she goes out. We're not her freaking parents, for Pete's sake."

Becca frowns. "Who the hell is Pete?"

"It's an *expression*! Geez!"

I half-listen to the gibbering, and picture Cammie lying on a brown leather couch, talking to a woman in a suit who's nodding and writing things down on a little black notepad. Relief washes over me.

And right at that moment, as the relief washes and I feel as carefree as is possible for someone in my current position, we turn the corner of the block that Second Chance is on and see police cars and an ambulance are blocking the entrance to The Coop.

We stop at the edge of the police-car wall. A cop in a uniform spots us and walks our way, a hand on the side of his belt. On his gun, I guess. "Girls, I need you to please step back." He puts a hand up like we're trying to push past him. "Please step back."

Becca props her hands on her hips. "Yeah, okay, we heard you the first time. What's going on?"

"Miss, I am not at liberty to say at this time. Please step back."

"We're stepped back!" Becca snaps. "What's goin' on? Hello, we live here? This is where we *live*." She sounds scared, and that scares me. Libbie looks terrified too, on the other side of me. I glance around and spot Mrs. Claremont, the lady who sometimes runs the front desk. She knows us. She's sitting on the back step of the ambulance with two police officers.

"Mrs. Claremont!" I yell. She looks up, sees Becca, Libbie, and me and bursts into tears. We back away from the jerk cop and walk toward the ambulance. The fastest walking I've done in four months, and my body hurts from the effort. I heave breaths in and out. "Mrs. Claremont! What's going on?"

She sobs into a white cloth in her hand, and I think about how gross handkerchiefs are. Then I think of my father, blowing his nose loudly on the ones my mother always ironed for him.

The policeman on her left speaks up first. "Mrs. Claremont, do you know these girls? Are they related to you?"

She shakes with sobbing, voice wobbly. "I know them. They live here."

"Are they related to you?" he asks gently.

She shakes her head. He looks at us again. "Girls, I'm going to have to ask you to move off the premises while the situation is handled by the authorities."

Libbie takes over. "Sir, what situation are we talking about, exactly?" She asks calmly, using a voice I'm sure she's practiced for sounding like a grown up in just such occasions.

"I'm not at liberty to say, miss. You'll need to leave the premises until the authorities clear them. That's all. Thank you."

Libbie looks desperately at Mrs. Claremont. "Please tell us what's going on. *Please*, Mrs. Claremont."

She only chokes on a sob and shakes her head slightly.

"That's it," Becca says, and grabs our arms. "Come on. We're 'leaving the premises,'" she says loudly.

We walk to the edge of the parking lot, then keep on walking. I'm getting tired. "Where are we going, Becca?"

"Around. To the side entrance. One with the low window that goes into the bathroom." She rounds the corner of the building and starts tromping through the overgrown weeds and grass. "Hurry up!"

I push through the mess of branches and knee-high weeds. Becca reaches the building first, followed by Libbie, and then me, pressing through the mess on legs that I'm sure will collapse. My flimsy flip-flops catch on twigs and yank at me. Three feet later my right flip-flop snags and sticks. I trip forward and gasp at the fact that I've almost fallen right on my stomach. I yank and my flip-flop comes off.

"It's right there! Come on! We'll go in through the window." Becca moves forward and I hurry to catch up, one shoe short.

"Ow!" I scream, as a sharp, jagged pain shoots up through my leg. "Ow! God, ow ow ow!" Libbie and Becca stop in their tracks and turn back to me.

"*What?!*"

I limp forward. "I – I stepped on something! Ow, it hurts so bad! It *cut* me." I can't see my foot under all the grass, but feel like I impaled it on a rake or something.

"You okay?" Libbie asks, frowning.

"Can you keep going? We're, like, ten feet away." Becca's voice moves me forward, despite the pain. She crosses the next ten feet in two seconds, and then stands at the window to the bathroom. I should know, then, by the way she stands, so stiff and straight, staring in, not saying a word. Because this is Becca we're talking about, and quiet isn't a thing she does. I probably should know better than to look when Libbie stops next to Becca and, after a brief, shocked silence, starts screaming a scream that just blends into the silence after a few minutes, like a far-off siren.

But I look anyway. I stand with the pressure on both feet and peer into the window at Cammie's lifeless, purplish face hanging two feet from us. Her eyes bulge at nothing, her hands hang limp at her sides. She is strung from the ceiling pipe by her neck, which is messily tied into the blue and purple silk Hermes scarf my mother gave me for my eleventh birthday.

I stand there not moving or thinking, until Becca abruptly sits, out of view of the window, and Libbie stops screaming for no reason other than that she maybe ran out of voice. I stand staring at Cammie while they both sit, and silently tell her how sorry I am.

Maybe it's five seconds later, maybe an hour. I'm not sure exactly, but sometime in there the pain in my belly goes from the normal too-much-oatmeal-feeling to a wrenching, unbelievably *strong* stab that tears down through me. I grit my teeth and groan.

Becca looks up. "Theresa?"

I grab my stomach and squat. The pain tears through again, and I let out a loud, desperate moan.

Libbie looks up, too, but I don't think she's really seeing anything. Becca stands, carefully avoiding the window view. "*Theresa!* What?"

The pain lessens a little, and I mean it when I say you just don't know how good it is to not have pain at all until it's so bad you forget what no pain felt like. "I'm hurt! My stomach! Becca!"

"This is it?" She grabs my arm. "You having the baby? Is this it?"

I clench my jaw. "I don't know! I think so. I'm not sure. Oh God, Becca! Help me! I don't know what to do!" I start to cry.

Maybe that's the magic Libbie needs to spring into action. She jumps up from where she's sitting Indian-style on the ground. "Becca, go get the ambulance. Tell them to bring a stretcher to get her! Go! Run!" She puts one arm around my wide waist and takes my puffy hand with the other. "We're getting help right now. Just try and be calm. *Breathe.* You're okay."

I nod, but the pain rips down again, and I yell through my tears. Becca is yelling to someone, then I feel a hot splashing on my legs and feet. "Libbie! Don't leave! Stay with me!"

She squeezes my hand. "I'm here. I won't leave you. I'm right here."

They load me into the ambulance on a stretcher and lift me up. Becca and Libbie jump into the back with me, and when the tech opens her mouth to tell us something about a one-rider limit, Becca cuts her off. "We're both staying with her." I guess she looks like there's no room to argue, because as the sirens start to scream and we pull out of the parking lot, they're both still holding my hands, one on each side.

I breathe out, and then feel the pain beginning again. Like a rollercoaster, this is the part where the car starts clanking up the take-off hill, and you feel yourself pressed back, hauled toward the top, up, up, up. And then comes the drop. I scream like I'm flying down a ninety-foot drop. "STOP THE PAIN!" I grit my teeth, then let out a really terrible animal roar.

"Give her something!" Becca shouts at the tech.

"We can't until we get her to the hospital and a doctor finds out what's going on," the tech says calmly, despite my screaming roars and Becca's shouted commands. "I need to get some information going on her to speed up her intake when we get there."

The rollercoaster is slowing down, back to the tunnel where everyone gets on. I nod. "O – Okay."

The tech opens a metal notebook and clicks her pen. She asks my name, then does that thing people do when they're trying to keep you calm. You know, where they say your name before they say everything else, with every single question.

"Okay, Theresa, how many months pregnant are you?"

"I – Nine."

"Who's your OBGYN? Theresa, do you have one?" She looks up briefly at me.

"Colleen. Colleen McDonnelly. She's at the Healthy Baby Clinic." I breathe out and try to savor the moments where the pain is so little. "Please call her."

"We'll do what we can," she says. "Your birth date, Theresa?"

"August fifteenth."

She looks up again at me. "The year?"

"1971," Becca cuts in. I stare at her, and then feel the rollercoaster start up again.

"Theresa, you're eighteen?" The tech looks at me, and I glance at Becca, and she opens her eyes wide at me for just a second, her way of silently ordering, "*Say it!*"

I tense and start to cry because I know what's coming. "Yes. I am." And then the pain arrives, and by the time it stops the doors are opening and men in uniform are lifting my stretcher off the back and setting it on wheels. As they roll me down a hall, I stare up at the lights on the ceiling, passing too quickly to count.

"We're right here!" I hear Libbie's voice call from behind us. "We're staying right here with you!"

I nod through my tears, which are coming constantly now. Because something's scissoring my insides apart. Because strangers are running me down a hall on a stretcher. Because I feel sticky and wet, but mostly because what it comes down to is I am completely alone in this, no matter who's running along with me.

They put me in a room with two beds, but nobody's in the other one. They stick in an IV I never even feel because it's during one of the bad pains. They put something else in the clear bag dripping down into my arm, and hook me up to about twenty machines. Then, suddenly, finally, blessedly, the pain is barely bad anymore. I look around the room with new eyes for the first time, breathing slowly and adjusting to the relief. An ugly room. It doesn't have curtains, and the walls are a gross yellow. I read somewhere that yellow makes people go crazy, or wait, no – that was Libbie telling me that. She read a story that this woman wrote a long time ago about being locked in a room with yellow wallpaper, and she started going nuts and crawling around the floor and stuff. It was freaky.

So I don't like the yellow walls. They don't have anything on them except for one picture from probably twenty years ago that shows a woman sitting in a rocking chair holding a baby in her arms. It probably isn't even her baby. Just some baby model or something. I rub my nose with the back of one hand and look at the fluorescent lights above. Yuck. Dressing room lights. The kind my mother and I would complain about when we tried on bathing suits. The kind we always said made us look fat. Then we'd go out for hot fudge sundaes after we finished shopping and laugh about how we weren't helping ourselves fit into bathing suits, but that it was worth it.

I want my mother. I wrap my fingers around the thin blanket covering me, and close my eyes and let myself *want my mother*.

"Alrighty, *mami*. What's going on? You're not starting a party all by yourself in here, are you?" I open my eyes and see a tiny, plump Spanish woman checking my IV bag. Her hair is pulled into a ponytail, and her scrubs have baby ducks printed all over them. When she looks at me, her brown eyes are warm and she smiles. I feel like holding onto her. Her accent is light but still warm enough to hear. "You must be Theresa."

I nod. "Who are you?"

"Oh, I am the angel of your stay, *mami*." She fixes her face into a fake surprised look. "Now don't tell me nobody told you about me? Sheesh! I'm just not appreciated around here." She pulls my blanket up higher, smoothing it out with delicate hands. "I'm your nurse, Isabella. You can call me Izzy," she says, winking at me.

"You're just *my* nurse?"

She laughs. "Well, today, yes, I'm all yours. So if you need something, you call *me*. If you want a drink, you call me. If you feel something change, you call me. If that baby of yours starts doing the cha-cha in there, you call me *quickly*. Okay?"

"What time will you leave?"

She looks at me for a minute and then drags the cushioned chair over toward my bed and plops down. "Does it look like I'm going somewhere soon? A hot date, maybe?"

I sit up a little in bed. I feel like maybe somebody is here with me after all. "I don't know. Maybe you have a hot date. I wish you did, so you wouldn't have to be here."

She lifts her left hand and turns it toward me to show the little diamond-studded gold band around her finger. "The only hot date I have these days is with the couch and the remote control. My husband, Dion, and me, we love that *Wonder Years* show. We make a hot date to watch it every week." She smiles. "But you want to know a secret? I have the best time."

"That's really nice," I say, and mean it.

She leans back in the chair and crosses her legs, getting comfortable. "So, *mami*, this is the deal. We're going to do this together, okay? This whole thing. We're going to sit here and chat a little, just us girls. Then a little later, we'll have a baby, yes?"

"Oh." I swallow down the panic of hearing that I'll be having a baby later today. "Okay."

She pats my hand. "Okay then. So, tell me about yourself. Where you from? How old are you? What's going on with Theresa today?"

I gasp out a laugh. "Well, you mean besides finding my friend dead in a bathroom and having my water break all over my feet in a field?" And that reminds me: "My foot doesn't hurt anymore. What'd they do?"

She shakes her head and clucks her tongue. "They fixed it, is what they did. Or tried to. What did you step on, *mami*? It cut your foot like it meant business. Nice gash, about this big." She made a circle with her fingers and shook her head again. "Doctor had to put in three stitches. He said it looked like you stepped on a broken sprinkler."

"How does he know?" Even I don't know what I stepped on. I forgot about the whole ordeal in the chaos.

"Just from the shape of it, how it cut so jagged. That's what the shot was for."

"What shot?"

"The tetanus shot they gave you while you were in the hall waiting for the room."

I never even felt the stitches. Actually, I never felt them do any of the fifty things they'd apparently done to me since lifting me from the field onto the stretcher. I tell Izzy this.

"Well, you've been through a lot. Give yourself a break." She stands to check the bag again. "I'll be right out there getting some things ready for later, okay? This," she says, pointing to a red button on the side of my bed, "is the Izzy button. Anytime you want Izzy, you push the button and POOF, there I am." She snaps her fingers, smiles, and walks out of the room.

My next thoughts are of Libbie and Becca. I press the red button and Izzy appears in the doorway. "Missed me already, huh?"

"Yeah, I did. And, um, do you know where my friends are? They came in with me."

"They're right where I left them, sitting in the waiting room, snacking on some yogurts I smuggled from the cafeteria. I can send them in for a few minutes, but you girls will have to keep the partying down to a minimum, mami, okay?"

I nod. "Okay."

One minute later Becca and Libbie come bursting through the doorway. Libbie rushes to my bed and grabs my hand, chipped hot pink nail polish leftover on three of her fingers. "I told them I wouldn't leave you, Theresa! I told them I wouldn't, and they *made* me sit in the damn waiting room while they got you 'situated,' or something like that. I'm sorry." She looks panicked.

"Libbie, it's fine. I'm fine." I kind of feel fine, too, but let's face it, each moment is different and for all I know, with the way this day is going, two minutes from now I could be screaming my head off and bleeding out of my ears.

She doesn't let go of my hand. "Okay. I'm here. We're with you. Okay?"

I pat her hand and think about how I'm comforting her when it might've been vice versa on a different day. A day when we hadn't seen what we just saw, and this whole having-the-baby thing hadn't happened at exactly the time it did.

Becca opens up the cupboards around the bed and pulls out a kidney-shaped plastic pan. "What the hell is this little thing?"

"It's for me to pee in."

She sets it down. "Gross."

"Or throw up in."

"Ugh." She plops on the chair Izzy pulled over. "So what's going on?" It's funny to hear her ask it like we're sitting in The Coop, eating pizza. Not in a hospital room waiting for me to have a baby, all of us trying not to see Cammie's eyes each time we close our own.

"Becca. What do you *think* is going on?" Libbie asks. "She's going to have it."

Becca leans forward and whispers frantically, "You told 'em you eighteen right?"

"I did. In the ambulance, remember?"

"Yeah, but did they ask again, in here?"

I think about all the things I haven't even noticed them doing, including actually jabbing me with needles. "No."

Becca narrows her eyes. "You sure?"

"Positive."

She leans back in the seat. "Okay. But you gotta remember to stick to that, okay? Don't forget, even if they try to trick you and ask when you're pushing a kid out or something, you remember to tell them..." She motions at me with her hands.

"I'm eighteen," I say. "I got it."

Libbie shoves one of the off-white blinds to the side and looks out the window. "Nice view you got here."

I sit up in my bed. And, really, this bed is a million times more wonderfully soft and comfy than the cots at the Coop. "Oh yeah? What do you see?"

She laughs. "The tops of four other buildings. Some really big air conditioners, and...wait...I think I see...yeah, I definitely see a homeless guy pissing down on the sidewalk." She lets the blinds swing back together. "Gross."

"We're homeless," I say, like it doesn't even matter. Like none of us even knew it before.

Becca rolls her eyes. "We ain't *homeless*. We got homes. We just don't wanna go to them. Plus, you don't see *us* pissing on streets."

"Knock, knock, ladies." Izzy's voice comes from the doorway, and we all look over. "Now, I told you about having parties in here without throwing me an invite." She shakes a finger at me. "Did you girls bring chips?"

Libbie smiles half-heartedly. Becca looks suspicious.

"Hm." Izzy presses her lips together and raises her eyebrows. "Lively crowd tonight." She comes over to my bed. "So, somewhere between now and an hour from now, your doctor will be in for you to meet, okay?"

I feel confused. Also, a stab of pain too real to be from panic...more like the kind you'd get from someone stabbing you once or twice with a marshmallow-roasting stick. "I already met her, like, five times."

Now Izzy looks confused. "No, *mami*. Your doctor is a man."

Now I feel panic. "Izzy, you don't understand. My doctor is Colleen. From the Healthy Baby Clinic. I told them that in the ambulance." I also feel like crying, even though, really, this has to be at the bottom of the list of Today's Reasons to Cry. My voice gets shaky. "Izzy, please call her. Colleen. McDonnelly."

But then I see what Libbie and Becca probably saw from the moment I mentioned my own doctor. Izzy's eyes change. Her lips pucker for a moment and she pats my hand. "It's okay, baby," she coos. "It's going to be okay. Dr. McDonnelly was called, but so far we haven't heard back from her. And this baby, well, she isn't going to wait around all night for the right phone call, you know?"

The pain starts to come again, lighter than before, more like a little echo of the old rollercoaster agony. Or maybe, God, maybe it's only the sound of the rollercoaster engines starting up again. This is truly what misery feels like. Maybe not so much the pain itself (that's more like a sick nightmare from some psychopath's fantasy), but sitting here, waiting, feeling this little bit of pain. Knowing what's coming just a little later on.

"Who's the new doctor?"

Izzy smiles brightly again. "Oh, he's wonderful," she says, dragging out the *ah* sound in her warm accent. "Just the sweetest man. Don't you worry, baby. He's a very good doctor. Been doing this kind of thing for, oh, you know, must be ten years now. His name is Dr. Starkist."

"Like the tuna?" Becca looks incredulous.

Izzy nods. "Yeah, I guess so. Like the tuna."

Becca makes a face, and Libbie gives her a look. "Don't start."

"What?" I ask.

"Nothing," Libbie shoots Becca another pointed stare.

Now both Izzy and I are looking at them. "No, seriously, what? Becca?"

She ignores Libbie. "Nothing. It's just tuna, is, you know. Nasty. Mercury poisoning and shit."

"For Christ's sake, she's not *eating* tuna! You make no sense."

Becca jumps to her own defense, talking fast so Libbie can't interrupt. "I'm just *saying*! Shit. It's just not a great way to start the baby's life. Like out it comes and the first person to lay hands on it is some guy named after tuna."

Izzy looks at me with wide eyes, as if she doesn't know whether to laugh or kick both of them out.

"We've had a kinda rough day," I say, in explanation, because we all need one badly at that point.

"And, I mean, second-rate tuna, too," Becca adds hurriedly and immediately looks at Libbie.

Who takes the bait. "*What*? What're you talking about? Second-rate tuna? What the *hell*?"

"I'm gonna just head on out to the hall and check on where our doctor is, okay?" Izzy moves toward the door, rolling her eyes at me as she exits.

I stare at the girls I've come to love more than any other friends I've ever had. I did have friends, in school and stuff. When I was really little, like four, the people across the street had a little girl my age. Josie and I started kindergarten together. Our mothers dressed us alike, both in red corduroy skirt overalls, both with hair in braids, both of us carrying new backpacks. Unintentional, of course. No way it could've been planned because planning would have meant talking, and talking would've meant friendship of some sort. My mother never made friends with Josie's mother, Tina. There we were, me and Josie, playing together every day straight through 'til sixth grade. And Tina, her mom, always being friendly and neighborish. But that was my mother for you: she never made a single friend, except for my guitar teacher, and even that didn't last. It was her way, I guess, of making sure no other women visited the house.

When I was little, though, I thought it was because she didn't like Tina, and it made me sad because I loved Josie. So I'd pester her to invite Tina over for coffee while Josie and I played in my room. If Josie was standing next to me, bowlegs and blonde hair, at my chosen time of pestering, my mother would respond with a warm, "Oh, that sounds very nice, sweetheart, but I'm sure her mommy is very busy with her beautiful garden." One of the stock answers for when Josie's eyes stared up at my mother along with mine. But if we were alone: "No, sweetheart. Josie's mommy is messy," she would say, looking into the mirror in her bathroom, carefully relining her mouth with lipstick at three-thirty in the afternoon, like she did every day right before my father was expected home. She called it Pretty Time, and I was allowed to come into the bathroom and watch only if I promised to be quiet and pay attention. So I did, and occasionally would use Pretty Time to ask her to be friends with Tina. Each time she'd point out some flaw that clearly ruled Tina out as an acceptable friend: messy, chatty, a gossip, never wore a drop of makeup to the grocery store, wearing those heels without pantyhose. Or, my favorite: "No proper lady would smoke cigarettes in broad daylight like a regular street whore."

In truth, Josie's mom was a young, free, smart woman who'd married a nice guy, had a nice little girl, and kept her house nice, and her garden nicer. Part of the animosity probably stemmed from the garden thing. With my mother, any display of ordinary petunias on someone else's property immediately distinguished them as unacceptable people. Our garden, giving credit where credit is due, was a wonderland of twenty different kinds of flowers at any given time of the year. My mother nurtured it like a long-lost child, and it showed its appreciation by making her front yard the most talked-about in the neighborhood.

Weird, to think it's still there, blooming and beautiful. While here I am, sitting in a bed in a yellow room, staring at two other homeless girls.

"Yeah, you heard me. Second-rate. I mean, it's bad enough he's named after tuna. But couldn't she even get Dr. Bumblebee or something? It had to be the one nobody even buys?"

Libbie sighs, exasperated. "Everyone buys StarKist! You wouldn't know what it was if it wasn't popular!"

She has a point, but Becca forever has to have the last word. "Still. It's tuna."

"You guys," I say, starting to feel the pain stronger. "I hurt again. I think it's going to be soon."

Becca throws her hands in the air. "Well, thank the Lord, Theresa. We only been here ten years waiting for this thing to happen. Can you maybe do some kind of baby breathing moves that speed it up a little?"

Libbie yells. "You're so freaking insensitive, Becca. If you're in a hurry to get somewhere more important than this, then just go!"

But she isn't in any hurry to go anywhere, ever. So they sit, Becca on the chairseat and Libbie on the arm, and we wait in silence. Unfortunately, in that silence, I feel the hum of whatever's about to happen next, and not having any distractions makes me feel trapped and nervous.

At almost exactly the moment I'm about to rip my own IV out and run, Izzy pops through the doorway with a tall, muscley, way-too-handsome-to-be-a-real-doctor black man. Green eyes contrast with his dark skin. He wears a blue dress shirt and blue tie under his white coat. And, of course, in the grandest unlucky freakshow that is my life, Dr. Gorgeous is the guy who's going to stare at my crotch at the most disturbing, grossest time of my entire existence.

"Hello, Theresa. I'm Dr. Starkist," he says, reaching out and shaking my hand. I peek at Becca and Libbie who must be thinking the same thing I am, but probably much worse. "I'll be your attending doctor for the birth tonight. How are you feeling?"

"Good," I say. Then immediately feel like an idiot. "Um, no. Actually, not good. Not good at all."

He looks like he's holding in a laugh. I feel the blush creep up my neck. God, I can't do this. Not with a guy doctor. Not with a hot guy doctor.

He opens a chart and flips a page. "Well, I'm guessing right about now you're starting to feel the beginnings of the pain again. The sedative we gave to temporarily calm you and provide a little break before dilation should be wearing off. I'm going to check your dilation now."

He snaps white rubbery gloves on and goes to the foot of my bed. I stop feeling panic and feel absolute terror instead. I clamp my legs together. "Izzy?" I say, pathetically, desperately.

She rushes to my side. "What he means is he has to check to see if your cervix has opened up enough, or dilated enough, to begin labor. It probably hasn't, *mami*, at this point. But we can get an idea of how close you are."

I look sideways at Dr. Starkist, who's waiting patiently at the end of the bed. "Um, what, I mean…*how* will he know how dilated I am? How does he check?" I dart another glance at him, and feel even stupider.

Izzy takes my hand. "It's just like a trip to the gynecologist. He checks with his hands, no instruments. With his fingers, like this." She makes her hand into a little gun with a two-finger pistol.

I tighten my thighs together under the blanket.

"The dilation is measured from zero, which means not at all open, to ten, which means it's time for that baby to get a move-on."

Now I'm sure I'm going to throw up.

"I'll need you to bring your feet up on the end of the bed, legs apart, and let your knees drop to the side, okay?" Dr. Starkist waits patiently. It's much worse to have him just staring like that, waiting. I want to yell. *Stop looking at me! Go away and do something! Read the paper or have a snack or something!*

Libbie and Becca, for the first time in all of history, are completely silent. Izzy follows my gaze and somehow understands what I don't even know I want. "Girls, I'm going to need you to head back to the waiting room until the exam is over. Patient privacy." She smiles encouragingly, and they don't protest, maybe because they're scared just sitting there and so imagining my fear is paralyzing.

I let my legs fall open and look at the ceiling and all I can think about is the first day I ever did this: spreading my legs. Well, not the first, I guess, but the first day I had to do it in a doctor's office, with that son-of-a-bitch geezer who called me a whore. Dr. Starkist puts something like Vaseline all over his fingers, and I start crying before he even touches me. Izzy holds my hand, squeezing it gently when I wince and cry out, but somehow it just isn't enough to stop the hurt that hasn't even really begun yet.

I cry for my mother without saying her name. I cry silently, even though I yell out from the pain. *Mama, mama, mama. I need you. I need you. I need you.*

Izzy squeezes my hand harder. "Is there a number where I can reach her for you, *mami?*" I open my eyes, which I've been squeezing shut tightly. Dr. Starkist is writing on the chart, and it's over, and Izzy has heard me saying my prayers out loud.

"Who?" Just to be sure.

"Your mama." She smoothes hair off my forehead. "Is there a number I can call her?"

I hold my arms around my body, resting on my belly, wishing there was. Maybe there is. Maybe she never really changed the number. I never even tried it. I feel a tiny flicker of hope, the tiniest spark that maybe I still have a way of hearing her voice right this moment when I need it so badly.

"951-625-2990," I say, and my heart beats faster because I'm saying something so real and not real at the same time. The numbers from a past life that feels like a million years ago but is really only a few months gone.

Izzy looks surprised. Maybe she expected me to tell her there was no one to call. Maybe there really isn't, but I want her to try. *Please Mama, please, please, please.*

She lets go of my hand and walks toward the door. "I'll try it right now, okay?"

"Can you do it in here? Can you call right here by my bed?"

She hesitates for a moment, standing in the doorway, arms crossed over her sturdy, curvy body. Then shuts the door, walks to the phone next to my bed, and picks it up. "Okay. Tell me the number again."

I give it, digit by digit, and with each number I feel like I'm a little bit of myself again. Like this whole crazy living-in-a-homeless-shelter charade was just something my mother concocted as a practical joke, and now it's time to go home.

"Yes, hello?" Izzy's voice cuts into my thoughts and scares me to death. She looks over and gives a thumbs up. "Yes, hi, my name is Isabella Vasquez. I'm calling from Mercy Saint Memorial Hospital." She pauses and I hold my breath. "I'd like to speak with..." She looks over with wide eyes and I whisper my mother's name. "Caroline Sepuchelio, please."

It's surreal. My mother is presumably on the other end of a phone only ten inches away. I reach out and stroke the coiled wire that connects phone to base.

Izzy puts a hand over the receiver and whispers, "It was a man. He's getting Caroline."

Daddy. My sweet father who loves me so much. Right there on the other end of that phone. I clutch the cord. Izzy smiles at me and then says, "Yes, hello. I'm calling from Mercy Saint Memorial Hospital. My name is Isabella, and – " Izzy stops talking then, and somehow, like something out of a dream that smacks you in the face in real life, I hear my mother's voice coming from the holes in that phone.

"Mama!" I yell, pure joy spilling out of my mouth. I motion to Izzy to give me the phone. I have to talk to her right away. She's so close!

The voice on the other end stops when I call out. And then, nothing at all. Izzy holds the phone there, in one hand, and my hand in her other, until the beep-beeping of nobody on the other end fills up the silent room around us.

Izzy sets the receiver back down on the cradle. I shake my head. "Try again."

She looks at me, so calmly, so sadly. I want to scream. I whisper, "Try, Izzy. Call again. You got disconnected."

I think for sure she'll argue. I mean, if it were me, and I knew what she does, what we both know, actually – I would've told her it was just no use. That's why I love her, love her so much, really, for picking up that phone and putting it to her ear again.

She hits redial and this time leans toward me, our ears sharing the phone.

My mother answers on the first ring. "Hello."

"Yes, hello. I'm afraid we were disconnected before. I'm calling from – "

The voice on the other end is my mother's, clear and crisp and businesslike as always. "Oh, yes. It's possible the phone lines in my neighborhood are the problem. Please hold on for a moment, and then continue." It sounds muffled, then as if she put a hand over the mouthpiece on the other end. I can see her doing it, those long, pink manicured nails covering the receiver. Izzy and I listen to her muffled voice speak to my father. *Disconnected call...something about a survey...could you please take out the garbage before it gets too late...thank you, my love.*

She's quiet a moment. Then her voice is back with us, hurried, angry, colder than any sound I've ever heard. "Now, you listen here. I don't care who you are, or where you're calling from. You tell whoever had you make this call that I will *not* accept another one from them. Do you understand?"

I breathe out. "It's me, Mama."

She's silent. And then, carefully, calmly, she ends my life. "Only my daughter calls me Mama, and currently my only daughter is home visiting from college. Do not call again."

For the second time that night, the beep-beeping fills the space around us. Except this time, it sounds like my funeral song. Slow, sad. Absolutely the end.

"Push!" Izzy holds my hand, and I squeeze my eyes shut, gasp for breath, and push againagainagain. I scream and cry and writhe in the bed, but no matter. The pain won't stop.

Sweat drenches my hair, tears drench my face. I feel wet, sticky, hopeless. Caught in the worst possible place for anyone to ever be. *I'm being punished. This is the true punishment. I thought the last few months were hard, but this is my real fate. I'm going to die.*

Voices around me, muffled, coming from all over. Libbie's among them. "I'm here, I'm here. Reesie, you're almost done."

"Push! Again!" Izzy holds my hand, and I push again, and don't even know how because I am dead. *Dead dead dead. This is what I get. This is where God puts girls like me. Deaddeaddead. Mama, mama. Please stop. Stop it. Stop it. Stop it.*

"That's it! Oh, here it is! *Mami,* one more! Push one more time!" Izzy's face is beaming, and I do push, once more, and then the pain is slowly fading into a fuzzy background. I see nothing but black and think, *this is death. This is my reward. Thank you, God.*

"She's waking up. Look." Becca whispers loudly, though I don't see her.

"No, you did that. She wasn't waking up before you started talking two inches from her face."

I look through the smallest slitted opening of one eye, and see Libbie and Becca on either side of my bed, staring down at me.

"And you're ten feet away and silent, huh?" Becca counters.

I open both eyes a little bit and work up a smile. They look down and two matching grins meet mine.

Libbie pats my arm. "Hi!"

"Hi," I squeak out in what feels like my morning voice, as my tongue peels away from a parched mouth. "Can I have a drink?"

Becca snorts out a laugh. "We all need a fucking drink, girl. You got any idea how wild that was?"

Libbie holds the cup with the bendy straw in it while I take five giant gulps. She rolls her eyes. "I think she might have some idea about how it was. And *watch your language.*" She jerks her head to the right corner of the room, and flaps a hand at Becca. I look toward where she is motioning, and there, in the corner of the room, peeking from a tiny pod of blankets, is a baby's face.

"Whose baby?" I mumble. They look at me. I remember but don't, and it makes sense, but doesn't. Yes, I was pregnant and there was a giant belly and something kicking me all the time. That part I recall. It makes sense my belly is flatter, and I'm not pregnant anymore, and there is a baby in the corner of the room.

A baby that is my baby. I stare at the bundle. "Oh."

Libbie strokes my arm. "Theresa, you did so good...you were like my hero. That's her, over there. See?"

I look blankly at Libbie, and am not oblivious to the look she gives Becca, across me, over my bed.

Becca says, "I'm gonna get your nurse so you can hold her, okay? Be right back." She leaves, and I stare at the pod in the corner.

Izzy bursts through the door, smiling brightly. "Good morning! How you feeling?" She checks the IV, then turns to face me. "Rough night, huh?"

I smile, despite the weirdness of this situation. "Yeah."

I watch her walk over to the plastic box, then wheel it toward my bed. "Ready to hold your little girl?"

"Sure," I say, not missing a beat, still feeling like it's all just something I'm dreaming.

She reaches down and carefully picks up the bundle. It's too tiny to be a baby. More the size of a football, all bundled in soft-looking blankets that have MSM stamped on them. She comes around and holds the bundle out toward me, and I'm afraid of breaking it.

I shake my head. "It's...really small."

She smiles. "A tiny little *chica*, but so healthy. Everything checked out for her. Five pounds, twelve ounces. Fifteen inches long. A cheerful little girl." She lays her back down and starts to unbundle the blankets. "Oh, and she needs a fresh diaper, right, *mi querubin*?"

She's talking to it, as she unwraps the last blanket to reveal the tiniest little person I have ever seen in my life. I never imagined arms and legs and bodies came in that size. Like a weird little rodent, naked pink and moving around, and oh my God it's my baby, my baby, it's mine.

"I'll hold her now," I blurt.

Izzy smiles and picks her up, bare and pink and with the tiniest diaper in the world around a tiny butt. She carries her over, and when my hands touch the skin, the softest skin in the whole entire world, I feel nothing. I don't cry, like in the movies, when they hand the baby over to the mother and she starts sobbing. I don't cry, or smile, or anything. I just hold her in my two hands, pressed up against my ugly hospital gown, and stare down at the sleeping, wrinkly, tiny face.

"Happy Valentine's Day," Libbie whispers.

The two of them sit on either side of my bed, leaning against my pillow with me, and for the first time I'm not the center of the cocoon anymore.

Chapter 13

W ell, this is it," Becca says, sweeping a hand toward the peeling
      brown house with the overgrown weeds in front. "Say hello to
      our new home."

She turns to face me and Libbie, and we smile because Becca never
feels proud of herself. For her to have that look, an actual smile with her
lips parted and her crooked front teeth jutting forward, like she actually did
something good in her life...well, it could've been a cardboard box and we
would have cheered.

"Wow, Becca," Libbie gushes. "I can't believe you found this. I
mean, it's like a real home for us."

Becca turns her face away, but we can see her smile still. "Yeah,
yeah, don't get all excited, it's a piece of sh-crap." She glances at our baby
sleeping in my arms. "But," she adds, "it's not the Coop, ya know?"

"We know," I say, and we really do. This is the thing about Becca:
when you need somebody really badly to step up and do something, she's
the one to do it. So she lied our way through the paperwork for the baby,
fast-talked our way out of the hospital, and two nights later, while we sat
in the Coop, where I'd pushed a second cot next to mine for the baby to
sleep in, she came in and announced she got a job at the Rite-Aid a mile
from there. Three weeks after that she came home and said, "We're
moving, bitches."

And here we are. Moving. The house really is a piece of crap. Like
something you'd see in a horror movie, hiding in the woods somewhere,
except that woods would make it nicer. Instead, it's just sitting on a pile of
dirt and weeds, and the paint is disgusting, brown and peeling. No porch
or anything. It actually looks just like the kind of blocky houses I used to
draw when I was a little girl. You know, with two windows in front and a

door and that's it. No chimney. I always drew chimneys. The window on the left is broken, and the doorway has a door with no screen. So it's just the outline of a screen door, I guess.

"So, what we waiting for? Let's go in. Go get our stuff from the Coop and be done with that hellhole once and for all." Becca stares at us expectantly.

Libbie voices our concerns, keeping her voice light so as not to rain on Becca's parade. "So…are you sure we can afford this? I mean, it's a whole *house*. How are we gonna rent a house when we're not even eighteen or twenty-one or anything?" She looks at me out of the corner of one eye. "What if people start asking questions or the landlord wants ID or something?"

Becca rolls her eyes. "I already told you! We ain't gonna get caught. Nothing's gonna happen to us. Jerry. The guy at work." She says the words slowly, like we need help understanding. "Said his brother rents out houses around here. When I told him we needed a place, he told me about this one. No questions asked. No ID. Nothing. People just want money, okay? They don't care who gives it or if they're grown up or not."

I'm starting to feel the beginning of what I think I remember is excitement.

Libbie looks skeptical. "You sure we can afford it, though?"

"Yes, Libbie! I'm sure. He said we can pay each week. I got a job. I can afford it. Sixty a week. I can do that." She beams, and I just want Libbie to shut up.

I think she sees this, because she grins. "I can get a job or something too. This'll be great." We all stand there like total dorks, smiling at each other, until Becca starts walking toward the sidewalk again.

"Come on, let's go. We're packing our stuff up and moving it in." She walks faster, back toward the Coop, three miles away from this new house of ours.

The thought of walking all that distance again exhausts me.

I shift the warm weight in my arms and stand still. "I don't want to go back yet. I'm really wiped out from the walk here."

Becca keeps on, but yells over one shoulder, "Stay here then. Go rest in the house. Libbie, come on, we'll get the stuff."

Libbie looks at me. "You sure you don't want to say goodbye to the good ol' Coop?"

I laugh. "I think I'll be okay."

She nods and breaks into a jog to catch up to Becca. I watch until they round the corner, then turn to face the house. "Well," I say to Valentine, even though she's sleeping, "This is it. We're on our way up."

I look down at that little face, one tiny hand balled up by her mouth, and feel like this really truly is a weird, never-ending game of playing house. Swallowing a sick feeling, I try to grab the excitement back.

I take out the key Becca gave me and turn it in the lock, but the door is already unlocked, so I just push it open. The first thing that hits me is how dark it is inside even though it's eleven in the morning. The second is the smell of rotten socks. And the fact there's already furniture inside. And the last thing is there's a guy wearing nothing but stained white underwear passed out, or maybe dead, on the ratty couch.

I freeze in place. *Ohmygod ohmygod this is somebody's house. I just walked in and I'm standing in somebody's house. They're going to have me arrested. I'm trespassing.*

I inch backward toward the door, desperate to get out without the guy waking up and seeing me, some strange freakshow of a girl holding a baby, standing in his living room.

"Hey." A calm, muffled voice comes from behind me, in the opposite direction of the sofa. I close my eyes and try to imagine what Becca would do, or even Libbie, if they were in my position.

I turn and face the voice. It belongs to a guy who's standing in pajama bottoms, shoveling Spaghettios into his mouth right from the can. I stare.

"What's up?" He moves into the living room and sits in a bean-bag chair smushed into one corner. Not even looking surprised that there's a stranger standing there.

I try to smile. "Um, hi. I'm so sorry, I mean, really, really sorry. It's this big, huge misunderstanding because my friend thought we were moving in here, and that's where they are right now, actually, getting our bags and stuff, and that's why I'm here, and I didn't know because we thought this was going to be our house, you know?"

He crams another plastic forkful of saucy pasta into his mouth and nods. "Cool."

Cool? So, was I not getting arrested? Would I actually get out of this without a mug shot and prison time and God knows what other humiliation? "Yeah," I say, feeling half hopeful.

He holds out the can. "Want some?"

"Um, no. Thank you, though. I'm fine."

When he smiles, he's actually cute. Maybe sheer panic kept me from noticing before. He has moppy blonde curls down to his ears and really nice teeth for someone who eats canned pasta like that.

"Know how to play Rummy?" He sets the can down and pulls a deck of cards from the pocket of his pants.

And, because this situation couldn't really be called that weird, not in the grand scheme of my whole life, I say, "Yeah."

He deals seven cards to each of us. I stand awkwardly without moving. He looks up. "Oh, sorry. My bad. Here." He pulls the bean bag chair out from under himself and sets it across, next to my pile of cards.

"Oh, no, don't do that. I can just sit on the carpet. It's fine." I move past the couch where the guy is still sleeping in his tighty-whities.

"Yeah, I know," he says, and smacks the bean bag a few times to arrange it. "We can *both* sit on the floor to play, and you can put her in the little groove in the bean bag. See?" He presses into the center of the bag and it suddenly looks like the cutest, safest nest in the world.

I set her down carefully in the little hole, and she stays asleep, thank God. The thing about this baby is, she really doesn't wake up that much during the middle of the night. But when she does, and screams, I want to leave her somewhere and run away into a cozy warm bed and sleep forever. But I never do. I always feed her a bottle and change her diaper and somehow don't throw her out the window or anything. I actually surprise myself with my patience.

I eye my cards, then looks sideways at the guy on the couch. "Does he always sleep in his underwear?"

He grins. "On the lucky days."

I grimace. "Ew…"

"I'm Clifton. Cliff. Whatever."

For some reason, this seems like the perfect name for him. I tuck a piece of hair behind my ear, and suddenly feel like my hair is too stringy, too dirty, too split-endy. I smooth it self-consciously with one hand and smile at him. "Hi. I'm Theresa."

He draws a card off the pile. "Hi."

We take a few turns in silence.

"So, you're moving in?"

What? With him? "Well, no, we *thought* we were. My friend Becca was misinformed, I guess. She thought this house was empty. We were going to rent it."

He nods. "It is for rent."

I raise one eyebrow. "Yeah…but you live here…so that means it's already being rented."

He picks up my discard and tucks it into his hand. "There's an upstairs. Two rooms. We rent the two downstairs."

Oh. Now I feel super uncomfortable. My mother would die if she knew I was staying in the same house as boys. Just die. I can still hear her talking about Lauren Sothers, who had a slumber party in seventh grade, and whose mother let her have boys at it.

"Over my dead body will you ever attend that hussy's party, Theresa," she said, jerking a comb through her dark hair, glaring at the mirror during a non-Pretty Time time. "Unbelievable," she huffed. "Her mother is just a breeding ground for slutty behavior. Trash. Absolute trash, both of them. Letting – no, *encouraging* girls to sleep overnight in the same room as boys."

"Mama, Mrs. Sothers said she'd be there the whole time. Please!"

She whipped around in her chair, the padded one that spun in place in front of the mirror, and glared at me then. *"Theresa!* How dare you even ask! Do you want to be associated with those kinds of people? Do you? How selfish can you be? You know how hard your father works to give you a good life. Consider what type of person you would look like to others! Knowing how well-respected we are, you would even consider asking me to allow you to go spend the night with trash?"

I'd hung my head and half-heartedly tried to argue. "She's not trash. Really, Mama."

She took my hand in hers and gently scratched up and down my arm – my weakness, the very thing I loved too much. "Theresa," she said, lovingly. "Any girl who'd sleep in the same room as boys like a common whore *is* trash. And you, sweetheart, are not. Our family is not. We are good people."

Now I blink my way back into the Rummy game and nod toward the underwear guy.

"It's just you two, then?"

"Yeah, for the most part," Cliff says. "Sometimes we have one or two other people crash here, depending on the day or the night or whatever."

"Oh."

"But, I mean, the rooms are still for rent. If you want them."

I smile politely. "Thanks."

This little encounter, this whole playing cards with a real-life cute guy in the guy's living room thing – it was the first time since Charlie that I'd even talked to a boy (well, besides Matthew, but he doesn't count.) I feel nervous. Nervous and ugly and super fat.

Because, you know what? Here's the big kick in the ass: my fat baby stomach is just a fat stomach minus the baby now. Yeah. Try and figure that one out. I see the baby, right there in front of me, and yet somehow I'm still fat.

I kept my suitcase packed with the clothes from home. Even when I went to the Salvation Army and bought those really hideous maternity shirts and wore them for what felt like five years worth of months, I still peeked into my suitcase whenever I was feeling down. I'd just open it up, and breathe in the smell of home and my room and my real life. And picture me wearing these clothes again when I wasn't pregnant anymore. When everything would go back to normal, and I could fit in my old jeans again. Then I'd shut the suitcase really fast because I didn't want the smell to leave it. I always worried if I left it open too long, or opened it too many times in a row, the good scents would leave and I'd be stuck with the new smell – of the Coop and stained pregnancy shirts, and not having a mom.

And now, the clothes don't fit. They don't fucking *fit*.

"Rummy." Cliff lays out four sevens and three queens. He smiles a lopsided half-smile. "Again?"

I feel disappointment burning that same old hole in my stomach, and suddenly just want some cold water. I look at the carpet. "No, I think I'm Rummied out. May I use your bathroom?"

"Sure. *Mi casa es su casa*. Literally."

Yeah…about that. I stand and look around.

"It's the little door off the kitchen." He points to the left.

I walk through the little kitchen, scarily clean for a house two boys live in, and slip into a tiny bathroom. I scan: No shower. Only a toilet and a sink. No toilet paper…ew. Oh wait. Yeah, there is, just not on the roller thing…it's on the floor…*ew*. I turn on the faucet to let cold water splash out, and then cup my hands to splash my face. No towels. Fantastic. I fan myself with both hands like a beauty pageant winner.

I open the bathroom door and walk back into the kitchen. Paper towels? No. My face is dripping, I'm in a stranger's house, and there are no towels. I open the little drawer next to the oven and stare down at a smiling duck oven mitt. Fine. I pick it up by one corner and dab really fast, like *that* makes it not an oven mitt and not touching my face.

When I walk around the corner, I can see into the living room. The guy in the underwear has turned to face the back of the sofa. And there, on the floor, Cliff is holding Valentine, my baby. He holds her tucked into one arm, whispering to her with a smile lighting his face.

"Hey there. Yeah…hi. I'm Cliff. You're a little sack of cuteness, you know that? Your mommy, she's pretty cool…she's in the bathroom. She'll be right back."

I watch as Valentine clenches and unclenches her fists and blinks up at him. She makes the little squirmy fussy grunting sound that means she's getting hungry, but I stay put, standing there behind the wall.

She fusses a little louder. Cliff puts his finger in her fist, and she closes her hand around it. "Wow, little girl, what a grip you've got! You're so strong! Shhh…don't be sad, your mom will be right back. I'm right here, too. I'll be your buddy."

I turn away and lean my back against the wall, thinking, *This is the weirdest life I have ever lived.*

So this is where we live now. Libbie and Becca took one room upstairs, the bigger space with the two windows, and I took the smaller one next to it. We share a bathroom with everyone else here, but at least it's not the Coop. My room has my own real bed, not a cot. Well, a twin mattress lying on the floor because we found it two Saturdays ago on the curb outside somebody's house. Free, not stained or anything. Becca dragged it home for me. She and Libbie sleep on blankets in their room, but I'm going to Wal-Mart to get them a present for being so great: two air mattresses. I already picked them out when we were there the other day food shopping. Twenty-seven bucks each, but they totally deserve it. Every other night they switch off with me. One of them sleeps in my room with the baby, and feeds her and stuff in the middle of the night, and I sleep on the blankets in the other room to get a full night's sleep. Tonight is Libbie's night. She's such a dork, too. She even made this little schedule she put up on the refrigerator with a Pizza Hut magnet that shows which night is baby night for who.

Valentine is really getting into things now. She used to be a little sack of mush that didn't know me from the lamp, but now she looks around, and you can tell she's taking notes on everybody, you know? She doesn't walk around or anything (it's going to be crazy when she does), but she sits up and laughs and smiles all the time. She's really cute, and I'm not just saying that because she's mine. Cliff got her this little floor mat with toys hanging above, so she can lie on it and play with the stuff. It's really nice. It's in the living room.

Josh, the other guy who lives here, is either stoned or asleep all the time, but he's making a real effort to wear boxers now. He's kind of weird, but I mean, he just does his own thing and once in a while has a girl over. The only really shitty thing is that Libbie and Becca smoke pot with him, and whenever they do I feel like maybe I'm crappy for letting them babysit Valentine. But really, it's not that big of a deal. Libbie always tells me I worry too much about stupid stuff.

I'm folding the tiny clothes into tiny piles in our room. I still don't fit into my old clothes, but I keep the suitcase, and I've been going for walks every day and being really careful what I eat. The maternity clothes were too big, so I had to go back to the Salvation Army and get smaller stuff to wear until I can get into my old ones again. Every time I look at the maroon suitcase, still so clean and neat from being tucked under a bed since I got here, it gives me hope. Reminds me that someday everything will go back to normal.

"Hey," Cliff says from my doorway. He's standing there, just like he always is, hands in pockets, moppy blonde curls too long around his face. I feel a little squeeze in my stomach when he smiles.

"Hi. Come on in." I shove the little folded piles to one side of the bed, and he sits back against the wall. It's not that this is weird, him sitting in here with me, because he does it a lot; in fact, really, he's the one I see most around here. Becca is always at work, and now Libbie is working at the Rite Aid too, almost every day, and Josh is kind of around but not around at the same time. Clifton doesn't work, but somehow, miraculously, always has money. I never ask. After all, he doesn't ask how *I* get money (from the envelope that is now down to $312).

"So, I was thinking we could go get dinner and maybe catch a movie," he says, never breaking eye contact. His eyelashes are very thick and long.

Okay. This is different. We never go out together. I mean, besides grocery shopping or other house-y stuff that has to get done. Suddenly, the house seems like a prison, and he's offering an escape route.

"Yeah? That sounds really great." I fold another little onesie. Valentine wears, like, five of these a day.

His face breaks into a smile. "Yeah? Cool. Will you be hungry in an hour?"

"You know me. I'm always hungry."

"Yeah." He laughs. "Me too."

"McDonald's?"

He picks up a pair of tiny jeans and folds them into a neat square. "Well, actually, I was thinking we could do something different."

"Like what?" We all pretty much live on McDonald's, Carl's Jr., or Taco Bell. I try to cook stuff at home, but the end result is usually not the best.

"There's this place down on 4th that's supposed to make some killer Alfredo sauce. You like Italian?"

I can't even remember the last time I ate something other than fast food. Was it when I first got to the Coop? I'm not going to count the soup kitchen's spaghetti because that just is no way Italian food.

"I love Italian."

Cliff grins. "Good. It's settled then. We'll go get some Italian and catch a flick."

Okay, but – this all happened too fast. "Is this place, I mean...what should I wear?"

He shrugs. "Doesn't matter. I mean, I'm just wearing this." He spreads his arms out, and I look at the jeans and checkered button-down shirt. He's dressed way nicer than normal. Great.

"Okay. I just wanted to make sure it wasn't, like, some place really fancy. I mean, it's okay if it is," I rush on, and God, I'm an idiot all of a sudden. "Whichever."

He scoots to the end of my bed and pats my shoulder. "It's a nice place. But you'll look fine. Stop worrying about it."

I blush. "I'm not worried."

"Good." He bounces to his feet. "Pick you up in a half hour," he jokes, shutting the door behind him.

Oh, crap. What just happened? I'm going to a nice Italian restaurant for dinner? With a cute guy who asked me to go to dinner and movie? Is this a date? Am I going on a date? I need Libbie or Becca or someone. I'm sitting on the edge of my bed and really, it doesn't matter what it is because I *have* no nice clothing, and can't go into this place looking like a total scummer. I walk over to my closet and whip open the narrow wooden door. All I see are t-shirts and a couple of sweatshirts. I could borrow Libbie's or Becca's, but they're so much taller than me...

No. I can't do this. I can't.

I fling myself out into the hallway and yell, "Clifton?"

He pops his head into the stairwell. "Yeah?" He's so cute, standing there waiting for me to come down. God! Why am I such a freak?

"Um – nothing," I say, and run back into my room. Okay. Jeans. Jeans are good. He's wearing them. I have kinda nice jeans. Where are they? I look around the room at the dirty clothes lying all over the place. Because, seriously, I never want to do any clothes at all after I get done with Valentine's non-stop laundry. So mine never get washed.

Oh. My. God. Valentine. Um, duh! The baby I have who can't exactly be left here alone! And even though I'm feeling panic about what to wear, and pretending to actually consider not going, suddenly, with it really torn away from me, a gushing disappointment socks me in the stomach.

I go back into the hallway. "Clifton?"

This time he climbs three steps and looks at me. "Are you okay?"

I sigh. I really wanted this. "Yeah. It's just that, we can't go." I feel burny in my sinuses and think, *Great. I'm seriously going to cry over this like a freaking lunatic.*

Clifton asks, "Why not?"

I wave my hands around like the lunatic I actually am. "Um, I can't leave the baby at home." And I taste the bitter sound of that damn word in my mouth as I say it. *Baby.* It ruins everything. Every time things go a little bit okay, and I start to feel a little bit of happiness, something forces that damn word back into my head or out of my mouth and it's all ruined again.

Clifton laughs. "No kidding. Probably tear the place apart, knowing her."

I try to smile at his joke, but all I feel is anger and resentment. *She ruins everything.* I will never be able to have a normal dinner or a normal movie or a normal date with a normal guy. Ever. Again.

"Yeah. So...thanks anyway."

He climbs five steps to stand one step down from me. We never stand this close. If I leaned just a little forward, we would touch. I shake my head, and he leans against the wall. "It just so happens," he says, and his tone is so happy that suddenly I feel like something is good. "That this restaurant does let adorable little girls in. It also just so happens we have an adorable little girl sitting down on the living room floor, all dressed to go."

My mouth hangs open. "We do?"

He nods. "We do. So...that means *you're* the only one not ready."

I could shoot through the roof with excitement. "Okay." On impulse I throw my arms around him and hug him tight, and he teeters on the step.

"Whoa! Didn't think I'd score a hug 'til after dinner. Bonus!"

I laugh and run into my room and just like that, my clothes problem is solved. I yank out the maroon suitcase and breath in the smell, and right there, four shirts down, is my pink and yellow halter top with the flowy bottom. I pull it out and feel the silky material. It's just as gorgeous as I remember it being when I'd unwrapped the box sitting under the Christmas tree.

"It's from Japan," my mother told me, and my father had put his arm around her. We looked so much like a perfect family I wanted to leave the silk shirt in the fluttering tissue paper nest just to hold out the moment. "Your father wanted you to have something special to wear to your end of the year party."

I hugged them both, and even though I got so many other presents, that shirt held the memory for me. And now, here it is.

I peel off my dirty, red t-shirt and stand in front of the half-mirror on the back of the door. My boobs are way bigger than they used to be. I could have breast-fed Valentine, but it hurt when I tried in the hospital, so I give her bottles. I slip the halter-top over my head and the silkiness flows down over my skin. It fits snug around the chest, but in a really, really great way that it never did before. The best part is, it flows loosely around my stomach, so nobody can tell it's really gross and puffy, with stretch marks around the belly button.

I run into Libbie and Becca's room and brush my hair, then take out the mascara from their makeup basket and put some on. No lipstick. Lipstick always makes me look like a pretend grown-up, like I'm trying too hard and it's just weird. I throw on flip-flops, the only kind of shoes I have right now, and go down the stairs.

At the bottom, I see Clifton stacking rainbow-colored plastic donuts on top of the white post with Valentine. I stare at her, and Clifton looks up. I'm not even going to lie. He looks surprised. I'm not bragging. I mean, I'm still just me, but it's the magic of this shirt or something. I know I look good for once.

"Wow. You look beautiful," he says, but I'm staring at Valentine.

"Her clothes." My normally messy little girl is sitting there on the floor in this super-adorable blue corduroy dress with white tights and little perfect shiny black shoes. Her black curly hair is smooth and shiny, pulled back in a little blue headband. "She looks so pretty. She looks..." I gulp because it really feels like nobody could've done anything nicer for me at this moment in my life. "Like a little angel."

Clifton grins and scoops her up as he stands. "Well, I figure now I get to be the luckiest guy in L.A., taking the two prettiest girls out to dinner."

I grab her bag and stuff two little diapers in it with a bottle full of formula, feeling like I'm in a dream. Like my own crappy real life is far away. I don't even mind that we're going to have to walk a billion miles in nice clothes to get to this restaurant. It's already a great night. I feel like Cinderella, and Clifton's my fairy godmother who managed to turn me into a beautiful princess for the night.

"You ready?" He holds Valentine, and she looks tiny and happy, a neat little girl my mother would've loved.

"Yeah, I'm ready," I say, slinging the diaper bag over one shoulder. My cheeks hurt from smiling.

We open the front door, and I stare at the City Cab sitting there on the side of the road.

"You didn't think we were going to walk lookin' this good, did you?" Clifton puts his free arm around my shoulders, and we walk out to our yellow horse-drawn carriage together.

Fairy tales never happen where you expect them to.

Chapter 14

The living room is a total cotton-candy dream. I take Valentine downstairs. As soon as we turn the corner, Cliff and Becca and Libbie and her boyfriend Dustin blow those puffy noisemakers that shoot out and then roll back in as you breathe into them. The balloons and the streamers throw pink everywhere, exactly the way I pictured a little girl's birthday party looking. I remember telling Cliff what I imagined for her birthday, three months earlier on that first date we had, and somehow, he made it happen. Here it is.

Valentine shrieks and grins, showing off her four teeth, two each on the top and bottom. We sing a loud, cheerful version of the birthday song, then Cliff comes out of the kitchen carrying a pink-frosted cake. The icing is swirly and gooey, a single candle smack dab in the middle.

Valentine stares at the flame.

"Blow it out, girlie!" Becca orders.

Valentine looks at me, eyes wide. She really is so cute. I lean in and blow the candle out, then kiss her cheek. "I made a wish for both of us," I whisper, and she hugs my neck tightly. We sit, the five of us, on the living room floor. Valentine waddles around, as we smoke weed and eat cake, until she rubs her eyes with balled fists and whines.

"Somebody in this room is way ready for some shut eye," Cliff says.

"Me!" Libbie, Becca, and Dustin chime together.

Cliff scoops Valentine up and kisses the top of her head. "All right, Birthday Girl, time for some good ol' napping. You're not as young as you used to be, you know," he adds. We walk up the steps together, him holding Valentine, her cheek smushed against his shoulder. She almost falls asleep on the way up.

"You have the juice?" he asks.

I shake the bottle of apple juice in my left hand. Valentine is funny like that: she won't drink milk anymore like babies are supposed to. She just guzzles apple juice all day long and every time she goes to sleep. It's kind of good, though, because the apple juice bottles are way cheaper than the gallons of milk. Plus, when she pees apple juice out, it doesn't smell as bad, so I can let her pee twice before changing her diaper.

He lays her down on the mattress she and I share sometimes, when she isn't kicking me and taking up the whole thing, and I'm not forced to sleep on the carpet next to her. She's sound asleep as Cliff shuts the door quietly behind us. I love this time of day, when she's sleeping and it's suddenly quiet, and I have time for my own stuff.

I run my fingers through my hair and breathe out. "Another nap time down."

I pick a gob of pink icing out of my bangs. "I'm going to take a nice, hot shower and de-frosting myself." I turn toward the bathroom, but Cliff tugs me back by one hand.

"Wait," he says, "I have something for you." He grins that wobbly grin where his eyes sparkle, and I want to melt. But seriously, nothing has happened between us. He takes me out on dates, me and him and Valentine, and we go food shopping and stuff together, but that's all. It doesn't make him any less amazing though. Or any easier for me to just sit around swooning over the guy who lives downstairs. *Ugh.* I am so pathetic sometimes.

"What?" I ask, trying to sound casual and not at all excited that *he* got *me* something. Also telling myself he probably doesn't even remember it's Valentine's Day, and the something is probably a really great coupon for baby wipes.

"Come on, I'll show you." He's still holding my hand. No big deal. It's not like our hands never touch normally. We go down the stairs, and around the bend and into his room. His smell is boy soap and Doritos. His room is green, pretty much, with a green quilt on the futon and some green sheets. Plus a desk with these little model airplanes all over it, and it's kind of weird because he's eighteen and still building model airplanes. But then I guess kind of not, because I'm fifteen and look how I spend my time. The door clicks as he shuts it and then goes to the desk.

"Did you build me a plane?" I only half-joke, because what if he *did* build me one and I've been making fun of it? Plus, I'm trying to lighten up the situation because it feels nerve-wracking, and God, what is *wrong* with me?

He takes a dark-red velvet box out of the desk drawer and turns toward me. "Nope, not a plane. Maybe next year." He's holding out the box, grinning like the cutest guy in the world, and I want to take it, but all I can do is stare at how sweet his eyes are, sparkly and wonderful and excited. "Here."

I wrap my hand around the softness of the velvet, and suddenly I can hardly open the box. My fingers fumble, I'm so excited. I push the lid up and lying inside, on this puffy bed of red silk, is the most beautiful necklace I've ever seen in my whole life. *Pearls.* He bought me pearls. I breathe out, and since there's really nothing good enough to say, I just look up at him. And because he's Clifton and he knows, that's enough.

"Happy Valentine's Day." He closes the five inches between us and kisses me, sweetly and softly, and his lips feel warm and not scary, wonderful against mine. He pulls back, eyes smiling under his curls.

"Happy Valentine's Day, Cliff," I say. Then I'm shocked because it's me who leans in for seconds. It's me who wraps my arms around him first.

Cliff and I have officially been together for nine months now. Becca is pretty upset. She says because she doesn't think it's a good idea, but I'm pretty sure it's because she's jealous she never has a boyfriend, and Libbie and I do. Plus, it's just me and Becca and Cliff and Valentine in the house now. Libbie is gone most of the time – working at Rite-Aid, plus she stays at Dustin's almost every night, so Becca has the room to herself. Actually, she has the whole upstairs to herself, besides Valentine, I mean. Cliff and I share his room, and my old one is now a real baby room – Clifton even painted it this really cool orange color when I was at work two weeks ago. The paint was left over from a job he was helping at, some bagel place thirty miles from here that needed a new look.

I faked my age when I went in for a job at the diner. They told me I could only hostess if I was under sixteen, so I said I was eighteen, that I just didn't have my driver's license yet. Now I get to waitress, and seriously, it's not that bad. The manager there, Linda, is a really nice woman. The kind you know goes home at night and has a nice life and just kind of comes to work to make a little extra money for her family, but doesn't really *need* it need it, the way I do.

The jackass landlord – he's a scum bucket, by the way. This obese, greasy guy with tiny, beady brown eyes too close to each other and the kind of mustache so tiny and stupid you want to take a razor and shave it off in his sleep – he raised the rent, and now it's six hundred a month, and with Libbie not paying anymore, and Jeff leaving too, that's like two hundred for each of us to pay, and that isn't even counting food and stuff. Especially Valentine – she costs so much with everything. We just pool it together, all the money, I mean. The thing about Becca is, lately, she hasn't been pooling any really, and neither Cliff nor I want to say anything about it because she's been so quiet, always staying in her room. Really, she's not the same. I can barely talk to her.

I finish up my side work at the diner and roll the last bit of clean silverware. I call the cab from the dirty cream-colored phone under the counter, and wait until it comes.

"On your way home, sweetie?" Linda asks, voice muffled as she restocks the little bakery case, reaching all the way in until pretty much half her skinny body disappears onto the shelves. Linda should probably eat some of the pastries we sell, but she never does. She and her husband are vegetarians and I guess all-around healthy eaters. Six out of seven days of the week, she clutches her stomach and says how the smell of the cow flesh on the grill is making her sick.

"Yup." I want to ask if I can take home an apple turnover for Cliff, but even though I've been here for like eight months now, I still feel pretty uncomfortable. Mostly around Linda, because she always smells so nice and her earrings match her necklace. I look down at my dirty apron and black tee shirt with the diner logo on my right boob, and sigh.

She pops out of the bakery case with a plateful of turnovers. "Well, don't forget to take some of these. There's apple and cherry here." She smiles and yanks a strip of plastic wrap over the dish, which is holding five unbelievably large turnovers. "Here." She hands me the whole dish. "Just bring the plate back when you're finished, okay?" She goes back to doing what she's doing, and it occurs to me that stuff like that, like giving away apple turnovers by the plateful, doesn't matter to women like Linda, who have plenty of apple turnovers to go around. I bet she never even thinks about it.

"Thanks, Linda." I hold the plate tightly as I walk out to the cab, which will cost me seventeen bucks, but, seriously, how else am I supposed to get to work? The bus doesn't come anywhere near our house.

I walk in to Cliff sitting on the bean bag chair with his arms behind his head, eyes closed. I think he might be napping, but as soon as the front door clicks shut, he opens his eyes.

"Hi," I say, quietly, because Valentine is nowhere to be seen, which means she's finally taking a nap. She mostly refuses to nap now, and doesn't just play quietly anymore, either. She refuses to sleep, in fact, then spends hours roaming around and tearing things apart, like the box of spaghetti she somehow opened and spilled all over the kitchen floor. Really, sometimes I can't handle it. Sometimes I just want to stick Velcro to her little ass and Velcro her to the carpet so she stays still for one damn minute.

"Hi," he says, and I know something is very wrong because his eyelids seem droopier than normal. His forehead has these wrinkles that are never really there unless he's worried.

I sit across from him on the carpet, back against the wall, and stretch out my legs. "What's wrong?"

"How'd you do at work today?" he asks, which he does every day. I open my apron and take out all the ones, the occasional five, and all the jingly, heavy change. I dump it in front of me to sort. "Forty-one dollars. After the ride home."

He nods and closes his eyes again.

"What's wrong?" I'm actually worried now. Was it me? Did I do something I don't remember doing that made him upset? He never gets mad, really. The thing about Clifton is he kind of goes with the flow every day, just worry-free and living, and helps me do the same thing, too.

"Becca's gone," he says.

I'm not sure what he means. I stare at him blankly.

He drops his arms and leans forward, legs spread widely, elbows on his knees. He makes two fists and leans them knuckle-to-knuckle against each other. "I was in the kitchen, and she came downstairs with two garbage bags and was like, 'See ya.' And I was like, 'You want help with that trash?' Cuz you know how we can only do two bags of trash a week and we already did two this week.

"But she goes, 'This ain't trash. It's my stuff. I'm movin' out today. Found a better place.' So I'm like, 'What do you mean? You can't do that, Becca. What about rent?' and she just went like this - " Cliff shrugs and flops one hand out in a really fantastic imitation of Becca, " – and said, 'Not my problem. You lovebirds can deal with that. Tell Theresa I said later.' And she walked out the fucking door, Theresa!" He raises his voice then, and my face must look just like his: wide eyes, mouth half-open, just shocked.

"Wow." She walked out on us? It doesn't make any sense, because we're a family, and when Libbie started staying gone all the time, me and Becca talked about how it didn't feel the same, and now she does the same damn thing? And didn't even say goodbye to me? My heart is pounding. I feel heat rising in my body suddenly. "That is so fucking *rude.*"

Cliff scoffs, "Yeah, no kidding."

We sit in silence for about ten whole minutes, then he stands and stretches. "So, I guess that's that."

"Yeah, but, like, what exactly? What?"

He stares down at me. "Well, how can we pay that much on our own? We barely make our regular rent with Becca's share, Theresa. What the hell do you *think* is going to happen now?" His voice is suddenly snappy and angry, like this is all my fault, and that makes me furious.

I stand so we're almost the same height.

"Why scream at me about it?" I scream, which I never do and especially not at him, but it does the trick. His forehead dewrinkles and he reaches out and pulls me into a hug.

"Sorry." He kisses the top of my head. "I didn't mean to get mad at you. I'm just fucking pissed at Becca. We'll be fine."

I feel better hearing those words. *We'll be fine.* I just need to hear that, you know? Because sometimes, like right at this moment, it definitely doesn't feel that way. But when somebody else says the words, it feels a little truer.

Linda gave me an extra shift every week at night, and Cliff has been working as much as he can, days. I stay with Valentine then, and he stays with her at night. So we've paid the rent three months in a row now, but Cliff used up all the money he had saved under his bed to pay this month's, which we paid two weeks late. It's already the end of February, and March is due. We didn't have any money left over for a cake or anything for Valentine's second birthday. I brought home a cupcake from the diner. She doesn't even know the difference anyway.

I swipe my hand over the table at work and shove the two singles and change into my apron pocket. Suddenly, I feel too sick and sweaty to stand. I plop down in the blue vinyl-covered booth, smack on top of a sticky little orange blob of mashed carrots, and take in a deep breath. The restaurant is cleared out now that dinner is over. I lay my cheek against the coolness of the table, and the sickness goes away a little bit. When I stand, though, my body feels too dizzy and sick to move. I drop back onto the booth seat and begin to cry, because I *know* this feeling. I've felt it once before. Panic swells in me like a marshmallow in a microwave.

I pay the cab driver to stop at the Rite-Aid. Libbie isn't there, and I'm glad. I pay for the stick and carry it to the taxi. The whole ride home I sing the ABCs quietly under my breath, letting my arm hang out the window in the cool air to keep from losing it. When I walk in, the house is quiet and still. The bathroom light bulb is burned out again, so I have to do it in the dark. Then I lay the awful white stick on the stove and turn on the little light above it. I wait the two minutes. When I see the second pink line appear in the clear window, as dark and awful as the first one, I slide down onto the kitchen floor and lay my head in my arms.

Cliff's voice wakes me up. "Holy shit, are you okay?" He's standing in the entrance of the kitchen, and I'm sprawled out on the floor. The dim light is coming in from the little window. I get the miserable feeling of slumber parties when the night turns to light and you still haven't gone to sleep yet. I'm clutching the pregnancy test in one hand, but suddenly I'm just not ready to tell him. I sit up. "Yeah. Sat down for a minute and didn't want to get up. Just tired."

He looks droopy in the dim light. He leans against the doorframe. "Okay," he says, rubbing his eyes.

I stand and move toward him, but the vodka on his breath makes me stop. "Cliff...were you drinking?" I whisper.

He lets out an annoyed sigh. "Yeah. And if I did, so what?" He glares, and I back up two feet to give us a little space from each other.

"When you were watching Valentine? What the hell, Cliff? She's two!" He runs a hand through his hair and says nothing. I feel angry and miserable, my fingers still wrapped tightly around the stick. "You can't do that! What if she got hurt or something? Were you even *watching* her?"

He explodes then, screaming at the top of his lungs. "It was after she went to bed, Theresa! Chill the fuck out! I'm so sick and tired of this shit! Aghhhh!" He throws one arm out and knocks the little porcelain ducks that Libbie got at Dollar Tree off the counter. They break all over the kitchen floor.

All that does is make me angrier.

"Great, Cliff! That's wonderful," I scream. Now we are both screaming and it's five in the morning, and the next thing I hear is Valentine yelling at the top of her lungs from upstairs.

"Ma-ma! Ka-liff? Ma-ma? Hellloooo?"

Cliff and I stare at each other. Then he turns on one heel and stalks into our room. "You get her," he spits out. I hear him lock the door behind him. Everybody has to have their first fight, I think, trying to breathe. This was just ours. What a doozy. I stare at the yellow shards on the floor, then open the cupboard and throw away the pregnancy test. Later, when he's calm and I'm calm, I'll just tell him. We've gotten through worse stuff together.

"O-meal?" Valentine asks, standing there in the doorway, her dark brown hair in a messy pony-tail, her diaper soggy and swollen under one of Cliff's white tank top undershirts that drags past her toes.

"Sure," I say, exhausted, getting down the box of oatmeal packets and taking out the last peaches and cream. "Sit at the table. I'll make it."

* * *

I walk to Rite Aid with Valentine. It takes us over an hour to get there because every few steps she sees something, like a pebble or a little flower, and wants to stop and talk about it. She's so smart. I mean, way smarter than most babies. Plus, really pretty. Her hair curls all over the place. It's just long enough to put into little pig tails on either side, but she always tears them right out five seconds after I put them in. The whole diaper thing is really getting on my nerves, but I just don't *get* potty training. I bought a little potty seat from the Salvation Army, and I read I'm supposed to make like a huge exciting production when she goes. But I haven't had the chance because instead of going on it, she just walks into the bathroom near the seat, then pees in her diaper.

Libbie is standing at the counter. We haven't seen her in probably two months. When Valentine spots her she calls out, "Libbie! Libbie! Pick me up!"

Libbie grins and comes out to scoop her up. Libbie is Valentine's favorite, besides Cliff any way. I'm pretty sure I'm in third place.

"Hey, my favorite girlie!" She kisses Valentine's cheek and hugs me. "How you guys doing?"

I smile despite the last hellish twelve hours. "Fine. We felt like going for a walk."

Libbie looks at me for a moment, then nods. "Well, it's really nice out. A walk is a fun thing to do."

"Yeah," I say, and it's awkward and completely uncomfortable, but then Libbie does the Libbie thing.

"So you've been kind of MIA, huh?"

"I've been what?" I ask.

"Missing In Action," she says, not making eye contact pretty successfully by playing with Valentine.

"Oh. Yeah. Well, it's been a really crazy past few months."

Libbie nods. "Me too," she rushes out. "Dustin and I are moving."

I feel shock. I know I haven't been around for a few months, but Jesus, I've been working and trying to pay the damn rent that Becca screwed us with. Still, I thought Libbie was just around the corner if I needed her. Moving away is completely different. My stomach hurts, and suddenly I remember the stick, and that makes it hurt even more.

"Moving? Wow. To where?"

She smiles and looks up for the first time. "We want to get out of here, you know? Just start new somewhere. Dustin's dad offered to let him work for his landscaping business if we go back home. His parents have this apartment over their house. They're going to let us rent it."

I force a happy smile. I should be happy. God, I'm so selfish. "Wow! That's awesome, Libbie. Where do his parents live?" I brace myself.

"Up in Washington State," she says. Then looks at my face and quickly adds, "It's not that far, actually. Just a few hours drive. And we'll come back to visit and stuff. We like the sun around here."

Valentine pulls on my leg and yanks on my tee shirt. "Apple juice? Mama? Apple juice?"

I reach into the little backpack and pull out a sippy cup of juice for her. "So when are you going?"

Libbie smoothes out her blue Rite Aid vest. "We're packing up now, pretty much. We're heading out next Saturday."

Valentine guzzles the apple juice next to me, making a little smacking sound with her lips, then shoves it up toward me. "Take it! Take it, Mama!" I grab the sippy cup. I hate that I can't have a single conversation without her yanking and talking at me constantly. I feel like pulling my hair out.

"I better get her home. She's driving me nuts," I say.

Libbie nods. "Okay," she says, and stands to face me. "Well...okay."

"Yeah," I say and turn away quickly because my eyes are burning. Partly from no sleep and partly from the hot tears just waiting to spill out all over.

"Theresa?"

I hold Valentine's hand and turn halfway toward Libbie, who's still standing with her arms at her side ten feet behind us. I don't say anything, because there's nothing to say. I just look at her. Valentine has one sharp little nail that digs into my palm as I struggle to hold onto her hand.

"Good luck," Libbie says, and puts a hand up in a half-wave.

"You too. Really." And I suddenly am completely overcome with how sad I feel, so I bust ass out of there, forgetting to buy the diapers I came in for, dragging Valentine with me. She talks the entire walk home. When I finally put her on the mattress upstairs, she conks out, and I fall asleep next to her.

When I wake, the sun is low and the room is dim, and that's twice in one day I've woken up at a weirdly-lit time. For a few minutes I just lie there in the silence and think about how absolutely wonderful it is to have it quiet with no little kid running all over me. Then I snap back to real life.

The downstairs is dark, and I sigh because Cliff probably took Valentine out for dinner or something, and I didn't get a chance to say I was sorry for this morning.

"Mama?" Valentine's voice is coming from our room, so I turn the corner and stand in the doorway. She's on the bed. It's strange because it actually takes me an extra long time, maybe a whole minute, to realize everything in the room is gone. The sheets. The hangers in the closet without a door are just hanging there, empty. The model planes. Cliff's planes.

"Mama, bounce!" Valentine is jumping on the bed. Then I see the piece of yellow paper on the empty desk, where the planes used to be. I pick it up, feeling confused.

Theresa, it says. *I just can't stand it anymore. You know? I'm sorry. I'm out. - Cliff.*

"Bounce, bounce!" Valentine squeals. She falls onto her butt and then jumps up to do it again. I set the paper down on the desk, exactly how it was, and really don't even think as I go into the kitchen. I reach into the cupboard above the fridge, and take down the bottle of whiskey Cliff stole a couple months ago. There aren't any clean glasses, so I rip the lid off one of Valentine's sippy cups and pour the stuff in.

The first four or five gulps burn so bad I'm sure I'm going to puke, but you know what? After that, it just gets better, and everything sucks a whole lot less.

Chapter 15

Valentine's small hand grips mine as we stop at the steps of the two-story brick building. She looks up from under long dark lashes and smiles uncertainly. "This is it, Mama?"

I sit down on the step, patting the spot next to me. When Valentine plops down, I draw circles in her palm. "This is it, kiddo. Pretty impressive, huh?"

She looks up at the building looming above us. "Yeah. I guess."

I poke her just enough to tickle. "You guess! What do you mean, you guess? Look at that place, it's just calling your name." I lean close to her and whisper, "*Vallllentiiiine. Vallllll...*"

She raises her eyebrows, always the cynic. "Mama. That's creepy."

I try again. "This place is just waiting for you to open those doors and announce, 'Here I am, ready to rock and roll!'"

She leans her head on my shoulder and sighs.

"Oh, Jellybean, what's wrong? Tell me why you're so sad on such a happy day."

"It's not a happy day, Mama."

"What do you mean? You get to be a big girl and have your first day in a real school. It's going to be amazing! And look at this place. It's beautiful. I wish I could go to such a nice school."

She perks up a bit at this. "You could come with me, Mama! We could go in together."

I force a smile. "No, no. I already went to school. Now it's your turn."

"I want to stay home. You can teach me there."

"Oh, but just wait 'til you meet your teacher and see all the books and toys and wonderful things they have in store for you. And..." I grin, more excited than her probably. "I have a few magical things to help you out in there."

Her eyes go to the pink and yellow Tweety Bird backpack I've been carrying the whole way. It cost more than I should've spent, but you only get a first day of school once, right?

"The backpack?" she asks, blinking.

I unzip it slowly. "Not just any backpack. It's full of things to help on your adventure. Things like . . ." I put a hand in and slowly pull it out. "A giant pack of fat-tipped markers in every color of the rainbow. And...a whole box of ready-to-be-sharpened Hello Kitty pencils with a matching eraser and a very, very pretty matching pencil case. But, wait! That's not all!"

Valentine leans in closer, her ear-to-ear smile making every hard-earned, hard-spent penny so worth it.

Next I pull out a pink hard plastic case and wiggle my eyebrows, getting a small giggle from my little girl. "This right here is your case of magic. You open it and bam! Everything you could ever need for a school adventure. Purple scissors, brand new crayons, a nifty clear blue ruler, a couple packs of fruit snacks in case you're too hungry to wait for lunch time . . . which, by the way, will be just another fantastic part of your new adventure with THIS!" I pull a Tweety Bird lunchbox out of the backpack and show it off, modeling like Vanna White on Wheel of Fortune. "You have to wait 'til its lunchtime to open it, though, okay?"

She leans forward and wraps her arms around me. "I love them! Thank you, Mama. I love them all."

"Good. Now, up we get, and on you go." I hold the straps of the backpack as Val slides her arms into them. "And I'll be right here on these steps waiting to bring you home after your first adventure is over, okay?"

Her smile drops. "Okay."

"Hey, hey, hey. No sad voices. No sad faces."

"I'm not sad. I just don't want to leave you, Mama."

"Val, there's no reason to be scared. It'll be a wonderful day."

She shakes her head. "No, I'm not scared now. I have my backpack of magic. I just don't want to leave you. Because . . . your face hurts, and I don't want it to get hurt more."

I touch my swollen purple lip, still slightly crusty with blood. A souvenir from a guy I'd thought maybe I could trust, but I guess not. Go figure.

I look down at Val. "Now, that's just silly. There's nothing to worry about. I'll be fine all day, and you'll have a wonderful time. I'll see your little tushy back on these steps in a few hours, okay?"

She nods and turns to walk up the last few steps and through the double doors into the school.

I watch until she disappears down the long classroom hallway before turning   away   from   her,   toward   home.

Valentine

The little squeaking sound woke Valentine. Her eyes opened. She stared at the door of her room and felt panic when she saw it was shut all the way. Mama always left it open a crack, so a little light came in.

The squeaking started again. Val suddenly felt more curious than scared. She slipped bare legs out of bed and padded across the carpet, carefully sidestepping the row of carpet tacks poking through near the wall. When she opened the door, the squeaking stopped. She walked down the narrow hall and into the cramped kitchenette. Her mother sat there at the two-person table with the mismatched chairs, face hidden in her hands, crying. The squeaking sound was coming from her mouth, which was also hidden by her hands.

Valentine forgot to be curious and felt scared all over again.

When her mother lowered one hand from her face to take hold of the glass sitting in front of her, she noticed Valentine standing there silently. The skin under her eyes was so dark, the whites of her eyes a muddled, streaky red. "Valentine," she said, trying to cover the smear of blood dried under her nostrils. "Go to bed."

Val stayed planted, but felt terrified. This was not her mommy's voice talking. This couldn't be her mommy with blood on her face and black makeup all dirty under her eyes. "Mama?"

Theresa slammed an arm onto the table. "I said go to bed!" she screamed. "Go to bed! GO TO BED!" She closed her eyes, shaking her head wildly back and forth.

Now this all seemed like the movie Valentine had seen on TV, where aliens came and lived in somebody's body and they just looked like the person but really weren't them. Val couldn't move. Her mother was an alien, she was sure of it.

Theresa's eyes, ringed black from the smeared eyeliner, stared at the wall. Her hand lifted the glass toward her mouth again. She swallowed, set it down roughly, and dropped her head onto the cheap plastic table.

Valentine took one brave, small step toward the still figure of her alien mother and whispered, "Mama?"

Her mother didn't stir. She kept her eyes closed, breathing deep, heavy breaths. Valentine walked a careful half-circle around the chair, until she stood inches from her mother's face. It was the smell that made her sure. Val's mommy always smelled the same, like a flower or something else nice. But this alien mother had a bad burning smell that made her eyes water.

"Mama? Are you in there?" Valentine's hands were getting sweaty. She gulped at how brave she was being. "Mama? It's me...your Valentine. I'm going to bed now, like you said. I just need a drink. 'Cause I'm thirsty...Mama?"

She put just her fingertips on her mother's arm and felt warmth. Aliens were probably cold. So maybe she was just sleeping, then. Val looked at the glass on the table with one clear, cool gulp left in it. She picked it up and tipped it all into her small mouth. When the liquid burnt her throat and her eyes started to water, she coughed until she cried.

Her alien mom slept through it all.

Chapter 16

The regulars at The Pit Stop come in at opening and stay 'til closing, and spend the time in between mixing up their own stories with those on the radio or on a tabloid in the grocery store line, keeping each other entertained while the hours pass. They chain smoke, stubbing out one dead butt and lighting up a new one in the time that it takes me to finish pouring one of their endless cups of coffee.

The burgers are served on toasted white bread instead of on buns, and the owner, Lilly Ann Berger, stops by pretty much never. Rushing in, a perfumed flurry of high heels and expensive skirts, barely taking notice of the employees in her hurry to pick up the monthly books and get the hell out of the obligation her father apparently thrust upon her.

I know all the regulars: Jeff, a middle-aged alcoholic who spends his days in the diner and his nights in a bar, drinking his credit card debt away; Steve and Jackie, an unmarried couple who order coffees by the potful, always split a short stack, and who always seem to be brooding over some daily mutual misfortune; Harry, an old sea captain who still wears his cap, but who rarely makes eye contact or remembers who or where he is for more than a few minutes at a time; and Delilah, a red-haired, red-lipped middle-aged woman who smokes cigarettes languidly as an old film star, always ripping on everyone else and then yelling, "Behave!"

I'm the youngest here, and sometimes the only waitress on duty. Jeff tells me I'm the prettiest, too. But if you saw the dark circles under my eyes, you'd know he was lying. The other girls here are okay, though. Bitches, sometimes. But still, okay.

Two weeks ago I turned twenty-four. Kelly and Gina brought drinks and enough lines to go around. I woke up the next morning on a booth in the diner, the register emptied of cash, three windows broken. I left before anyone came in. The manager reported a break-in and so in the end nobody knew, but it was a close one. Really close. I can't afford to lose this job.

I press the start buttons on the coffee makers – I'm forever brewing fresh pots – then go outside by the dumpsters for a break. I sit on the edge of the concrete step next to the oil drum that the cooks dump the deep-fryer grease in, and light up a joint with a Bic I snatched off one of the regular's counter spaces.

I never get to just chill out anymore, ya know?

"Sure you wanna keep on doing that? Your kid's gonna be a retard," a voice says behind me. Gina squats next to me on the step.

I stare at the side of the building and take another puff. "There ain't gonna be any kid."

"Since when?"

"Since I'm not gonna have another. That's when." I cough – these fucking things will kill ya, she's right about that – and take a sip of Sprite.

She stares at the side of my face. "You mean you got rid of it?"

"I will. Made an appointment for week after next."

"Jesus, Theresa." Gina sighs. "How many of those you gonna have? You're gonna wreck yourself inside, you know that?"

"God, I hope so." And I do. I really do.

"No, you don't. You're young. What if you want to have kids with somebody later, when you get married?" Gina is thirty-five and unmarried, though she says by choice. "You wanna wreck yourself so bad no babies can ever grow in there anymore?"

I stare at the wall to avoid her eyes, all judgment. "What do you think?"

She shakes her head and stands. "Foolish. You're being a foolish girl. You keep having these to get rid of your mistakes – what is this? The third time since you started working here? – and then someday when you wanna have one, you won't be able to anymore. Don't be stupid." She reaches down and pinches the joint out of my hand. Takes a deep hit before throwing it down and stepping on it. "And, on top of that, you're gonna have a bunch of little retards running around if you keep this shit up."

Now I'm just pissed. "You owe me for that! And if I ever want your shit advice, I'll ask for it. I'm going home now. Close up for me."

Gina says nothing else, just nods and walks back inside. I untie my apron and get into the beat-up Toyota one of the regulars sold me for a couple hundred bucks and a handjob. I drive without the radio on for some peace and quiet, windows down, back to the apartment under the church. When I open the door, the house is dark.

"Valentine?" I call, quietly, not really wanting an answer. I drop my purse on the plastic table and head into the kitchen to pour a drink. When the glass is acceptably full, I take two large sips to shake off Gina's words, her tone. The horrible idea of little retards coming out of me.

Truth is, Valentine has been asking me to keep this baby. Wants someone to play with, I guess. Can't blame her. Who doesn't?

I open the door to the bedroom we share.

Amy Grant blares from the radio, "Every heartbeat belongs to you." Val is dancing on the unmade bed in a green Ninja Turtles t-shirt and pink cotton underwear.

She stops dancing and smiles when she looks around and sees me. "I was just practicing."

I take another gulp and lie down on the bed fully clothed. God, it feels good to close my eyes. Every time I open them in the morning, I start counting down to this moment at night.

"For what?" I ask, but the ease of the drink is already running through me, and I don't really care what she's practicing for.

"For Broadway, Mama." She unlaces my waitress shoes and pulls them off one by one. "For the part of Annie, in Annie Oakley." I hear her shuffling around, arranging my shoes neatly against the wall. She unbuttons my work shirt. "Lift up, Mama. Let's take this off so you can go to sleep."

I force an eyelid open and prop myself on one elbow, swallowing the last of the glass. "Just leave it tonight."

Valentine straightens the cover and fluffs them smooth over me. Maybe I should have another kid. A sister or brother for her to take care of. I just don't know anymore. Maybe it'd be like something nice for her. A gift.

She hums and strokes my hair as finally, finally, I fall asleep.

Chapter 17

The whirring of the trains rumbling over the tracks calms me down. You'd think the sound would totally freak me out, but it doesn't. I walk to the edge of the platform. There are people everywhere – way too many people. I wish it was just me here, but hey, gotta take what I can get now, right?

"I really fucked up," I say aloud to no one.

I think for a moment of Valentine as a child. A sweet little baby. I remember the smell of her hair as a toddler, sweaty and sugary at the same time. She was always a good kid.

"Hell. She practically raised her brother," I tell the woman standing next to me. She turns quickly and moves away. "She was like his mom. And he didn't come out retarded, like everyone predicted. He came out smart and cute. I almost died that day, having him. All my blood just poured out, poured and poured, and the doctors couldn't stop it. A real mess. I was sick for two weeks. It wasn't worth it, but Valentine always thanked me for Jonathon, like he was a birthday gift. She was always a weird little kid."

A few people are looking and listening to me now.

I run my hands over my sundress. It's the nicest one I own. Purple with yellow and white daisies printed along the skirt.

"My mother would love it," I say, wobbling slightly on bare feet. I left my shoes at home.

A man's voice calls out from behind me, asking if I'm okay. But the roar of the train approaching the bend in the tracks is already filling my ears, drowning him out.

I count to five, enough time to see the big light coming round, to see that long flash of red and blue metal flying straight toward me.

"She'd love this dress," I say loudly over my shoulder to him and everyone else. "My mother."

And then I take a step, and let my body fall forward.

Caroline

"But she dreaded the dark, dreaded shadows, dreaded black things. Darkness to her was the one thing dreadful."
— *H.G. Wells,* The Time Machine

Chapter 18

The beatings, you should know, came completely unexpectedly in our marriage. They began exactly three days into our honeymoon and continued through nearly forty years of marriage.

I'm actually very blessed. Abigail and Patrick are happy children. Their father never let them want for anything. Our home is beautiful, as well. I guess I'm rambling because I'm so goddamn sinful. But you must understand it's because I am so ungrateful that I must now live with this terrible thing I've done. Yes, I could have confessed, told the whole story, but that would've been selfish – so selfish. Truly, there *is* no punishment greater than living alone with one's own sickening guilt. Therefore, I will rightly get what I deserve for the rest of my life. It's just that…I want you to know *how* it came to be like this. Because there was a time when I wasn't what I am today. And if you can see that, well – I just pray that you can.

When Bruno and I first met, in the fall of 1961, I was a junior nursing student at Berkeley. He was a patrolman at the time. I met him by chance, after another attempt to drink away all my stresses. Truly, I hadn't any real cause to be upset; my grades were wonderful, I was preparing to graduate, my parents were happily vacationing in Florida for the season. I think perhaps the only reason I felt unhappy was because three of my girlfriends were engaged, so I was to be a bridesmaid three times in the coming year – without ever being a bride. I know that sounds foolish. After all, I was successful in my own right, but how can a girl truly be successful in her own right when everyone around her is succeeding in a completely different way?

In any case, to relax I drank gin and tonics at a little place called
Buddy's, where no students went, where nobody knew me. The lone girl in
the whole place, sitting primly on a bar stool at the very end, trying not to
make eye contact with any men.

On that particular night, Bill, the handsome, dark-haired bartender
who always looked like a prince in a black Buddy's tee shirt, took my
empty glass in one hand and wiped the bar in front of me with the other.
"You want something to eat, Rolin? Maybe an order of fries?" He always
called me that – Rolin – ever since one particularly bad night when I'd
fought with him about cutting me off, and in the midst of the argument I'd
told him I wished I were a man so I could kick his ass. He had laughed and
pointed out that my name wouldn't earn me any respect in a bar brawl. So
then we had spent the next hour deciding on a manlier version of Caroline,
finally settling on the middle cut of it: Rolin.

I shook my head and tried to stare him down. "I'll have another."

He turned away and washed out the glass. "No, you're all set for
tonight, sweetie."

"*Billlll*," I whined. "Don't do that. Bill! Come on. You know me."

He disappeared into the kitchen, then returned holding a basket of
French fries and a bottle of ketchup. He set them up in front of me with a
napkin and a fork. "Eat those."

"I can't," I argued half-heartedly, because by that time, I was almost
completely gone. For that, I give him credit, because the truth is he never
cut me off earlier than he would anyone else. "If I keep eating your fries
I'm going to be as big as a whale by winter break."

He wiped down the rest of the bar. Only one other customer remained:
a man with his head down on his arms at the other end.

I picked up the fork and stabbed a fry. "I need ketchup."

Bill came over and opened the bottle sitting next to my plate and
drizzled it onto the fries. "One, you need to eat, otherwise you're gonna
lose it all over the floor again, and I don't think either one of us wants that.
Two, you need to eat because you have too much gin floating around in
there with nothing to soak it up. And three, you don't need to worry about
eating a bunch of fries. You don't look half-bad even on the worst nights."

He put down the cloth and leaned against the bar, across from me. I
held out a fry at the end of my fork, and he opened his mouth. "Besides,"
he said, chewing, "the only bodies you should be worrying about right now
are the ones sitting in the hospital waiting for you to take care of them.
Don't you have a practical exam tomorrow?"

I groaned. "Yes." Suddenly the room was spinning and the fries
seemed sickening. I clutched my stomach with one hand and grabbed the
bar with the other. "Ooh boy."

Bill was around the bar in a flash, an arm around my waist. "Oh boy is right. You're in for another sick one, Rolin." He picked me up easily and carried me over to the one booth in the place, laying me down flat on my back on the red vinyl seat. "Hang on." He ran to the back and brought out his jacket, which he pushed under my head. Then he stepped back to survey the situation. "You're too much, you know that?"

I closed my eyes, but that only made it worse, so I struggled to focus on the water spot on the ceiling. "Don't be mad. Are you mad at me? I don't want you to be mad. Bill?"

He shook his head. "You can't keep doing this, though. You're going to do yourself in."

I was almost asleep, almost away from the spinning. "Who cares?" I mumbled, and suddenly he was there, above me, braced parallel above my body as though he'd fallen but caught himself with his arms braced on the edge of the table and the booth seat. I stared up at his face, inches from mine, and it felt like he was floating above me. His green eyes stared right into mine.

"I care," he said, eyebrows furrowed. Then he quickly pushed with his arms to spring back into a standing position. I closed my eyes, thinking how handsome he was up close, how strange it was that I'd never before noticed the arc of freckles running across the bridge of his nose.

When I opened them again, the bar was dark except for a dim light from the back room. I felt absolutely parched. I had to have water. I stood up shakily and squinted at the Felix the Cat clock on the wall: 4:54. Almost four hours of sleep. So I was good to go. I took a few shaky steps forward and peeked into the back room. Bill sat at a metal table writing in a notebook.

I leaned against the doorway to stay upright. "Hello."

He turned, took off a pair of black-rimmed glasses and set them on the desk. "Morning, Sunshine."

I attempted a laugh. "Yeah, hilarious."

"Do you feel as terrible as you look?"

I pulled my hair back into a ponytail and crossed my arms. "Probably much, much worse." I nodded toward the notebook on his desk. "Still on the one about the Kansas town?"

He nodded sadly. "Stuck as a truck in mud." He wrote short stories, mostly about the lives of different small-town folks, though I couldn't say for sure because I'd only read two, and he didn't know I'd read any at all.

"Well, don't worry. You'll get it. Anything I can help with?"

He looked thoughtful for a moment, but then he set the pen down and stood. "Yeah. You have a practical in five hours. Go sleep." He walked toward me and put his hands on my shoulders to turn me around and propel me through the door.

The motion made me want to vomit.

"I'm going home to sleep for a few hours."

Bill stopped steering me back to the booth and turned me to face him. "No. You haven't slept it all off. You can't go driving in the middle of the night like this, watered right off your rear end."

But I could feel my pillow and my soft, fluffy comforter already. "I'm fine. Look at me." I did a strange little jig, and Bill burst out laughing.

"That was everything but fine. If anything, you just convinced me you couldn't possibly drive a car."

I made a grab for my purse. "Bill. Really. I'm going home. The booth is luxurious and all, but I want my own bed. I'll be just fine." I proved my point by tripping over my own feet and hitting my thigh hard against the tabletop.

I sucked air in through my teeth. "Yow!"

He picked up my purse and my pink cardigan and slipped an arm through mine. "Yes, you're in great shape. Let's go. I'll drive." The soreness of my leg paired with the shakiness left no fight in me at all. It wasn't the first time he'd brought me home, anyhow. Actually, on almost a dozen occasions he'd poured me into the backseat of his car, sleeping like a liquored baby, and driven me back to his apartment in town. Most times I woke up in his bed, clothes wrinkled and sweaty, before I sneaked out the door, giving him a pat on the head where he lay sleeping soundly on his couch. The apartment was small, almost completely unfurnished, except for the brown couch, two stools borrowed from the bar, and his bed, which oddly enough was always clean and soft.

He locked the back door behind him as we went out into the chilly morning air. The fresh smell of dew and grass immediately cleared the sick feeling out of my gut. I opened my purse and handed Bill my keys. "Here. Let's take mine."

I didn't have to point out my reason for this; his car was at death's door, knock-knockin' away. It sometimes didn't start at all. Mine was a gift from my parents – a shiny yellow Chevrolet Impala bubble-top, barely a year old, my favorite possession thus far.

"How am I going to get home, exactly?" He smiled as he unlocked the passenger door and held it open for me.

"Just drop me off at the dormitory, take my car home with you, and come get me later. Easy peasy, lemon squeezy," I said, all smart-alecky, feeling a million times better than back in the dark bar.

He turned the engine over and listened with appreciation. "Oh, and bring you back here, is that it?" He shook his head. "Nope. You're not drinking again tonight. No, ma'am. You've had enough to last you a month."

I opened my mouth to argue, but the sun was rising, the sky was turning all shades of beautiful colors, and a new day lay ahead of me. So I just rolled my eyes and looked out the window. "Uh huh. Let's get coffee."

"Now that sounds like a good idea," he said, and we pulled out of the parking lot.

We flew toward Milly Mucker's Diner, ten miles outside of town. Even though it was only five in the morning, we rolled the windows down and let the cold air blow in, and for a few minutes, I actually felt like life was good. Like maybe I wasn't a hopeless mess with no prospects and no future. So what if I was going to be an old-maid bridesmaid three times before I ever got to be a bride? I was only twenty, after all. There was still time.

These thoughts were broken by the sound of a police siren close behind us. I whipped around.

"Bill! How fast were you going? Pull over!" I was frantic. I'd never sped in my life. I had never received a ticket.

He calmly pulled to the shoulder and turned the ignition off. But he looked concerned. "I wasn't going that fast. Really. This bugger just has it in for us, I think."

We watched as a uniformed police officer, a large, barrel-chested man in his early thirties, climbed out and approached Bill's window. He bent and looked in at me. "Good morning, folks. In a hurry?"

I smiled my brightest smile. "Actually, no. We were just on our way to Milly's," I said, keeping my hands tightly clasped in my lap.

The officer stared at me for a moment, then looked at Bill. "Awfully speedy for someone on their way to breakfast at the crack of dawn." He looked around the interior. "This your car?" he asked, frowning at Bill, who narrowed his eyes. His jaw clench tightly.

"It's mine!" I chimed in, cheerfully, and reached for the paperwork. "A gift from my mother and father...for good grades," I added, on second thought. I handed him the registration my father had tucked under the dash in case of emergencies. The officer barely glanced down, just held it all in his hands.

"Awfully nice gift. You must be a special young lady." He smiled, and seemed charming all of a sudden, much less intimidating. "You go to school around here?"

"Berkeley," I answered, glad to be on a friendly basis and out of interrogation mode. "I'm a junior there."

The officer folded the papers back up and handed them in through the window. "Caroline Maureino. Hm. I'll have to keep an eye out for that name."

Bill exhaled loudly. "Is that it? Can we go?" He sounded so rude.

The officer glared. "You, young man, had better keep that lead foot in check." He winked at me and straightened up.

Bill turned the engine on without responding, and pulled away, just inches from the patrolman's body. "Bill! You could have run him right over! What is *wrong* with you? He let us off the hook!"

He stared out angrily at the road. "Yeah, after pushing his weight around. And trying to move in on you."

I laughed hysterically. "Move *in* on me? Bill, you're out of your darn mind." I laughed harder and hung an arm out the window to feel the breeze. But when I glanced over again, he just looked angrier. I tried to make amends. "Come on. Don't be mad. He wasn't trying anything. Besides," I added, "he should first smell the gin on my breath and then decide if I'm the right kind of girl for him."

Bill smiled despite himself, and I felt a small victory. "Gin breath or not, you're still sitting there, pretty as pie, beaming like the damn sunshine. A sitting duck for some schmuck cop whose only intention is to use everything he's got — which wasn't anything besides a badge, by the way — to get what he wants."

The wind blew through my hair, the sun rose completely, and I smiled because I'd heard him say something new. "You think I'm pretty as pie, do you?"

He looked at me sideways and grinned. "Right now?"

I smacked his arm lightly. "You're a devil, you know that?"

"Yes, I do," he said. "To both questions."

Bill dropped me off after coffee and flapjacks. After the exam, I sat in the common room of my dormitory flipping through a magazine, fielding twenty questions from my dormitory girlfriends, Pauline and Georgia. I scored a ninety-three on the pharmacology exam, in case you're curious.

"You didn't even come in at all last night!" Pauline breathed, looking scandalized, bright red hair poking out from under a silk kerchief. "You were gone the whole night *again*! If the dorm hen finds out, you're splitsville from this place, Caroline!"

"Oh hush, Pauline," Georgia interrupted. "More importantly," she added, with a grin, "who were you gone all night *with*?"

I kept my habits pretty well under wraps, simply because the girls came from respectable families, like mine. Knowing I was out all night in a bar, drinking until I passed out...well, it wouldn't have put me in the best social position in the world. So, in the spirit of a good cover up, I had introduced them to Bill one morning, and he'd confirmed he was the man behind the curtain. The perfect cover for me.

"Just Bill," I said, shrugging, and waited for the reactions.

"Ooooo, Caroline! What did you two do all night?" Pauline loved all things scandalous. She enjoyed nothing more than juicy gossip, the possibility of a taboo situation.

"We slept," I said.

Georgia snorted. "You slept all night with that specimen, did you? Snored a bit, perhaps?" She laughed, and Pauline joined in. "You *are* a sneaky one, Miss C, I'll give you that. But no warm-blooded American girl would keep her hands to herself with that boy on an overnight. I know I wouldn't," she added.

"I get the point. Thank you both kindly. But we slept. That was it." I felt annoyed all of a sudden. Annoyed I couldn't have a moment of solitude without them hounding me about a man every moment of my life. A little annoyed, I think, that Georgia, whose wealthy, dashing fiancé worked for her father's company, had the gall to say anything about good ol' Bill. Geez Louise, isn't one catch enough for her?

"Caroline!" A freshman girl came running into the common room, calling my name, all out of breath. "Caroline!" she whispered frantically. "There's a *police officer* downstairs to see you! He said he knew you from an encounter this morning." She stood wide-eyed, waiting for my response.

Pauline and Georgia sat stone-still, mouths hanging open.

I loved it. I stood calmly and addressed my stunned girlfriends: "Pardon me. I have a gentleman caller." Then I exited the room in what I imagined to be the sassiest of fashions, and was halfway down the steps before I realized it must be the same police officer from that morning there to see me. I ran my hands down my blue wool skirt and turned the corner.

He was sitting on the reception chair in the lobby of the dormitory building, policeman's hat in his hands. When he looked up and saw me, his face broke into that charming, toothy smile he'd flashed that morning. He stood. "Caroline Maureino."

I didn't know his name, so I glanced at his uniform badge. *Sepuchelio.* I held out my left hand and attempted to seem composed. "I don't believe you've introduced yourself, officer."

He looked embarrassed. "I'm sorry. You're right. I'm Bruno. Bruno Sepuchelio." He tapped the metal name badge. He wasn't tall, just a few inches more so than me. But broad and muscular, his presence looming and protective. His black hair was slicked back, shiny, his eyes dark, like two black olives peering out under thick black eyebrows. All in all, undeniably handsome. While I considered this, he took my proffered hand and kissed it. "And you, Miss Caroline Maureino, are the girl of my dreams."

I stood there, his lips still pressed to my hand, and all the while never taking his eyes off me. And I thought: Finally, the storybook romance I've been waiting for. Finally, it's *my* turn.

Our courtship was quick: just a tad over three weeks, in fact. Bruno brought me flowers nearly every other day during that time. The girls in the dorm gushed when he came to pick me up after work, in uniform. He took me to dinner every free night I had, and we ate steak and shrimp and spaghetti Bolognese while chatting and laughing about our respective days. It felt like a dream, I was so happy. On the last Friday of the semester, he drove us to the ocean, where we held hands and walked along the beach, bundled in scarves and jackets. As we looked out at the choppy, gray water, he went down on one knee and opened a red velvet box that held the most gorgeous, shimmering diamond I'd ever laid eyes on.

I said, "Oh. Yes!"

He scooped me up, swung me around, and kissed me. That night, after he dropped me off, I squealed in delight with my girlfriends while they took turns holding my hand up to the light to see the ring.

Then I called my sister, Elizabeth, and told her the news. Out of an entire population of thrilled, screaming girls, she was the only one who sounded skeptical.

"But Caroline – it's only been three weeks. Are you sure?" She asked gently but firmly, the way she did about anything that was on her mind, worrying her.

I smiled very hard on the other end of the phone. "I'm so sure, Lizzie! I'm so, so, so sure!"

She was quiet for a moment. Then her voice changed to the delighted, high tone of the other girls. "Well, then, we have a wedding to plan!"

After relaying the details of the beach proposal for the one-thousandth time, I hung up and went to my room for some peace and quiet. I flopped down on my bed and thought about the whirlwind the past few weeks had been. Who would've imagined the police officer that'd pulled Bill and me over would be the man I would marry? What a story to tell our grandkids.

I lay there imagining that story-telling. Then thought of Bill's role in it. Good old Bill, who knew nothing of any of this because in the three weeks I'd spent wrapped up in all the excitement with Bruno, not a drop of liquor had passed my lips.

I grabbed my car keys and drove the familiar route to the bar.

When I walked in, Bill saw me and grinned, though his eyes seemed sad. "So you kicked the drinking habit. Good girl!"

I took my usual seat at the bar.

"Though, I have to say, would it kill you to come in and see me, even if the night doesn't end in vinyl heaven?"

I realized I'd missed him, despite these last exciting weeks. Missed him a lot. I'd always imagined my affection for him to be a liquor-induced, Florence Nightingale Syndrome. Except one where the nurse falls for someone instead of vice versa. But, here I was, sober and clear-minded, and he was still sweet and familiar and wonderful Bill.

"I'm sorry. It's been a wild three weeks."

He poured a Coca-Cola with extra ice, my drink of choice when I wasn't truly drinking, and popped the straw in for me before pushing it across the bar. "No harm done. I'm sure you have a fantastic recounting of your wild adventures. Lucky for you, I'm stuck behind this bar with no escape from your voice for the next," he glanced at the wall clock, "four hours. Tell away."

I took a sip of the Coca-Cola, preparing to tell the entire, unbelievable tale of how a girl who was practically an old maid went from no prospects to fully engaged in less than a month. The door opened and shut at the end of the bar. One of the regulars sat down at the far end, saw me, and waved.

"Look at that, Bill. Told you she'd show back up. No need for you to be worrying like that, going on like a clucking old hen," he called out. Then coughed violently and lit a cigarette. He addressed me. "You sure had him in a tither, little lady. Glad you decided to show your pretty face again."

Bill slammed a beer down in front of him. "Thanks, Stan. That'll do. Drink up."

When he turned to face me again, his cheeks were pink. I was both shocked and highly amused. "Are you...is that...you're blushing! My, oh, my. You were like a clucking hen?" I teased. "Worried about me? Annoying, vomitous old me, Bill?" I fanned myself in a fake swoon. "Aren't you the sweetest!" I reached out and squeezed his face. He caught my wrist and held it.

I stopped laughing when I saw his expression. Still holding my wrist firmly, he turned my hand over gently in his own and stared into my palm for a moment. Then leaned in across the bar, still holding on, until his face was inches from mine, and said quietly, "Yes. I was worried about you. Happy?" He let go of my wrist. When he turned to clean up the sink, I realized I'd been holding my breath.

Holding it for what?

He turned and faced me, old smile back in place, the slightest bit more mischievous than normal. "So are you going to bore me with a story, or what?"

Silently, in the only way I could find to do it, I held up my left hand. He looked and saw, then understood. "A ring," he said.

"Yes." I put my hand back down, under the bar. Feeling deflated, confused. I didn't want to talk about the ring. I wanted him to hold my wrist again, to lean close once more. Silly. I pushed the thoughts out of my mind and focused on the situation in front of us.

"An engagement ring, that is." He didn't make this a question, but his eyes were asking me to confirm it.

"Yes."

He set the towel down on the bar and nodded. "Well, Rolin," he said, "that really is a wild three weeks." He made an attempt to smile, but it fell completely flat. "Who?"

I felt too sad to muster up any excitement about telling the story now. I felt drained. I wanted to make a joke about him raining on my parade, but how do you say that when the rain has no other choice in the matter?

"Well, it's a very funny story," I said at last, trying to put the cheer back into my voice.

"I would imagine so," he murmured. Then it really was too sad in there, and I wanted out immediately.

"You know, Bill, actually, I've got to go for now." I slid off the bar stool and walked toward the door. "I'll just tell you about it some other time. Soon." I turned and walked out the door, and the minute it swung shut behind me, my eyes overflowed and the tears came down in rivers. I walked as quickly as I could to my car. As I unlocked my door, I heard the bar door slam, and suddenly Bill was there, spinning me around to face him, holding me tightly, my back pressed against the car.

"Rolin," he said, and I cried harder. He cradled my face in his hands and wiped away tears with his thumbs. "Don't cry. You aren't serious, are you?"

I sniffled loudly and choked out, "He asked me to marry him, Bill. He wants to marry me."

He pressed his body up closer, so that we were touching from toes to chin, and whispered, "No, Rolin. No, don't. I want to marry you. Me. Don't do this."

I stared at him for a moment, our foreheads touching, and his arms around me, and suddenly my life felt wonderful and terrible – a feeling I now know comes from having everything that you want in the whole world at exactly the wrong time. "But I already said yes, Bill! And you never asked!"

He pulled away suddenly, and the cold air hit my body again, remarking loudly on the absence of his warmth against me. His voice rose slightly. "I didn't ask, Rolin, because I'm broke as a joke right now! Why the hell do you think I'm always here, working? Don't you think I'd rather be taking you out dancing and to nice dinners and buying you pretty dresses? I just can't yet! I can't, but I'm working so that I can! So I can ask you to marry me and not have you ever want for any of those nice things you're used to." He flung his hands in wild gestures as he spoke. "How can you not see that? Look at me. *Look at me*, Rolin!" He put his hands on either side of my face and held it firmly up to his. "I love you. Okay? I love you. Don't do this."

I put a hand gently on his chest, and he let go of me. "You never said anything, Bill. And I was such a mess. A mess every night, drinking and looking downright horrible, and nobody ever asked me out on a date, much less to marry them. You didn't ask me! You didn't say anything." I felt confused and angry, but most of all, dangerously close to heartbroken.

"Jeepers, what else did you want me to say? Did you want me to get down on one knee and propose with no job but a night owl shift at a lousy bar, and an apartment with no furniture?" He raked his hands through his hair and turned around in agitation. When he spoke again, his voice was calmer. "What did you want me to do that I didn't already do?"

I shook my head. I didn't even know. His love had come out of nowhere. But then, it didn't really, I suppose. He took care of me, he confided in me, listened to me, and knew me. He was the best friend I'd ever had, other than Lizzie.

"I never knew." I said.

"How could you not know? In a year and a half, not once did it occur to you that I didn't have a date with anyone else? That I never brought a girl home, other than you? That I stayed late at the bar while you slept in the booth for *a reason*? I'm sorry I never said it maybe like I should have. I'm sorry I never kissed you under the stars or anything else I wanted to do. I didn't want to make an offer that would seem inadequate!"

I nodded. "I understand."

He stepped forward, right into my space, until my back was hard against the car again. I breathed him in and held my breath. He slipped his arms around my waist, then looked up at the sky for a moment before moving his mouth an inch from mine, and whispering, "It's starry out *now*. I'm kissing you now."

And he did. Softly, holding me tightly pressed between him and the car. I closed my eyes in the lost, wonderful, liquid feeling of that kiss. Cupped a hand around his neck, feeling the close-shaven tickle of his hair on my palm, and held on. He wasn't my first kiss, by a long shot, but I had never lost faith in my legs to hold me up until then.

When our lips finally parted, I'd lost both words and breath.

He pressed his forehead against mine and breathed as heavily as me. "See? I love you."

The gravity of these words slammed me back into horrid reality. I thought of my fiancé suddenly. About how just ten hours ago, another man had been holding me this way, asking me to marry him. A man whose proposal I'd accepted and committed myself to. I turned my head away slightly, but Bill saw. His eyes changed as he took one step back, putting miles of space between us.

"Don't, Rolin. Don't."

My chest felt too tight. I took shallow breaths, my eyes stinging again as I reached for my keys, set on the top of the car when Bill had surprised me. "I made a promise, Bill. I accepted. It's too...it's just too late."

He stared. I turned away first, getting into the driver's seat, peeling out of the parking lot.

I'd like to say I didn't even look back. But the truth is, I watched his figure get smaller and smaller in the side mirror as I drove away, my heart breaking into smaller pieces with every mile marker I passed.

Chapter 19

W e were to marry on January twenty-sixth. In light of this, and the fact that he'd already bought a neat little ranch-style house in a new development, and I was to be its sole keeper, Bruno and I decided that my finishing college was not necessary. I packed up my dorm room alone over winter break. The girls threw me a lovely farewell party in the common area. The remainder of December and all of January was spent in a blur of wedding preparations, dress fittings, and floral arrangements. I didn't go back to the bar, and Bill never sought me out. Life moved forward, as it does. As it should.

The wedding, for all its quick arrival, was elaborate and beautiful. Bruno insisted on a thank-you getaway for my parents – he bought them tickets to France and arranged for a week's worth of fine lodging. They were in love with Bruno from the moment they met him. Which is was what I'd expected. The coldness in their own marriage had permeated Lizzie and me since we were children, always feeling like we had to bridge the gap between them, though they smiled at each other over dinner. Bruno was exactly, as my father phrased it, "The old-fashioned kind of man with deep pockets and an abundance of wits about him." My mother's conclusion: "Imagine what handsome children you'll have, Caroline!"

Lizzie seemed less smitten. She was polite to him, of course, but I knew she wasn't being herself. I caught her staring once when he was at the kitchen table playing cards with my father, two afternoons before the wedding. She stood against the sink sipping a glass of iced tea, and when I walked into the kitchen, she flinched, looking wholly and completely guilty.

"Lizzie," I said, once we were sitting out on the patio, our hats and gloves matching. "You look like the cat who ate the damned canary."

She didn't smile. "Caroline, how well do you know Bruno?"

I'm her sister, only fourteen short months younger, so I knew exactly where she was going with this. "Oh, Lizzie. Don't you like him?"

"Sure I do!" she said defensively. "I just don't *know* him. And, gosh, I'm not sure you do either. I mean...what if he isn't at all who he says he is? Aren't you worried about finding that out later?"

"I love what I do know. I'm sure we'll both learn things about each other as time goes on, but I'm looking forward to it. Isn't that what's so wonderful about being in love? Discovering all those new things about each other."

She nodded and looked at the sky. "Three weeks. Holy Moses! Are you in trouble?" She glanced at my stomach, and lowered her voice to a whisper. "Is that it, Sissy? Are you," she gestured wildly, "in an unfortunate *way*? Because you still don't have to marry him if you aren't entirely sure he's the one." She stared at me with such earnest love and concern I had to start laughing. But Bill's face flashed into my mind, and I pushed the thought out quickly.

"Jiminy Crickets, Elizabeth! I'm not in any trouble! I haven't even done anything that could *get* me in that kind of trouble," I added meaningfully. I raised my voice again. "I love him, Lizzie. *I love him*. He's a good man." The more I said it, and the oftener, the truer it felt.

She set her mouth into a line, her way of ending a conversation without being completely tactless. We sat in silence for a few minutes, then she sighed. "All right, Caroline." She linked her arm in mine. "If this is really what will make you happy, then I am thrilled for you, Sissy." She smiled sincerely at me.

"Thank you." I was very grateful she'd stopped interrogating me on a subject that had already been gnawing away at me during quiet moments, when the flurry of planning wasn't consuming my thoughts.

Three days into our honeymoon in Cozumel, we were as happy as newlyweds could be. The hotel suite my parents had booked for us was gorgeously decorated in a nautical theme, blue wallpaper with tiny white anchors up and down the walls, and our own mini-kitchen. Our cruise had taken us down the Pacific coast, and since we'd boarded the ship just hours after the reception, our wedding night was a water-bound one, among other things. I'm sure I was nervous and irritating, completely neurotic about our first time together as a married couple, and my first time, period. He was a little impatient, I found, and nothing agitated him more than when I cried. Details unnecessary, we did consummate the marriage, but it was nerve-wracking and strange to me. I didn't look forward at all to repeating the act, and so, in an effort to keep us out of the hotel room, and therefore out of the bed, I enthusiastically planned activities. Swimming, boating, fishing, snorkeling – we had appointments for all of these. On the third day, Bruno seemed strangely unlike himself, as I read our morning schedule over a room service breakfast of fresh fruit, French toast, and ham.

"This says we can rent bicycles for an afternoon ride. Doesn't that sound fun, sweetheart?" I turned the brochure over to find the phone number. Bruno didn't answer, which made me look up. "Darling, did you hear me?"

He set his fork down hard. "Yes. I heard you. I'd rather not go bicycling." His voice seemed unfamiliar, formal and edgy.

"Oh. Then of course we don't need to go. What would you like to do instead?" I helped myself to another spoonful of strawberries.

He didn't touch his fork again. Just laid his hands flat on either side of his plate, palms down on the tabletop. "I'd rather stay in with my new wife," he said, unsmiling. "I'd rather enjoy the benefits of being with the beautiful girl I married."

I felt my stomach churn. I'd managed to avoid this for the last two and half days, trying to make sure our wedding night was the only miserable experience we had together throughout the trip. I can't for sure say what was wrong; he was still so handsome and charming, but I felt uncomfortable and nervous, therefore unable to be accommodating, much less happy and enthusiastic. He had attempted, the past two nights, to start something, but each time I'd simply gone limp, forced my breathing to be slow and even, and fooled him into thinking I was plum tuckered out from the day's excitements. This was the first time he'd addressed this fact. That, paired with his unsmiling, brooding face, made me feel twitchy.

"Darling, that sounds lovely," I started, smiling brightly. "But wouldn't you like to enjoy the sights while this gorgeous weather holds out?"

He drummed his fingers on the tabletop. "No, not particularly. I would, like I just said, like to enjoy my gorgeous wife." His lips twitched, but it wasn't his usual smile. "We can see the outside later. Besides, it's nothing compared to the sights in this room."

Charming, no doubt, but I suddenly felt sick to my stomach. Maybe talking about it would help? Maybe I was being completely silly, expecting him to understand me without even trying to explain. "Bruno," I said gently, slowly. "I'm feeling very nervous these past few days...the excitement of the wedding and all...and just nervous in general about our

– " I struggled with the discomfort of speaking the words to him. "Our love life."

He stood up suddenly, knocking the chair over, and I jumped in surprise. The next thing I knew, he had me by one arm, up against the wall, squeezing my throat with the other large, meaty hand.

"We don't *have* a love life!" he spat from between clenched teeth. The panic I felt compared to nothing before in my entire life. "You're an ungrateful, dried up bitch, you know that?" He slammed me against the wall, then turned suddenly and left the room.

With his hand off my throat, and the air coming again so I could breathe, I had the good sense to realize my legs were about to collapse. I slid down against the wall, dragging my palms along the striped wallpaper to slow the descent, until I was sitting with my knees drawn up to my chest. Only then, once I was safely on the floor, did I allow myself a gasping, shocked cry. I put a hand on my neck, where his had been, and felt for something I expected to be there: a cut, perhaps? An open, bleeding wound? I felt nothing different.

I sat there, that afternoon, for over an hour, legs shaking too badly to stand. At last, I pushed up, washed my face, and reapplied my makeup. Then headed to the door, to be anywhere but in that room. When I opened it, Bruno stood on the other side, holding a bouquet of irises and stargazer lilies.

He held them out to me. "I saw these in the window of the sweetest floral shop, and they reminded me of you," he said, the old smile back in place. I felt a sudden wave of confusion mixed with absolute fear. "Let's put them in some water, Darling, so they last at least until the end of our honeymoon."

He strode past me, my hand still holding the hotel room door open, and laid the bouquet on the bureau. "Well, don't you want to see what else I picked up?" He grinned mischievously, holding up a wrapped box I hadn't even noticed before.

I let the door fall shut on its own. My legs had just stopped shaking only minutes earlier. The washcloth I'd used to dry my face after washing off the smeared mascara and rouge still lay crumpled and wet on the sink. Yet, here he was, holding out a present. If I hadn't been absolutely sure of my sanity, I would've been convinced I'd imagined the entire incident.

"Go on, Darling, open it." He held out the pink-wrapped rectangle with a perfectly-folded lace ribbon.

Silently, I took it from his hands and peeled the wrapping paper off, then opened the white box. A crystal vase lay inside. I stared at it.

"To...put the flowers in," he said, sounding uncertain. "Is it not right? We can go back down to the market where I bought it and pick out another one."

I realized, at that moment, exactly how life would be from then on. Exactly how I was expected to behave. But the frightening aspect of this role gripped me, and I hesitated.

"Darling?" he asked. "Let's go right now and get another one, of your choice. Whatever you'd like." He put a hand in his pocket and jingled the room key and some loose change.

I shook my head slowly. He frowned, and suddenly I felt desperate to play along. "No, no. This one is *lovely*. It's...it's exactly what these flowers need." I took the vase out of the box and went into the bathroom to fill it with water. I turned the faucet on high and shoved my wrists under to feel the shock of the cold, running stream.

"If you're sure, Darling," he called from the room.

I quickly dried my hands and filled the vase, emerging from the bathroom with a bright smile. "Oh, yes," I said. "I'm sure."

And that is exactly how it went, you see. The beatings escalated, naturally, but he was careful only to leave bruises that would be covered by the right blouse or the right stylish set of sunglasses while we were vacationing in a sunny location. Sometimes months would pass without a single incident. At first, early on, I fooled myself into thinking it was just temporary, some nightmarish situation I had only imagined. Later on – and now, of course – I just accept it for what it is: my life. The life I chose. The one I have wholly and completely accepted.

Chapter 20

T he knock startled me. In the afternoons, especially the mid-week afternoons, I was always alone with the baby. Lizzie came around once in a while, but she was so busy with her nursing job and going out with girlfriends that our lives often seemed like two very different branches poking out of the same tree. I missed her, my sister. When she came we'd sit together on the back deck while she played with Abigail on a blanket, and she'd tell me the most hilarious stories of pompous doctors and silly, rowdy patients. Or of the outrageous blind dates she endured for the sake of her friends' feelings.

Abigail was healthy and beautiful, the perfect little girl. Bruno adored her from the moment her little crow head popped into view, and I couldn't have asked for a more cooperative first child. She rarely fussed. Some afternoons I'd tuck her into her umbrella stroller with a little flowered bucket hat on, and we would walk to the park to watch the older kids play on the swings. Other days we stayed around the house, and she played happily in the living room while I dusted and vacuumed and took down the china from the cupboard to polish.

So when the three-tap knock sounded off from the foyer, I was startled because nobody visited us except Lizzie, and she was at the beach with her girlfriends for the weekend. Abigail cooed and kicked and flailed, lying on the afghan on the olive-green living room carpet. I peeled off the yellow rubber gloves I was wearing to clean the oven and tiptoed into the foyer. We didn't have a peep hole. I suppose we could've had one, if I'd asked, but the house didn't have one when Bruno bought it. I suppose some part of me liked the surprise of not knowing who might be calling on the other side of the door.

When I opened it, the surprise hit me full force. Bill was standing there, one hand in his pocket, the other holding a magazine. I hadn't seen him since that terrible day in the parking lot outside the bar. I stared for a moment. Then the fact that we were standing right across from each other in such a strange, unlike-us environment made me laugh out loud.

His lopsided smile still lifted the right side of his mouth. "Happy to see me, Rolin?"

The name rang hard in my ears. Guilt overcame me for absolutely no reason. I told myself I'd simply say it wasn't right for him to be here; that it was inappropriate.

"Come in!" I said instead. When he stepped through the doorframe the nearness of him took away my good sense. I stretched up and kissed his cheek. "Hi, Bill."

He looked down with the same gaze he used to give me over the bar, half amused and half sad, but wonderfully magnetic all at the same time. "Rolin."

I shut the door behind us, wondering what Mrs. Gibson next door must be thinking. That old biddy would be chatting it up about my goings-on with everyone else on the street come dinnertime. Yet, I didn't even care enough to think of it again.

"What're you doing here?" I wanted to know. It's strange when something from the past is standing smack dab in the middle of your new life. Like finding a frilly church sock under the bed when you've been old enough to wear stockings for years.

He didn't move past the foyer, didn't step away or give me any space. "I wanted to show you something." He held up the magazine. "Can I come in?"

I laughed nervously. "Well, you *are* in."

He turned his head toward the end of the foyer, which led into the kitchen. "I mean *in*. To sit down a second. Or are you too busy keeping house to entertain guests?" I followed his gaze to the apron covered in oven grease that was neatly protecting my lacy white blouse.

"Still a smart ass, I see." I walked into the kitchen. He followed, and I snuck at peek at him sneaking a peek at the furnishings.

"Still living the high life, too," he said, but a smile took away a little bit of the sting.

I pulled out a blue crystal pitcher of iced tea and poured two glasses. The ice made cracking sounds that seemed to echo through the kitchen. When we sat at the kitchen table, I realized my nervousness was actually giddiness at the prospect of having a conversation with another person who wasn't a cooing, chubby infant.

Another person that was Bill.

"So," I said, crossing and uncrossing and recrossing my legs.

"So." He looked around again. "Nice place."

I nodded, suddenly self-conscious in the way only Bill could ever make me feel about something. "Yeah. It's all right, I suppose."

He snorted. "Right. Anyway," he said, patting the magazine with his long fingers, taking a long gulp of tea, "I got published."

I looked for a long moment, to take in the sheepishness suddenly on his face, because it was so rare. Then I squealed with delight, and began to make the great big fuss he deserved. "Bill! You didn't!" I picked up the magazine. "What is this, anyway? You didn't resort to writing smutty bodice rippers."

He grinned and flipped some pages. "Oh, it's a literary magazine. For short stories and the like."

"About what?"

He turned to a particular page and smoothed it out. "I don't know. Everything. Life. Just everything."

"Well, show me!" I scooted my chair closer, around the table.

He laughed. "It's right there."

I looked down at the page and saw it was a story. "Blue Moon" by William Eaton, illustrated around the edges, set into a dark, nighttime background. I blinked quickly and stared at the page.

"So? Don't tell me you don't have anything to say. I thought that was a medical impossibility." He laughed. The tears spilled over my lashes, and plopped down on the page. I felt Bill turn his head to look.

"Rolin? What the hell! Why are you crying?" He leaned closer, until his face was inches from mine, peering like a curious kid. "Are you okay?"

I laughed then and looked up. "I'm so proud of you, Bill. I'm just…so proud of you." I waved a hand over the magazine. "This is amazing."

He nodded, then threw an arm over my shoulders. "So you're proud?"

"Yes. Very." I wiped my cheeks on my shoulder. It was like *I* had succeeded somehow. Like his victory was mine. He wasn't mine, to share proud moments with. I knew that. But he felt a little bit mine.

He squeezed my arm. I felt his chest rise as he took a deep breath. "Thanks. I wanted you to be. It was quite the chore finding you. But worth it."

I stood and his arm slid off my shoulders. "More tea?" I asked, even though both our glasses were still half full.

He leaned back in the chair. "No thanks. I was thinking maybe something like dinner."

I went to the sink and turned the faucet on. This was not the Bill I knew. That man would never strut into a married woman's house and ask her out to dinner. I said this exact phrase to him.

He was tipping the chair back onto two legs as I delivered this rebuke. He set the chair back down firmly on all four legs and stood. "The Bill you knew was a fool." He moved closer to me. "The Bill you knew was wimpy and stupid and never stood on his own two feet."

I squarely faced him. "The Bill I knew was decent and honest and caring."

He stopped a foot from me. "No. Just spineless."

I threw the dishtowel down onto the counter, now angry as all hell. But why? Why was I furious? "The Bill I knew was – he was wonderful."

"He blew the bottom out of the loser barrel."

"Well, I don't think so! And I loved him!" I froze in the silence after I said that. Then, from the living room, like a small, incessant warning siren, Abigail began to cry.

Bill's eyes shifted toward the living room, and changed altogether. "Ah. Clearly," he said, then walked toward the sound of crying.

I followed him into the room where Abigail lay fussing on a quilt spread out over the carpet. Bill reached for her first, and tickled her pudgy belly. When she whimpered again, he began to sing gently. For a moment, a real, live moment, I leaned against the archway and saw a different life. When he finished the song – one I didn't know, but that I'd loved hearing – he pressed his hands against his knees and stood to face me.

"It's great seeing you, Rolin." He jammed his hands in his pockets. "I'm gonna take off."

My throat felt tight, constricted, but I nodded anyway. "Thanks for…"

"Yeah," he said, then turned to leave.

I rushed over to meet him in the entryway. He turned so quickly to face me, just as I rounded the corner, that I ran right into him. My chest pressed briefly against his.

I stepped back, burned. "Bill?"

He raised his eyebrows at me the same old way, and butterflies filled my stomach, surprising me. I hadn't felt those in a long time. My body had closed up, a silent, stony place only entered in moments of obligation. I reveled in the feeling that drifted through me.

His gaze didn't stray from mine. "Yeah?"

I shook my head. There wasn't any good reason to do so, I suppose. But somehow it felt like the only way to say what I wanted to say – *don't go, don't disappear* – was to shake my head like an insistent toddler. *No. No.*

Of course, Bill understood. He always did. He raked his fingers through that messy, thick black hair and sighed. "See me again, Rolin."

I tried to put on a friendly smile and make my voice carefree. "Oh. Are you in town long, then?"

He stepped a foot closer, until we were nearly touching again. I looked up into his clear, green eyes. "I'll be around," he said, voice low.

I nodded. "Well then...we should catch up. Soon," I added.

"My phone number's in the back of that issue. Your copy to keep. Courtesy of the author," he said, grinning. "Call if you want me."

He let that phrase – *if you want me* – hang there between us. Our faces too close, my heart beating so loudly I was afraid he could hear it. Then he turned and stepped out the front door, closing it behind him.

I turned back to my baby in the living room, but she was fast asleep.

Chapter 21

Time moves fast when children are involved, as any mother will tell you. Patrick was born a year later. The first boy of Bruno's family, he held a coveted position in the extended Sepuchelio clan. Bruno's brothers envied him the first male grandchild – someone to carry out the name. Bruno was proud, of course, but so very busy on the force. By the time Patrick began school, Bruno had made chief of police in the department. It was a big to-do, as he was the youngest to ever be promoted to that position. But good at his job, and loved by all.

The promotion kept him away. He was gone nearly every night of the week. For the first time in six years, I was alone with my thoughts. With the children at school all day, Bruno at work all the time, the house stayed clean. Dinner practically made itself. So I picked up gardening. I joined the Women's Recreational Committee in our town, and together we planned outings and fundraisers for the Boys and Girls Club. I was busy, too.

It was on the day of a committee meeting, in fact, when I was rushing around, unpinning curlers from my hair, hurrying to put rouge on before heading out, that the doorbell rang unexpectedly.

It was Bill.

I never called him, you should know. I kept his magazine issue tucked under a box of potpourri in the bottom drawer of my nightstand. But I'd never opened it, and never called him.

When I went to the door on that day, he stood there. The same old Bill, handsomer than ever in black-rimmed glasses, his hair long and shaggy nearly to his shoulders. He wore blue jeans and a faded red flannel shirt hanging loose.

I yanked the last curler from my hair as I opened the door, and for a moment we just stood there, a carbon copy moment of years before.

"Hi, Rolin," he said.

I realized I was still holding my breath. "Bill." I exhaled.

He grinned, and his smile was the same. His green eyes under serious dark brows were the same. His goatee was different.

"You grew a beard."

He laughed out loud then, and I wanted to fling my arms around him and squeeze him tight.

"Come in," I said.

"Yeah?" He raised an eyebrow, and then glanced over his shoulder at the house across the street. "You've got a peeping neighbor. You sure about this?"

I gazed past him to see our new neighbor, Tina, peering out of her front window. She saw me looking, and yanked the curtains together quickly.

Suddenly I felt completely suffocated. If you've ever been out on a gusty day – when the wind is blowing so fiercely you feel that your lungs actually cannot keep up, that you cannot draw a good, clean breath – you know how I felt right then. *Goddamn neighbors, goddamn neighborhood.*

"Goddamn petunias," I said out loud. "Come in." I flung the door wide open, staring pointedly across the street at Tina's house.

Bill nodded, looking impressed. "Well, all right. There you go, Rolin. Goddamn those petunias. There's some life left in you after all."

I turned, angry, and walked toward the kitchen. "What's *that* supposed to mean? I'm *alive*."

Bill followed and leaned against the counter island. Strange, I thought, how he fit perfectly into my home, my life, like nothing ever changed. Like it hadn't been over half a decade since we were face-to-face.

He plucked a red grape off a bunch sitting in my fruit bowl and popped it in his mouth. "How's life treating you, Rolin?"

I still felt steam pouring from my ears. Why so angry? I didn't know. Bill always could get my goat when he tried. I glanced at him casually chewing, a small smile on his face.

That beard looked good on him.

"You're looking well," I said.

He swallowed and grinned. "You think so? Thanks." He surveyed me head to toe, eyes gliding slowly – too slowly, for Pete's sake! - and said *nothing.* I wanted to punch him right-square in the jaw.

"What are you doing here, Bill?" I asked nastily.

For a moment his confidence faltered, his gaze shifted to the floor. I felt victorious. And then horrible.

He looked up again, shrugged. "I can go."

We stood like that, silently, his lanky frame leaning against my kitchen counter, me with arms crossed in front of my pale pink linen dress. I thought of the committee meeting and felt anger and frustration and hatred for all of those women sitting there, waiting to plan other people's lives. Waiting to plan mine. I wanted to throw a brick through my china closet, sitting so beautifully against the dining room wall in front of me.

Instead, I said, "Want to go to a diner?"

Bill smiled widely, lighting up my kitchen, my house, my whole life. "Sounds perfect."

So we went. He left the house first, straddled his black motorbike, zoomed down the street. I waited two minutes and then hurried out to the car, glancing across the yard just in time to see Tina peeking out again. I waved, exhilarated and cocky, and ducked quickly into my sedan.

Goddamn petunias.

Three weeks later, as I was polishing the wood china cupboard, the doorbell rang again. I checked the timepiece on the wall and felt confused. Bill wasn't due for our lunch for another twenty minutes. Gently setting aside the fork I was working on, I rose from my chair and opened the front door.

It was Bruno. And he looked unhappy, brow furrowed, hands on hips, impatient.

"Why's the door locked, Caroline?" he said, pushing past me as I stood, still holding the knob.

My heart beat faster. He was unreasonable. I knew the signs, the little clues, when he was in a dangerous mood, and it made me instantly jittery. Sometimes it was a hint as small as his posture – he became rigid, holding himself very still. A horrible brooding green sky before hail started falling, before the tornado ripped through.

I shut the door calmly and swallowed.

"I must have locked it accidentally this morning. I was watering flowers earlier." I carefully rounded the corner into the kitchen, where he was rummaging through a bottom drawer. "You're home very early," I said, trying to inject my voice with pleasantness, happiness to see him.

He grunted.

"Should I make you some lunch? A tuna sandwich?" My palms began to sweat. Silence was never a good sign. I knew there was nothing to fear when he was raising his voice – that always meant he would yell, say what he needed to, and then move on with the day. The silence shook me. I walked toward the cupboard on the far side of the kitchen. Sometimes, if I just ignored it all together, nothing happened. But sometimes, it made it worse.

I pulled a wheat loaf from the bread drawer and sliced two pieces. He continued rustling and clattering behind me. I drew a deep breath. "Can I help you find something?"

Silence.

I pulled a Tupperware container from the refrigerator and spooned tuna from it onto the bread.

Finally, he spoke. "Where's the spare bottle opener?"

I turned quickly, relieved to hear him say something, to break the silent tension.

"The spare one? Hm. I'll have to check. I thought it was in that drawer..." I saw his eyes flash, and hurried to cover my mistake. "But obviously not, since you just checked. I'll look around. Maybe the basement." I rattled on nervously, not wanting to give him a chance to do anything but listen.

I moved toward the basement door, but he caught my upper arm with one stubby, beefy hand. I tried to control my breathing so that I didn't sound panicked. Sometimes crying made it worse.

"Why is it, that with all the space you have, with all the time you have every single day, you can't keep track of one single item in this house?" He squeezed my arm harder.

I shook my head, looking down. I could still head this off. I could turn it around. It was always like a puzzle: Just find the right piece – the right move, the right *word* – to turn it around.

I forced out a light sigh. "You're right, darling. I don't know how I can be so silly sometimes."

Sometimes acting innocent and absentminded made him laugh a situation off, squeeze the back of my neck gently and wink, saying he didn't know what to do with me. A loveable screw-up, I was.

Not that day. He moved lightning fast, slamming me back against the kitchen sink. No turning it around, by that point. I knew that all too well.

His hand circled my neck, and he breathed out heavily. "Stupid." He spoke calmly, quietly, teeth gritted together. "So stupid. Don't patronize me." He held the hand steady against my neck, my back arched over the sink. The faucet dug into my spine, holding me hostage.

I closed my eyes. The first blow landed on the side of my head, against my left ear. I clenched my jaw, kept my eyes tightly shut, and didn't make a sound. The second landed hard on my mouth, his knuckle slamming my lips against my bottom teeth, breaking open the skin on my lower one.

"Stupid," he said again, hand tightening on my throat.

And then the doorbell rang.

I opened my eyes. He released me as quickly as he'd grabbed me, and strode to the entryway. My legs felt like gelatin, as they always did, and I grabbed at the sink behind me to steady myself. I touched my lip with the tip of my ring finger and stared at the red smear there.

"Caroline!" Bruno's voice – his real voice – was back, and he was calling for me.

"Yes?" I frantically wiped at my lip as he rounded the corner.

He snagged his car keys off of the counter, where he'd dropped them while rummaging through the drawer, and picked up our good bottle opener. "Darling, I'm going to take this one to work." He chuckled. "I promise, I'll bring it back. Sorry I can't stay for lunch."

I nodded, covering my mouth with my fingertips so he wouldn't see the blood.

He leaned forward and pecked me on the cheek. "Oh, and there's some hippie on our step, selling magazine subscriptions. I don't want anything, but order yourself whatever you'd like. Maybe renew your *Home and Garden*, hm?"

I continued nodding like a Mickey Mantle Bobblehead, until I heard the front door shut. I glanced in the hall mirror, smoothed my hair down, and went to the door to speak to the salesman.

But, of course, it was Bill.

He was sitting on the front step, facing the street. He turned when I opened the door. My hand flew to my mouth again. I had forgotten about lunch, forgotten about Bill, during the entire episode.

He jumped to his feet, faced me, and held out a copy of *Time*, playing the part. "Ma'am…"

I began to cry. He glanced behind him, probably checking for that goddamn nosy Tina, and then gently pushed me into the house, shutting the door behind him. I gasped in a breath and tried to calm myself. His sad eyes were too much. A fresh set of tears leaked out.

"Rolin," he began, sighing heavily. I lifted a hand and put my fingers to his lips. I couldn't bear to hear him say anything right then.

I stared up, one hand covering my own bloodied mouth, the other covering his. And in that moment, I gave up. Or perhaps just finally gave in.

I slid my hand from his mouth to the back of his head, and leaned up on tiptoes. Pressed my lips against his, and they pressed back, warm, dry, soft.

And my world changed again. He wrapped his arms around my waist, pulling me closer, his fingers pressing into my sides. I leaned heavily into him, and he held me, trailing his fingertips along my jaw. His hands were soft, delicate, long and lean.

When we parted, we stayed wound in each other, breathing heavily. Hot, runny, liquid. In my stomach, the million butterflies only Bill could give me. I leaned in once more and touched my lips to his, gently. He kissed me back before tucking a piece of hair behind my ear.

I stepped backward slightly, to give myself, *us*, some space. But I didn't want space. I wanted to be close to him, engulfed by him. But I stepped back anyway.

His olive gaze met mine. He straightened suddenly, staring at my mouth. I remembered the split lip, and touched it.

"No," he said, shaking his head. "*No*. He did that?"

I turned away. "It's nothing much." I shook my head, tried to clear my mind, solidify my insides once more.

He put a hand on my shoulder and spun me around. "Rolin. *Goddammit*. No."

I sighed, trying not to cry. "It's just what it is, Bill. I've got – *we've* got – this." I flung a hand out toward the living room, toward the life I'd chosen.

Bill wrapped his arms around me, and I buried my nose in the soft skin below his throat, between his collarbones. I inhaled deeply, then let my lips part on his skin, pressing gently against his throat. I felt him swallow. His pulse thumped against my mouth, quicker.

"Rolin," he said, voice low, almost a whisper in my hair. "Come away with me."

"I want to," I muttered against his neck.

He took me by the shoulders and held me at arms' length. "Then let's," he pleaded. "We'll go anywhere you want." He looked down at the floor and pink spread across his cheeks. "I - I have money now. I'll take care of us."

He was worried, you see. About whether or not he'd be good enough, whether or not he could give me everything I'd want. All I wanted, as I stood there in my stylish living room, with my unfinished silver sitting nearby, and my bloodied lip, was him.

And I couldn't have him.

My eyes caught on the portrait we'd had taken of the children for Christmas the year before. Abigail and Patrick. I loved them, more than anything else I'd ever known in life. They were the one true thing, untainted by the misery of my situation with Bruno.

I locked eyes with Bill. "The children," I said. "We can't. You have to live down here, on earth." *With me*, I thought. "Your head – it's in the clouds."

He closed his eyes for a moment, and then nodded quickly.

I began to cry. Rather than move toward me, Bill took a step back, toward the door.

"No!" I reached out. "Bill, please."

He watched me hard for a moment and then threw his hands up. "Rolin! What can I do? What do you *want* me to do? Tell me. Anything."

And because we could never have our life together, could never run away, sit on a beach somewhere, go to a diner at four in the morning, stand watching a river flow by on a lazy day, because we could not grow old side by side, I said what I wanted, selfishly, right then: "Stay with me."

I flung myself at him, and he caught me. Our mouths were forceful, *starving,* years apart making our hands desperate to be on one another. I pulled him onto the living room carpet.

This, I thought with wonder, as his hands ran along my body and we lost ourselves, this was what it felt like to want someone. To want *this*.

We didn't speak much for the rest of the afternoon – just lived in each other, desperate, we both knew, to hold on to a fleeting, wonderful dream.

Chapter 22

I held the brown paper grocery sack in one arm, balancing it partially on my knee, as I unlocked the apartment door. Before I could push the door open, an elderly woman popped her head out into the hall two doors down.

She waved to me. "Good afternoon, Sarah!"

I gave a small wave, holding the door open with my foot. "Good afternoon, Mrs. Davis. How's that cold feeling today?"

She gave a small, theatrical cough and shrugged. "It's sticking with me, I suppose. That's what happens when you get old. I recommend never getting old, Sarah."

I laughed. "I'll try my best, Mrs. Davis. Thank you for the wise words." I pushed through the doorway with the groceries, and shut the apartment door firmly behind me.

I pulled turkey cold cuts from the bag and began fixing a sandwich at the small Formica table. Wrapped in a hug from behind, I turned my face toward the assailant. Bill kissed me softly.

"Hi," he said. "Pickles?"

I reached into the sack. "Kosher dill. Would I forget pickles?"

He kissed the top of my head and came around to sit across. "You might. If you're feeling particularly obstinate."

I laughed. "True. But today we feast on pickles."

We ate our sandwiches on the couch, side by side, watching the news anchor bring us the latest on Patty Hearst, rich girl turned bank robber. You couldn't escape the scandal following her arrest.

"Urban Guerilla, huh?" Bill said. "She's bad, if you ask me. And right around the corner from us."

I agreed.

"You think she was really brainwashed?" he asked, getting up to fish in the fridge for a cola.

I shrugged. "Who knows? Maybe she's completely sane and just got sick of the expectations."

"And decided to wield an M1 carbine and hold up a bank? Is that what happens, then, when you ladies decide you've had it?" He poked me in the side.

"Perhaps," I made my fingers into a gun and pointed it at him. "Don't push me."

He wrestled me to the floor, and we rolled around for a few minutes, me struggling to gain the upper hand, him pretending to struggle against me.

"It's not fair! I'm not as strong when I'm laughing!" I shrieked hysterically as he poked my ribs. "Laughing takes away my strength!" We collapsed together, and he slid an arm under my shoulders and pulled me close. We stared at the yellowing ceiling.

"You take away my strength, Rolin," he said.

I looked over at him. Still so handsome, even pushing thirty-five, crow's feet just beginning around the eyes. I kissed his cheek, making a loud smacking sound. "Only if I cut your hair, right? Like Samson."

It was shaggy, long over his eyes, but I loved it that way, and frequently begged him not to cut it.

"Ha. I wish you would, Delilah. All I need is to stop shaving for a few weeks, grow a full beard, and I'll be able to really pull off the terrorist thing. Maybe Patty would like me."

I flipped over, landing on top of him, straddling his legs. "Well, she can't have you."

He stared for a moment, silently reminding me of a fact we both hated, and I regretted saying what I did. It gaped, like an open wound with no salve to apply, no bandage to cover it up.

I leaned forward and kissed him. "I love you."

He pulled me down against him. "I love you, too."

We lay like that for a while, and then I rolled off and stood up. "It's two-thirty."

He sat, running his hands over his face, pushing glossy dark hair back. "I know."

"I'll see you tomorrow." I put on my sweater and tied my printed silk scarf around my neck.

He walked toward the small room in the back he used as an office. "Tomorrow."

I wanted to stay, to pull him out of that cloudy mood, to make him smile again. But the children were due off the bus at three-fifteen, and the drive home took over a half an hour this time of day. The distance was necessary, though. It was out of Bruno's jurisdiction, for one, and it allowed me to know people, to say hello, to be a familiar face in the neighborhood, in the grocery store – even if everyone knew me as Sarah.

It allowed me the ultimate selfish luxury: two lives for the very expensive price of one.

Bruno was gone most of the time, attending every event, policeman's ball, ribbon-cutting ceremony – always smiling for the camera and being the town hero. Some days he didn't come home until the wee hours of the morning, and some nights he didn't come home at all. Just slept, he said, on the couch in his office at the station.

He had mistresses, of course. I'd spotted quite a few of them, at various times, riding along with him in the patrol car while I was out running errands. Or hurrying out of his office when I absolutely had to stop in to drop blueberry muffins off and make my appearance as the chief's doting wife.

His habit of spending spare time with other women had its advantages. For one, he rarely wanted to be home, leaving me as much free time as I could have hoped for. For another, since he was obtaining it from other places, he rarely pushed me to be intimate. Lastly, since we saw each other so very little, he hardly had cause or opportunity to beat me any more.

It was a good time in my life. The children were both healthy, active in school, busy with friends, content to play after school and come in by dark. I made sure to leave each morning as soon as they left, and return home each day by the time they arrived on the school bus. Even I found it odd that I'd never been caught.

I suppose it was the unusual circumstances of our busy, separate lifestyles, and the fact that I felt so happy in my other life, that made me truly absentminded. I was completely unaware, to be honest, until one afternoon, as I tied an apron around my waist, preparing to make meatloaf for dinner. I'd gained weight. I pulled the apron away and stood in front of the mirror in the powder room. I lifted my blouse, and there, where my trim, flat tummy should have been, was a bump. Nothing largely noticeable, really, but enough for me to know – for any woman to know – about her own body.

I calmly tucked my blouse back into my skirt, asked Abigail to watch her brother while I ran out for some ingredients I'd forgotten, then drove straightaway to our apartment in San Francisco.

I opened the door, flustered, fumbling my key in the lock. Bill startled, sitting on the sofa. He stood immediately. I'd never come unexpectedly like that, in the late afternoon.

"Rolin," he said, looking surprised and happy, and slightly concerned. He wrapped his arms around me, hugged me tightly, and then sat down again, looking expectant.

"Hi," I said, holding my arms tightly around myself, trying to keep my wits about me. "We need to talk."

Chapter 23

When the school nurse called on Friday afternoon to inform me Patrick was feeling too lethargic to continue with his school day, I didn't pay much mind. Four days later, when both he and Abigail were moaning in bed, covered in blistering, red splotches head to toe, I cursed my life.

"Oatmeal, Mom!" Patrick called weakly from his room. "I want another bath!"

I sighed, wanting to tear my hair out. I'd hoped to somehow spare the kids the usual childhood diseases. Yet, there I was, in my own brand of hell, with two aching, miserable children lying in bed and a screaming, sobbing toddler clawing at the mesh of her playpen like a rabid little raccoon.

I threw a handful of Cheerios into the playpen. Theresa didn't even glance in their direction.

"Mom! Bath!" Patrick's voice was impatient and whiny, and suddenly I could not breathe. I stumbled to the front door and whipped it open, running off-balance to the edge of our driveway before stopping, out of breath, pulse thumping frantically.

Outside, it was quiet. A breeze was blowing. The sky was blue. I tentatively looked around. Silence. My mind went to our apartment in the city. I closed my eyes and felt the peace of the small, three-room flat with the sunny green and yellow kitchen I had carefully painted. I gave myself exactly to the count of thirty before turning and walking back into the house.

I'd just settled Patrick into his bath, brought Abigail a cool washcloth to put over her forehead, and carried the trays of dirtied cups and dishes back into the kitchen when the phone rang. The sound set Theresa off again.

I wedged a finger into one ear and pressed the phone to the other. "Hello?"

"Hi. It's me," Bill said.

I faced the window and watched the trees move gently in the breeze. "Hi," I said, knowing why he was calling.

"I thought you fell off the face of the earth. You haven't called in almost a week." He laughed uneasily. "It shook me up a little, Rolin."

"I know. I've wanted to, but the kids are sick." Theresa let out a blood-curdling scream, mouth opening into a toothy, gaping hole of noise. I raised my voice over the racket. "They have the chicken pox!"

"Are they okay?" Bill sounded alarmed. "Do *all* of them have it?"

"She doesn't," I said.

He sounded a little relieved. "You sound really burnt out. Are you getting it?"

I leaned against the counter and focused on the leaves outside. "No. I'm just..." I lowered my voice. "Well, I'm damned near blowing my brains out. They've been sick for four days, I've been up all night, every night. They're nowhere near the worst of it yet, and...and..." I felt my throat clog up with the familiar lump and felt ridiculous for being such a baby.

"Okay, Rolin, that's it."

I sniffled. "Okay, what?" I heard the jingle of car keys, and I pictured them, hanging on the small metal hook I had mounted by the phone.

"Okay, I'm coming over. Unlock the door. I'll be there in a half hour."

I shook my head, then remembered he couldn't see me. I suddenly hated the playpen and the yelling, pudgy baby in it. The spotted kids upstairs, and everything else, because it was a reminder of why I had to say the exact opposite of what I truly wanted: "No, you can't. Don't do that."

"Mom! I need a drink again! Please!" Abigail called from her room. Bill was silent on the other end of the phone line.

"I have to go," I said, chest heavy, my sinuses stinging from trying so hard not to cry.

"Okay," he said, and I hung up.

An hour later, I'd left a more comfortable Patrick in his bed, smothered in Calamine lotion, content to read a stack of Spiderman comic books. I'd sat with Abigail for nearly thirty minutes, talking about schoolmates with her, trying to distract her from the perpetual itching.

"I'm going to nap now, Mom, okay?" she said.

I retaped the oven mitts around her wrists, a precaution she'd complained about, but one I knew was imperative to prevent scarring later on. She'd thank me later.

"Good idea." I closed her door gently. It was only as I stood out in the cool hallway that I realized the inside of the house was as quiet as the outside. Theresa had stopped screeching. Perhaps even fallen asleep, I thought gleefully, turning the corner and entering the living room.

There she lay, asleep, sprawled across Bill's chest and shoulder, one fist clutching his black tee shirt, the other jammed into her mouth. He smiled when I walked in. I wanted to yell at him for being reckless, for risking my entire life, for being here when it was an unspoken rule that our life and home was in San Francisco, never in the living room of this house.

I opened my mouth.

"Shh," he whispered, pointing unnecessarily to Theresa. "Why don't you go take a nap? I know you could use one."

I thought of Bruno's late night schedule. Of the chances he might just stop home on patrol, something he hadn't done in years. Of Abigail or Patrick walking out and wondering who this man was. Of twenty ways to tell Bill he had to leave.

I whispered back. "Bill...you just saved my life."

He grinned. "Don't be a cheese ball. Go on."

I took a shower instead, relishing the hot water and the smell of my lavender vanilla shampoo, and the fact he was sitting in my living room, holding the baby while she slept, with no expectations of me at all.

When I emerged, hair wrapped tightly in a towel, I felt like a new person, ready to take on the world. Bill had kicked his sneakers off and was sprawled length-wise across the couch, Theresa sleeping flat on her belly across his chest. He breathed deeply, asleep himself. I sat on the love seat, afraid to move, to stir in any way, and ruin this perfect moment.

Chapter 24

We were foolish, I suppose, in the way people get complacent and somewhat cocky when, after a long time, there are no repercussions for their actions, and it feels like maybe all the worry is for nothing.

Bill began coming over frequently, a few times a week, spending the mid-morning and early afternoon with Theresa and me. Most days we just stayed around the house. I would make lunch and he would play games or draw or color pictures in her Sesame Street coloring book. They both loved Oscar the Grouch best.

She was so animated and creative. They both had an imagination that could barely fit indoors. On this particular afternoon, they were playing in the living room, and I was fixing bologna sandwiches when Theresa came running into the kitchen, her black curls bouncing wildly around her heart-shaped face.

"Bill says I can learn to play the guitar too!" She squealed happily, small teeth gleaming brightly in a smile. "Come see our song!" She tore off again, and I set the meat aside and walked into the living room. Bill winked at me, and then pointed at Theresa, making his face serious. "Okay. Sure you're ready for this?"

She nodded, all business, and he began strumming out chords on his acoustic. Theresa tapped a hand on her leg, matching the nod of Bill's head with each tap. I smiled. Their mannerisms were uncanny. He hummed for a moment and then began to sing:

And someone saved my life tonight...

He raised his eyebrows at Theresa, and she piped in: "Sugarbear!"

Bill winked at me and kept singing, voice smooth, solemn, with just a little rasp. Theresa bounced in her seat and sang out the next line, her preschooler's lisp catching slightly, making me and Bill smile.

Together, they sang the last two lines, her small, high voice matching his in words and pace. He played the last chords out and then stopped, and Theresa clapped. They smiled up at me, two sets of sparkling, half-moon-shaped green eyes.

"I'm a butterfly, too!" Theresa said, delighted.

I clapped. "Amazing!"

She stared at me. "Why're you crying?"

I wiped my fingertips gingerly under my eyes. "I'm just happy." I looked at Bill, and he reached out and grabbed Theresa around the waist, lifting her onto his lap.

"Our singing brought her to tears, Sugarbear! That must mean we're either really good, or..." He howled like a wolf. "Really, really bad. Which do you think it is?"

Theresa giggled, and began howling, and before I knew it, both of them were wailing like timber wolves at the ceiling. I was laughing and trying to put bologna sandwiches together, and it was another snapshot, another memory, another moment that led up to the worst day of my life.

Bruno showed up for dinner. Most nights, he wasn't around for meals or homework or bedtimes. In fact, the children really didn't pay him any mind, whether he was there or not. They just seemed to take for granted that he most likely wouldn't be there, and even if he was, he didn't do much besides drink a beer in the recliner and "unwind." But that night, he was animated, spooning their mashed potatoes enthusiastically onto plates, and asking about their days at school. It was uncharacteristic, and put me on edge.

"Abby, how's the play coming along?" he asked.

She told him all about her part, one of the leads, and how the drama teacher loved her, and how she couldn't wait for opening night.

"I can't wait to see my leading lady up there," he said, flashing her a smile.

"And how about you, Baby?" he looked at Theresa. "How was your busy day with Mommy? What did you get up to?"

Theresa put her fork down and dabbed daintily at her mouth with the napkin. "Bill taught me how to sing and play the guitar."

My heart stopped. I felt my breath catch in my chest, and squat there, a stone wall, keeping me from moving in even the slightest way. Theresa had mentioned him once before, to me, asking when he was coming to play again. It had been in front of Patrick, and he'd asked her who Bill was. She told him, "My friend. He plays with me while Mommy cleans."

That had been the end of it, because at three, she'd had imaginary friends, and Patrick paid no attention to her ramblings.

But she'd never so much as spoken his name to Bruno.

Bruno took a gulp of his whiskey sour. "Bill, huh? Who's Bill?"

Theresa smiled. "My friend that comes and plays with me."

Bruno winked across the table at Abigail and Patrick. "Oh yeah? What's this Bill look like? Is he your size? Does he have a big, red, clown nose?" He laughed.

Theresa shook her head seriously. "No, Daddy. He's bigger than me. And..." She looked Bruno over, her eyes narrowed, concentrating. "And I think he's bigger than you, too. His head is higher up. Like this!" She stretched up her arms and wiggled her fingers at the top.

Bruno nodded, feigning approval. "Sounds like a big guy. Where'd you meet him?"

"He's Mommy's friend." She looked at me expectantly. "Mommy...where did I meet Bill?"

Bruno set his fork down and looked at me. The air surrounding the dinner table changed, and I truly felt terror at that moment. Afraid to look away from my plate, to put my own fork down – afraid I was shaking so badly everyone could see. But when I looked down at my hand, it was steady. That made me brave. I looked into Theresa's eyes.

"Well, goodness. You ruined the surprise!" I chided, my voice wobbling slightly. I turned my eyes to meet Bruno's. "Bill is giving her guitar lessons. I thought...I thought it best for her to have a musical skill going into school, since Abigail is our actress and Patrick is our athlete." I forced a thin-lipped smile and nodded again, to reaffirm that it was the truth, to wash away doubt.

Bruno didn't smile. He stared at me in silence until I looked down at my plate. I counted the kernels of corn scattered about – seventeen – before looking up again. He tilted his head slightly, watching me, and then spoke to Theresa without taking his eyes off mine.

"And how are the guitar lessons going, Baby?"

"Super!" she said cheerfully.

"Great. And how often do you have these lessons? Is it every day?"

Theresa shook her head sadly, but Bruno didn't see. His unblinking eyes stayed on me as I watched my little girl think about the question. She didn't have the concept of calendar time down yet, though she should have since she would be entering kindergarten in just a few months. She pursed her lips and tapped her chin with one pointer finger, a cartoon character thinking.

"Mondays," she announced at last.

"Mondays," he repeated.

"Yes, Mondays," she said, resolutely, though if he'd been home at all in the last few weeks he would know she'd taken a shine to the word Monday, and repeated it in a sing-song voice while in the bathtub, renamed her favorite baby doll Monday, and announced nearly every day: "I love Monday. Today is my favorite day."

But he knew none of this. So her innocent, cheerful resolution was all it took to snap him back to his dinner. He broke eye contact with me and took a bite of the biscuit growing cold on his plate.

"You should've told me. I think lessons are a wonderful idea." He didn't sound like himself yet, though, and I felt far from safe.

"Can I take lessons, too?" Abigail piped up. "I think I should know music, too! What if I'm on Broadway some day?"

I opened my mouth to respond, but Bruno spoke first.

"Absolutely, Pumpkin. Caroline," he said to me. "Can you set up lessons for Abigail as well?"

I nodded without thinking. "Yes. Sure."

Bruno leaned back in the chair and brushed his hands together, taking his napkin off his lap and dropping it on the table. "Great. Call tomorrow morning. See if he can stop by before next Monday."

I nodded again.

"Oh, and be sure to let me know which day it'll be. I'd like to meet this Bill fellow." When I glanced at him, his face was the ugliest damn thing I had ever seen, the face of a scaly crocodile lying in the water, beady brown eyes just waiting for its prey.

I dreaded the morning.

That night, as I absentmindedly applied Noxema and removed my makeup in our bathroom, I went over my options. Whenever in doubt, I simply made a list with the choices that I had to consider, and everything felt clearer, more manageable, less overwhelming.

Option A: I would call Bill in the morning and ask him to come and pretend to be the children's guitar instructor. My face flushed hot at the thought of that one; he'd be humiliated. Bruno would meet him, shake his hand, and Bill would be able to pull the whole thing off without a hitch.

I scoured my memory for flaws in the plan. Bruno had seen Bill just twice: once on his way out the front door, when he had mistaken him for the magazine salesman, and once, all those years ago, when he'd pulled us over on the way to the diner. Would he remember his face? If so, would he make the connection?

I splashed warm water over my own face, eyes squeezed tightly shut. I could hear the sound of the evening news drifting up the stairwell. Bruno always watched to the end, and most times fell asleep in the living room. *I have time to think this over*, I told myself, trying to calm down.

Option B: I would tell Bruno that Bill could not take on any other students, and that, in fact, a family emergency had come up, and he would not be able to provide lessons for Theresa anymore, either. But Bruno would be suspicious. Nearly three decades on the force had made him critical and suspicious of everyone, me included. He would watch me, for who even knew how long.

I patted my face with the towel and went to tuck in the children and turn the lights out. I rounded the corner in the hallway but stopped when I heard Bruno's voice coming from Theresa's bedroom. I inched to the doorway, leaning onto my toes so my slippers didn't make a shuffling sound. Peering in, I saw Bruno was on his back on Theresa's twin bed, arms behind his head, legs straight out, crossed at the ankles. Theresa was posed identically next to him.

"Just songs," she was saying. "Like, one about being a butterfly and another one I can't remember."

"And he comes on Mondays to teach you?" Bruno asked, eyes on the ceiling. I put one hand to my throat trying to quiet my heart. It was so loud, giving me away.

"Yup," she said, making the 'p' sound pop at the end.

"Does he ever teach Mommy how to play?"

"Mmmm...no, not really. Mommy just watches. And we put on shows for her sometimes!" Theresa bounced a little at the thought.

"That's nice. How long has he been coming to give you lessons?" I closed my eyes. Bruno was in interrogation mode, and there was no turning him back when he was like that.

Theresa considered this. "What do you mean? Mondays?"

He shook his head and turned his eyes from the ceiling to look right at her. "No. I mean, do you remember when you first met Bill?"

Theresa shook her head, slightly confused. "No. I don't remember. I never met him. I just...I always knew him."

I backed away from the door, not wanting to hear anymore. I already knew what Bruno was thinking – and he was right. So what could I do?

Tiptoeing back to my bedroom, I pulled the covers up over myself in my bed and turned the light out. A few minutes later, Bruno came in. He said nothing, just changed into his pajamas. I watched his silhouette against the large paned window, the outside lit up by the blue of the moon. His dark, stocky frame climbed into bed. I tried to make my breath even, sleeping, but it was short and spastic. I knew he could hear it.

"Caroline," he said, voice breaking through the dark.

"Mm?" I couldn't bear to turn, and instead clutched the covers and kept my eyes closed tightly, facing away.

"Caroline. How long has Bill been giving lessons to Theresa for?" He was asking genuinely. It wasn't a trap.

I exhaled. "Um…maybe a month?" I regretted saying it. I should have said longer. Or shorter. I didn't know. I kept adding lies, and Bruno was like a hound dog, sniffing them out, running them down, catching them. For all the lying I did, you'd think I'd be a bona fide pro, but I gave myself away the same as I had since I was a child, with a shaky, uneven voice.

"Caroline?" He moved closer. The bed shifted, his weight sagging my side, rolling my body nearer.

"Yes?"

He pressed my shoulder down, forcing me to lie face up. His face hovered over mine.

"Tomorrow, you're going to call this person – this guitar teacher – and you're going to tell him Theresa has decided not to play any longer. That he does not need to come anymore."

I lay still. Bill's face appeared in my mind right then, a perfect, life-like vision of him, smiling, brushing my hair away from my face. Laughing.

"And Caroline?" Bruno's voice made Bill's face disappear, wiped away. I was back to darkness, the press of Bruno's hands roughly moving down my body.

"What?" I said, voice much more tearful than I had anticipated. It sounded clogged, desperate, heavy.

He clutched my waist hard in his meaty paws and shifted his body parallel over mine.

"If I even hear his name again, I will kill him. And then I will kill you. Understood?"

I nodded, even though he wouldn't see or care. I lay there, a fallen marble statue, not feeling, not seeing, head turned to face the moonlight, as he punished me, more brutal that night than any other I could remember.

In the phone booth near the children's school, I huddled, incognito, my head covered in a paisley kerchief, sunglasses covering most of my face. I dropped coins in and dialed Bill's number.

He answered after one ring.

"Bill," I choked. I would count every word of this conversation. It would imprint in my mind and replay, a horrible, scratchy recording, many times over the years.

"Rolin. What's wrong?"

"He knows," I said, gasping aloud at the reality of it.

Bill was silent for a long moment. Then, "Are you okay? Did he...are you safe?"

"I'm fine." I pushed away thoughts of the night before.

"I'm going to come get you," he said, and then hesitated. "And Theresa. And Abigail and Patrick, too. There's not a lot of room here, but we'll figure something out. We'll figure it out together, Rolin."

Option C. So he gave me Option C, but I'd already mentally crossed that one off my list last night. And the only time I cross things off is when they are truly done.

I pictured him leaning against the yellow wall, the winding telephone cord tangling at the base. Our coffee maker to the left of him, probably brewing as we spoke. The worn copy of *The Bell Jar* I had yet to finish or move to a more appropriate place, collecting dust on the top of the refrigerator. I began to cry.

"I know you're scared. Don't be scared. We'll be okay," he said. "I'll come now, okay?"

"No!" I yelled through my tears. "No, Bill. The kids – they have a good life! I can't *do that*. I can't do what you're asking me to do!"

Bill's breathing puffed heavily into my ear, a static sound. "What are you asking me to do then? What can I do? I'll come. We'll go. We'll take the kids. Theresa will start school – "

"No," I said again. Like a faucet handle wrenched sharply to the left, my tears stopped. My feelings skidded to a screeching halt. I felt nothing at all as I spoke. "It's not going to happen. They have a good life. They have their own futures, Bill. I'm not going to take that away. For mine. For...for ours."

His voice changed, hardened. "What're you saying?"

The musty, sweaty smell of the phone booth surrounded me. My voice steady, and said, "I'm saying we're over and done with. That we won't see each other again."

"Are you kidding me? I married you a long time ago. Maybe not the regular way, but I've been faithful to you. Always."

I said nothing.

"Are you *kidding* me, Rolin? Is this a goddamned joke? The choice is yours right now! You're going to choose him, *again*, over me?" His voice cracked. I wanted to die right then, knowing he was crying, that his heart was sick and pained, that I had caused it. Again.

"I have to go. If he catches me talking to you, he's going to kill us both."

"Oh, bullshit! He's not killing anybody. He's just trying to scare you!"

"Yeah! And it's working! And I've got three kids to take care of!" I slammed my palm against the clear plastic of the booth, punctuating my anger. For a solid minute, neither of us spoke. I dropped another quarter in the slot and listened to it clink down in the silence.

"I want Theresa," Bill said. They stuck there, those words, implying what we'd never said aloud, what I'd never dared to mention, not through my entire pregnancy nor the four years he'd held her, fed her, bathed her, sung her to sleep.

"What?"

"I want her, Rolin. I love her."

"You…you can't *have* her, Bill. Are you out of your mind?"

He screamed at me then, a voice filled with tears and confusion and anger, the first time ever, since I had known him. He never raised his voice. "No! Are *you* out of *your* mind? I love her, and I love you. You can't do this to me again. Rip everything out from under me, like we don't have a life together. Like I don't love that little girl! *You cannot do this!*"

Right then, at that moment, I truly considered what he was saying. I considered Abigail and Patrick, and their happy lives: well-adjusted, never abused, active and popular in school, bright futures ahead. Bruno was a lot of things, but he was never a bad father, in the larger sense of the word. He provided for them, secured their futures, gave them the opportunity to thrive and succeed in life. I wanted the same for Theresa. I wanted it for all of my children. If I left, I would never see them again. Bruno would make sure of that, if he even let me live. Was it worth sacrificing them for my own selfishness, for my own future? I knew the answer even as I denied it to myself, refusing to believe what I was doing.

"I love you," I said. "I love you so much that every day that I live from now on will hurt me. Every single day."

I hung up the phone before he could answer and walked out of the phone booth, leaving him behind.

Chapter 25

In the months following that phone booth conversation, Bill tried twice to get me at home in person, and dozens of times to get me on the phone. I didn't open the door. When I answered the phone, I simply hung up if I heard his voice. When it rang, I always expected him, but after a couple of years, the calls stopped. My death felt complete.

Bruno often had patrolmen in the department stop by the house mid-day to check in on me, even six years later. They knew it was crazy, but I always pretended it was a pleasant surprise, offering lemonade or a slice of pound cake, and made the entire interaction as comfortable as possible.

Abigail graduated magna cum laude from her private school and had received a full scholarship to her first-choice university as a dual theater and art history major. Patrick was near graduation, doing well on both the football team and in the classroom. He'd be quite the catch, though his temper sometimes got the best of him and resulted in my visiting the school to meet with other parents or teacher or coaches or staff members.

Theresa was preparing for her eleventh birthday party, chatting excitedly to me in the kitchen as I iced a cake. She was expecting just ten classmates, five boys and five girls, and was nervous about the refreshments.

"Do you think we have enough pretzels, Mom? It doesn't look like a lot in the bowl." She swished the salty sticks around the crystal bowl.

"I think it's plenty, sweetheart. There's lots of other snacks besides pretzels." I shook white sprinkles across the top of the cake. I had become excellent at baking and pastry design, thanks in large part to a summer course taken at the Y. I had, in fact, become an expert at baking, pastry design, sewing, crocheting, and above all, gardening. I spent four to five hours a day outside when the sun was shining. I could never quite get all the weeds.

I held the cake out for her inspection. It was iced in pastels, purples and pinks and greens, with candied ribbons on all four corners. "How does it look?"

"Beautiful! I love it!" She was giddy with excitement. "How do *I* look, Mom?"

I carefully stuck the light blue candles in, one at a time. Out of the corner of my eye, I saw her twirl, skirt swirling around her. She had done the exact same thing in the dressing room when she'd chosen that dress.

"Mom?"

I counted the candles. "Hm?"

"How do I look?" She stood expectantly, holding the edges of her dress like a curtsy without the bow.

"Beautiful, sweetheart. You look beautiful."

I felt her deflate next to me. "You aren't even looking, Mom."

I glanced at her, eyed the dress, and smiled. "You look like the Birthday Princess," I offered, turning back to the cake. She seemed content, then ran off to her room.

The truth of the matter is I'd stopped really looking at her around her ninth birthday, when her face became the spitting image of everything I'd thrown away. The straight, narrow nose with the bridge of freckles across it. The thick, dark lashes framing green eyes. All of it was poison to me, doing nothing but worsening the aching nestled deeply in my bones. So I looked away.

The doorbell rang as I slid the cake onto the center of the table. Theresa's heavy running steps slowed as she neared the foyer. I heard her open the door, and then close it. I pasted my hostess smile on, expecting her to lead her friends into the kitchen. Instead she came in alone, arms around a gigantic basket of pastel roses.

"Mom! Look!" She set the basket down on the counter and stood back. "Aren't they perfect?"

They were. I was surprised, since Bruno had become more and more addicted to his job and the obligatory nightcaps with the crew as he neared retirement. He hadn't even remembered that very morning, in fact, that it was her birthday. I'd reminded him as he shaved, and he'd grunted an acknowledgement. In any case, it meant nothing one way or the other, since her presents were purchased, wrapped, and ready to go, and her party was planned.

Theresa grabbed at the little envelope buried in the roses. "Look! There's a little card!" I peered over her should as she opened it and read the words aloud.

For my sugarbear, my beautiful butterfly, on her 11th birthday.

I grabbed the card out of her hand and read it again. It was his writing. No mistaking the narrow scrawl that always leaned a little too much to the right. I'd seen it once a year for the last six years, on each of her birthdays, in an unsigned card. But never with flowers. I had thrown each of these out as they arrived, and she'd never seen even one.

"Oh my God. Who do you think it's from?" She squealed excitedly. "Do you think I have a secret admirer?"

I nodded, forcing a smile. "It looks that way."

The doorbell rang again and that time it really was guests. Theresa busied herself laughing and chatting and serving punch, and I stole off to the bathroom to sit, clutching the small rectangular card, knowing he'd held it perhaps just hours before. I flipped it over to read the logo and florist's information.

Bay Area Blooms. San Francisco, California.

He was still there.

In the bottom right corner, nearly camouflaged in the floral design, the tiniest of words were penned.

Still. Always.

I stared dry eyed at the gold and navy stripes on the shower curtain before tearing the card into small pieces and flushing it down the toilet.

I would later tell Theresa it must've gotten misplaced in all of the party litter and chaos.

Chapter 26

I pulled to the side of the narrow road leading from the train station to the main highway and jammed the car into park. The sound of the trains coming in at a distance whirred far off, already feeling like my past. She would be standing there, on the platform, by that time, perhaps waiting for me to come back.

Both Patrick and Abigail were grown and out of the house. Theresa was the last, and she was out too, now. Bruno was practically non-existent. I had moved into Abigail's room after Patrick left, and we slept separately, ate separately, lived separately, but for the teenager holding us together in the other room. He came home only two or three nights a week, and had stopped hitting me, forcing himself on me, or even acknowledging me nearly a year earlier. The doctor had told us, in a small, white office with two matching burgundy chairs that cirrhosis had reached a dangerous level and would take his life if he did not abstain from alcohol. When we returned home that afternoon, I'd poured him a whiskey sour with dinner the same as always, with a heavier hand than usual. It was just a waiting game. But I wasn't waiting any longer.

I put my blinker on and eased back onto the highway, making a right. I drove too fast, speeding toward San Francisco, wondering if he was still there. I rushed up the cement stairwell, familiar in smell and sound and feel, knocked on the door of our apartment and waited.

Bill answered, a pencil held between his lips. His hair was short, dark, curling slightly around his forehead. He wore rectangular glasses and, as he always did in my dreams, a plain black tee shirt. I bit my lip, self-conscious. The years hadn't been as kind to me. He looked nearly untouched by the decades. I looked like an old woman. Girls probably still smiled at him on the street, and though I had never asked, never worked up to nerve to broach that portion of his life, I was sure he could've had other partners during the decades of lonely nights.

"Bill." I whispered. "You cut your hair off."

"I did." He stepped back, holding the door open. And just like that my life filled with color again, Dorothy stepping out of her black-and-white farmhouse and into the Technicolor Land of Oz.

We sat at the table, and he made me coffee – two spoonfuls of sugar and lots of milk, the way I always drank it.

"Is that okay?" He pulled the chair out across and sat down. Not next to me, but across.

"It's perfect," I said, sipping it.

He sighed and ran a hand through his hair. I was secretly thrilled to see some gray pulling through around his temples. "Why, Rolin?"

He'd never minced words. I nodded. "We need to talk."

He leaned back in his chair, arms crossed, full attention lent to me. I took a moment to gather myself – this was the one chance I had to pull it off, to keep my voice from wavering, from sounding unsteady in any way.

"Theresa ran away from home. She met a boy." I tried to make myself cry, but at that moment nothing would come, so I settled for rolling my eyes and flipping a hand up carelessly. "They think they're in love."

Bill leaned forward, brow furrowed. "How did that happen? She's gone?"

"Yes," I said – not a lie. "She left a note. Said she was going out East with him. Said they were meant for each other." I swallowed and waited.

Bill didn't say anything at first. He stood, looked out the window, opened the refrigerator, and then sat back down. "Okay."

"Okay what?"

"Okay, you want me to go find her."

I had to tell myself not to rush, not to make him think anything was wrong. I pressed my lips together.

"No. That's not why I'm here."

"Well, why are you here?" He sat back again and stared at me expectantly. I felt unnerved. He was so handsome still, his eyes so familiar. I wanted to reach out and touch him.

"I'm here…" I started, but then stopped, because I didn't trust myself to pull it off any longer. "I'm here…"

Before I had to redeem myself, to explain, to say the words aloud, he stood and pulled me out of my chair, wrapping his long arms around me. I leaned in, smelled him, and buried my face in his neck, his pulse thumping softly on my bottom lip.

"It doesn't matter, Rolin. It doesn't even matter." I heard him sob. I leaned back and wiped my thumbs across his cheekbones, pushing the tears away.

"Don't cry," I said. My eyes were dry, stoic, unshakeable. I hadn't cried once since the phone booth. The faucet handle had been permanently pulled out of its socket, it seemed, my tears turned off for good.

"So much time is gone," he said, holding my head against him. He kissed my forehead. "It doesn't even matter."

I looked around the apartment. Some things had changed. A new clock here, colored paper squares stuck to the table for something he was working on, but nearly everything else was the same.

"You kept the kitchen color," I said.

He didn't reply, just nodded while tears rolled down his cheeks.

"Did you...are you with someone?" I forced the words out, stones scraping the side of my throat, my insides shaky at the real possibility.

He shook his head. "No."

I tried to make light of it. "No? Not at all? I mean, with a face like yours?"

He didn't laugh. "No. No one. Never any one else, Rolin."

I felt our hearts against each other, the pounding blending together.

"It's been a long time..."

"I waited, Rolin," he said, simply and pulled me tighter.

"I won't leave again," I said, and felt him nod his head on top of mine.

We stood like that, holding each other, unmoving in the small kitchen for a long time. And when the sun began to go down, Bill cooked us chicken parmesan with angel hair, and I set the table. I didn't care what time it was or that it was dark or that Bruno may or may not be home. I stayed the night, and many nights after, in Bill's bed, only returning to that house in the suburbs when I absolutely had to. My garden shriveled and died. The silverware tarnished untouched in its mahogany case above the mantle. The china collected dust, surrounded by angel figurines I'd always hated.

I'd like to say I thought about the lies. Thought about Theresa, in those years afterward. But I rarely did. Bill never mentioned her again after that day. He never played that song again, and we both knew why. Bruno stopped looking after a short time, and Abigail and Patrick looked in all the wrong places. Though for a while I was afraid they would, in fact, find her, with all the effort they were putting into it. Lizzie, deeply entrenched in her role as a preacher's wife in South Carolina, took it the hardest, refusing to believe that a girl could just disappear. So I told her a different lie than all the others, one that would make Theresa unredeemable. It was the only way, really.

Life is expensive, and I was the only one who had the means to pay the tab.

Chapter 27

I was making a cup of tea when the cell phone rang. The grandchildren had given me the phone over a decade ago. Patrick had encouraged it.

"It'll make it easy for us to keep you company, Ma," he had said, implying that, with his father's recent death looming over our family, I'd need constant companionship to keep from going off the deep end.

I fiddled with the buttons to answer it. "Hello?"

"Mom?" It was Abigail. Any mother will tell you, one word from an upset child, one word when they aren't themselves, and you just *know*.

"Abby. Everything all right?" I sipped my tea and made a face. Too weak. I dunked the bag in again and swirled it around with the spoon.

She was quiet on the other end for a moment before speaking. "Oh, Mom. Are you alone?"

I glanced around the empty kitchen, wondering why she was asking. Feeling a slight panic course through me, like a teenager caught sneaking out, though I was nearly seventy. Both the children lived hours away, and I never had visitors.

"Yes," I said. "What's wrong, darling?"

Her voice sounded strained, almost angry. "Mom, I need to tell you this, and I want you to stay calm. Try not to get too upset, and I'll come be with you soon." She paused. "Theresa died."

I sucked in a breath. My tea sat in the porcelain cup, the dark tendrils swirling ominously.

"I found her, Mom. She died a couple of days ago. Her funeral was this afternoon."

My chest began to hurt. I clutched one hand to my housedress, gripping the small slippery phone with the other. "You know this?"

She sighed. "Yeah, Mom. And...she had two kids. And they're beautiful." Her voice cracked, then, and I felt my heart pulling from my chest, pulling out and suffocating me with pain.

"Where?" I gasped out.

"Up around the Bay Area." She took a deep breath, voice thick with tears. "Mom?"

"Yes. I'm here." I pushed the teacup away, hands shaking, brittle and thin-skinned. The hands of an old woman.

She cleared her throat. "Mom, I'm bringing them home with me. And...we're going to come there. Not today. Not this week, but soon."

"Yes," I said again.

"Okay," she said. "I've got to go. I love you, Mom, but..."

"Goodbye, darling. I'll speak to you soon," I said, not wanting her to trail off, not wanting the implication to come through the tiny phone and smack my face.

We hung up. I sat for a moment, as my tea grew cold, before I stood and shuffled into the living area, completely remodeled from the room I'd hated for so many years, though the pictures of the children and their little ones stayed the same.

I stared at him, snoring softly on the recliner, green slippers worn and scuffed. He'd never lost his thick, wild hair. Instead, it had turned completely white, practically all at once, not too long after Theresa had disappeared.

I perched on the arm of the chair and watched his steady, peaceful breathing, before gently shaking his shoulder.

He stirred, slowly opening his eyes, peering up grumpily. "Right in the middle of a good dream, Rolin," he mumbled, stretching his arms in front of him.

"Bill," I said, laying my palm across his warm forehead. "We need to talk."

Punishment is *not* having to confess your worst decisions, your biggest sins, your most horrendous wrongs done to others. It's living with the secret of it, forever, alone.

1992

The sun rose higher over the ocean, making the water sparkle like the sea was made of diamonds. The beach was always empty at this time in the morning, save for the few dedicated runners. They passed so quickly one would hardly know they were sharing the beach without the treaded prints of athletic shoes left in the damp sand. On the pier, a very old fisherman sat on the bench, looking out over the railing at two figures skipping and twirling along the water's edge. The woman would run and scoop the little girl up right before the tide could graze her feet, and the little girl would scream and laugh every time. Occasionally they stopped, and looked at the sand, sometimes picking up and examining pieces of the beach.

Valentine held her mother's hand as they walked to where the sand still bubbled from the remnants of the waves. She looked up at her mother's face, so beautiful and youthful, eyes narrowed as she stared out over the ocean, and then down at the little girl beside her.

"What're you looking at?" Her mother asked playfully. "Do I have a boogie?"

Valentine burst out in a fit of laughter. "No! You're gross!" She grinned up at Theresa. "I was looking at your face. You look pretty."

Theresa stopped walking and knelt in front of Val. She brushed her bangs off her face and then kissed the little girl on the cheek. "Oh, Jellybean, so do you. You look absolutely beautiful." Theresa kissed her cheek again, and pressed her into a hug before standing up straight again.

They walked along another half mile before stopping at a place that held a sea of washed up shells. Valentine bent down to sift the shells through her fingers, looking for a seahorse, a sand dollar, or something equally holy.

"This one is the most beautiful of all, don't you think?" Theresa held up a perfect pink conch shell. Not a single chip flawed the creamy, swirling pattern. Val made an "Oooohhh" sound and reached out to touch it. "Let's save this one for home," her mother said, putting it in the beige cloth bag that hung from one arm.

Val used her bare toes to push the fragments of shell around in the sand. "Mama, do you think that every one of these broken ones looked like that before they got broken?"

"Yeah. I do. They're all just as magnificent as this one when they start out."

Val looked at the tiny, sharp pieces in her hand. "What happens to them? Why do they get so broken?"

Theresa sat down on the sand and brought her knees against her chest. "Well. They all start out beautiful and whole, Jellybean. But then the seawater and the rocks and the sand wear them down until they're nothing but shattered pieces. Only a remnant of what they used to be at one time – something beautiful."

Epilogue: Valentine

I slipped my feet into sparkling gray ballet flats and took a peek in the mirror. White capris, a silver cardigan against the coolness of May in New England. The woman at the salon had cut my hair into a neat, layered bob, and I was happy with how professional it looked. My long, wavy, girlish hair finally gone.

"Beautiful," Abigail said, walking up behind me. "Just beautiful. Rory has the car running. Do you want to drive together?"

I smiled at her, and how she mother-henned the two of us, even now. We'd moved out shortly after I finished my degree, a few months after graduation, when the agency had hired me out of my internship as a full-time case worker. Two years later, Jonathon was thriving in middle school, on the honor roll and the track team. And today, graduating eighth grade. Abigail and Rory had wanted us to stay with them longer – forever, I suspected, knowing her love for cooking big breakfasts and putting fresh sheets on beds – but there was something magical about finally getting our own apartment, just me and Jonathon. The day we moved in, he'd surveyed the place and then chosen the smaller bedroom.

"You can have the big one," I'd offered.

"No way. You take it. You got this all for us." He'd looked up, eyes gleaming brightly, and I remember wanting to capture how proud he was, how much he clearly loved me.

We'd spent the first week making it ours, decorating, painting with the help of Rory and his stretch rollers. Putting curtains up with Abigail's guidance.

I smiled now at the thought of it. Home.

"Think I'll drive myself, if you don't mind," I told Abigail. "I'm swinging by Jessica's to pick her up."

"Oh. Okay, sure." She twisted her hands at her waist. I knew she was grappling with the idea of Jessica as she always did, even four years after meeting her. "Well, of course she has to come over for dinner and cake after."

I kissed her on the cheek. She was making an effort since they'd gotten off to a slightly bumpy start: Abigail tense in her conservative ways; Jessica a beautiful, bubbly liberal trying her best to win over my only aunt.

And I appreciated it. "Of course. She'd love that."

Outside Jessica's apartment I checked the time on the dash clock and honked again. Jonathon was already at the school, he and his buddies probably fooling around in the gym in their caps and gowns.

The front door of the brick apartment swung open and Jessica appeared, a green and yellow sundress grazing her knees, blonde hair loose down her back. She moved lightly, quickly, waving and grinning at the car. "You belong on the west coast," I always told her. "That tan is so out of place here." But she was Boston born and raised, and swore she could never settle anywhere else.

"It's graduation day!" she sang out, whipping the car door open, gliding into the passenger seat. Jessica always loved a celebration. She'd ordered a cake for nearly every small and large event in the last four years. Had wrapped presents for Jonathon on random days, barely containing her glee when he turned the corner and spotted them.

"Hi, you!" she said to me, clicking her seatbelt into place. "I just sent the last of his graduation announcements out. Angela texted me. She'll be here on Tuesday and probably hang out for the whole week. Do you think we can swing a milkshake run, super fast?"

Jessica also always jumped from one topic to another naturally, super fast. But I'd learned to follow the various threads from nearly the first afternoon we'd spent together.

"Hi," I said back, squeezing her knee, feeling happy. "Thank you. That's great. And yes. Milkshakes, absolutely."

THE END

Acknowledgements

The earliest thanks goes to my uncle, Jim Detrick, without whom I would have never started believing in my ability to write stories, and who sat with ten-year-old me, scribbling on kitchen napkins, one scene at a time, about Jake Drummin and his dog Pooky. Also to Aunt Jamie, who manned the other side of the kitchen counter and supplied us with bologna sandwiches and witty dialogue suggestions, and occasionally huffed when we used the word 'busty' to describe a woman.

Nesting Dolls was a long time coming, and the girls who helped me in the early stages by reading chapters and drafts and commenting include Monika Manter, Theresa Tulaney, Kristi Watkins, Tina Walton, and especially Bryce Russo, who's single-handedly put up with my novel aspirations for two solid decades.

At East Stroudsburg University, where the earliest scenes started taking shape, a big thank you to Professor Bill Broun's writing class and his encouragement. At Wilkes University, where the novel really became something perhaps worth reading, I am forever indebted to my mentor and friend, Lenore Hart, and also to Bonnie Culver, Jim Warner, and the 2010 Creative Writing program graduates, particularly Dania Ramos, Kacy Muir, Lynne Spease Reeder, and Megan Kaleita Patton, who took time to read, help, and nurture.

I owe serious thank-yous to Connie Harris, who encouraged me to bloom at Lackawanna Trail High School. Another enormous thank you to Kari Stuart, literary agent, whose patience and confidence in me helped me believe in my potential, and who on numerous occasions told me to have some Oreos and come back to it when I was feeling better.

I am forever grateful to Northampton House Press and publisher David Poyer for delivering my novel into the world, and to Heather Harlan, my editor, who provided some great suggestions that changed it for the better.

My family has always cheered for me, way before I ever was all fancy with a book and stuff. My mom, Susan Mangiafico, sacrificed a lot so that the three nesting dolls inside of her would walk a different life path than she did. Thanks also to my sisters, Shannon Nordmeyer and Sherrie Vertolomo, who have no problem telling me when things make no sense and to stop being dramatic. I love you.

Lastly, I will always be grateful to my husband and biggest fan, Ryan, who will insist until the day that he dies that this is his favorite book of all time, no bias, of course. I love you.

Northampton House Press

Northampton House LLC publishes carefully selected fiction, as well as lifestyle nonfiction, memoir, and poetry. Our logo represents the muse Polyhymnia. Our mission is to discover great new writers and give them a chance to springboard into fame. Our watchword is quality, not quantity. See our list at www.northampton-house.com, or Like us on Facebook – "Northampton House Press" – to discover more innovative works from brilliant new writers.

CPSIA information can be obtained at www.ICGtesting.com
Printed in the USA
BVOW03s1848220514

354321BV00006B/329/P